Ruby

& Spear

Ruby & Spear

TODD WALTON

BANTAM BOOKS
NEW YORK TORONTO LONDON SYDNEY AUCKLAND

RUBY & SPEAR

A Bantam Book / April 1996

Grateful acknowledgment is made for permission to reprint from the following:

"Late Afternoon" from the book of poems *On Bear's Head*, by Philip Whalen, © 1969 by Philip Whalen, published by Harcourt, Brace & World, Inc. and Coyote.

"The Temple of the Animals" from the book *robert duncan: selected poems*, by Robert Duncan, © 1959 by Robert Duncan, published by City Lights Books.

"Cézanne at Mont Sainte-Victoire" from the book *The Hours of Morning*, by William Carpenter, © 1981 by the Rector and Visitors of the University of Virginia, published by The University Press of Virginia.

"Mulch Cloud" from the book of poems *The Dark Continent*, by David Meltzer, © 1967 by David Meltzer, published by Oyez.

"I Saw Myself" from *Selected Poems*, by Lew Welch, © 1976 by Donald Allen, published by Grey Fox Press.

Cover art © Photonica

Book design by Caroline Cunningham

Library of Congress Cataloging-in-Publication Data
Walton, Todd.
Ruby & Spear / Todd Walton.
p.   cm.
ISBN 0-553-37813-9
I. Title.
PS3573.A474R8   1995
813'.54—dc20   95-17037
CIP

Published simultaneously in the United States and Canada

Bantam Books are published by Bantam Books, a division of Bantam Doubleday Dell
Publishing Group, Inc. Its trademark, consisting of the words "Bantam Books" and
the portrayal of a rooster, is Registered in U.S. Patent and Trademark Office and
in other countries. Marca Registrada. Bantam Books, 1540 Broadway, New York,
New York 10036.

PRINTED IN THE UNITED STATES OF AMERICA

FFG   10 9 8 7 6 5 4 3 2 1

for Linda Gross

Acknowledgments

Enormous thanks to my agents Linda Chester and Laurie Fox, and to all my dear friends for their love and support.

Part One

Late Afternoon

I'm coming down from a walk to the top of Twin Peaks

A sparrowhawk balanced in a headwind suddenly dives off it:

An answer to my question of this morning

PHILIP WHALEN

1

Once, when I was young—oh, fifteen—I stood on the western edge of my father's driveway, focused intently on his finest gift to me, a shiny orange rim mated to a whitewashed backboard—a fresh net awaiting my throw, the summer sun warming my bare skin. I was a rosy tan white boy, longing to flee the oppressive confines of suburban dependency. Nearly all my heroes were great black men who could fly. Elgin Baylor, Oscar Robertson, Wilt Chamberlain, Earl the Pearl Monroe.

My greatest wish was to drive the lane, that narrow corridor leading to the goal, to leave the ground and soar high into the air, there to float in defiance of gravity before releasing a delicate shot that kissed the board and tumbled through. I could jump and shoot. But to float, to fly, that was what eluded me.

And on that day, that once in my life, I transcended my wish. I ran toward the basket and leapt into the air, discovering as I left the earth that I had forgotten the ball. It was still in the hands of the love of my life, the sweetest sixteen I've ever seen. She was leaning back against my father's Skylark, her body bare save for shorts and the illusion of a T-shirt, the basketball cradled against her breasts. But as I winced to think that my fabulous ascent would be for nothing, she passed to me, the ball finding my hands and lifting me high above the rim, where I gave it down into the hoop, my view of the world changed forever.

She is still there, thirty years gone by, kissing me back from death with her rapt attention, vanquishing the shame I feel for doing what I love.

2

My name is Victor Worsley, Vic to my few friends, *Worsely* to my legions of detractors. I'm a sportswriter, basketball my main game. Perversely compulsive, I write longhand in fast black ink, seven columns a week. I've been doing this for fifteen years without a break. I used to write at a desk in a quiet room far from my fellow human beings. Now I write everywhere—hotels, coffeehouses, train stations, park benches. Anywhere but in my office.

However, on Tuesdays, my favorite day of the week in San Francisco, I do go down to the *Chron* to taunt my editor, the lugubrious Lucas McCormack, a man terrified of offending anyone. Poor Luke will no doubt be fretting about the widening rift between yours truly and Jim Hathaway, coach of the Warriors, the most annoying man in my life. Why? Because he won't let the men play without strict orders from the bench, and it's killing the game. It has become a point of honor with me now. I want him to give the game back to the players, to free them to improvise.

But the real reason I go downtown, *ever*, is to flirt with Greta Eagleheart, our divine section manager. And I do mean divine.

Greta is a most successful mélange of peoples, a Nefertiti with the cunning eyes of a fearless wolf. I've known her for three years, dreamt of loving her from head to toe, but always feared to take things past office repartee. It seems impossible to me that a woman possessed of so delightful a personality would be mateless for so many years, but office gossip insists it is so.

Dazzling in a silky blue dress, she greets me today with her weekly tally, her voice a tender growl. "I liked you Wednesday, Friday, and Sunday," she says, her smile turning to a frown. "But you were just too mean on Tuesday and Thursday and Monday."

"What about Saturday?"

"Are you asking me out?" She takes a step closer. "I had plans to go for a hike along Half Moon Bay, but I'll gladly miss it for a date with you."

"My column," I cough, unused to such candor from her. "I mean, what did you think of my Saturday column?"

"I know what you mean," she says, her smile fading. "Still, a person can hope."

This is new. She's never been so direct. So why don't I ask her out? What am I afraid of?

"There's someone here to see you." She nods in the direction of my cubicle. "She wouldn't wait out here."

I give her my most ferocious glare. "Since when do you allow people to wait in my office? What if she wants to kill me? And besides, there's no place to sit."

"Vic," she says dolefully, "she's just a nice old lady. Don't you worry. I checked her out."

"What does she want?"

"Maybe *she* wants to go out with you, too." Her phone rings. "I gotta get this."

Having made a colossal fool of myself with Greta, as usual, I enter my paper-ridden cell and behold a grim little woman with dark chocolate skin and white frizzy hair, her ears spiked with shards of green glass. Her simple gray dress is belted with a strand of red rope, her tiny feet lost in bright red high-tops. She stands at my desk, holding herself rigidly, furiously searching my face.

"Mr. Worsley," she says gruffly, "I'm Ruby Carmichael. Did you get my letter?"

"Letter? God, I get so many letters, Miss Carmichael, I . . ."

"That's *Mrs.* You'd have remembered mine. With the picture of my child? Spear?"

"I haven't been in for a week. When . . . ?"

"A month ago." She squints at me. "Please don't lie to me, Mr. Worsley. I may be old, but I'm not stupid. I was a schoolteacher for twenty-five years, mother and grandmother to more children than I can remember. So I'll know if you're lying. It's something I'm good at."

"Please sit down." I indicate a chair wedged between two towering stacks of newspapers. "Just move that thesaurus anywhere."

She sits down and opens her tiny yellow purse, bringing forth a little jar of greenish goo, a bit of which she dabs onto her lips. "Don't look much like your picture," she says more to herself than to me. "Put on a bit of weight since then."

I move the piles of yellowing paper off my chair and sit down at my junk-strewn desk, wishing I'd stayed home, though a week without seeing Greta wouldn't be much of a week at all. "It's actually better that people don't know what I look like," I reply, unable to meet her gaze. "It allows me my anonymity. Not to mention my life of lonely debauchery."

"If you say so," says Mrs. Carmichael, squinting critically at the faded poster on my wall of Julius Erving flying above the parquet floor of Boston Garden on his way to dunk over Larry Bird. "But I'll tell you something. If you'd seen that picture I sent, you'd remember it."

I buzz Greta. "Hello, G, it's me. Long time no see. Would you please find me the letter from Mrs. Ruby Carmichael? From a month ago."

"It's more like a package," Ruby shouts, leaning close to the intercom. "I drew a hummingbird next to Mr. Worsley's name. To bless it." She smiles ever so slightly at me. "I believe in spirits. You?"

"The truth is, Mrs. Carmichael, I don't read my mail. There's too much of it, and it's almost all in the form of, shall we say, argument."

"Why do you keep it?"

I frown. *Greta* keeps my mail carefully filed in an underground room, convinced it will one day prove valuable. I can sense her gloating all the way down and back with Ruby's precious package. "To be quite honest . . ."

"I studied your last column about the Warriors needing to trade a name or two for a big man, a *true* big man, you said, and that's when the spirits said Spear was finally ready to be that man. He could be as great as there has ever been."

How great would that be? What might be as great as Michael Jordan threading his way through huge defenders, pushing the ball through the center of the ring, landing flat-footed, arms raised in grateful triumph?

"The best?" I sneer. "The *best* there has ever been?"

Ruby winces. "Didn't say anything about *best.* I said 'as great as there has ever been.' *As* good, though I admit he's a bit rough around the edges. Nothing *you* couldn't iron out, I'm sure."

"Me?" I point to myself. "I? Iron out your son's faults?"

"Not actually my son. Left to me by my neighbor. Before she went off to die. Spear was two, his brother Godfrey was five."

"His name is Spear?"

She bows her head. "Spear Rashan Benedentes."

"Look, I'm a writer, not a coach. I . . ."

Greta enters triumphantly with the unopened package. "Nice hummingbird." She winks at Ruby. "Bringer of joy."

"You know something about birds," says Ruby, her eyes shining. "Good for you. But don't forget, the hummingbird can't bring joy to a place without flowers."

"Don't I have a meeting soon?" I ask, pleading with my eyebrows. "Like any minute now?"

"Nope," says Greta, handing me the envelope. "Your day is clear."

I glare at Ruby's hummingbird. "Listen, I'm sure Spear is a wonderful ballplayer, but I'm a writer, not a trainer. My relationship to the game is theoretical. I played twenty minutes for a college so small anyone could be on the team if they *wanted* to. Nowadays I play one-on-one with an old friend. No touching. Bad backs."

"Just look at his picture. Please, Mr. Worsley. Just take a peek at my child."

"I don't want to."

"Why not, Mr. Worsley?"

"Because I can't help you, and I don't want to disappoint you any more than I already have."

"Just take a peek." She clasps her hands. "You won't disappoint me. The spirits have made all this perfectly clear. This is all part of your destiny."

"Look," I say, tiring of her babble, "there's nothing I can do for you. I'm a writer, a humorously cynical commentator, okay? When I play in celebrity fund-raisers, they *let* me shoot, but we all know I'm as slow as a tortoise by professional standards. The worst of them can block my shots without bothering to jump. I'm nothing, okay? I'm a stupid little white guy, okay?"

She glowers at me. "Not okay. You know the game. You see how it works. I've been reading you for ten years. You taught me to see what my boys were doing. You opened my eyes. You helped me understand what they loved. I know you'll want to help my Spear once you see him." She takes a deep breath. "I took the picture myself."

I feel absurdly vulnerable as I open her envelope. I hate saying no to people. I hate letting people down. I hate turning out to be so much less than they expect me to be. Better to remain a disembodied voice, a swarm of words on a page that never sticks in anybody's mind for more than a week.

I bring forth a glossy photo of a powerfully muscled man flying high in the air, his skin ink black, his hair a wild spray of dreadlocks, the ball held delicately in his gargantuan hands. His eyes are closed, his every cell launched toward fruition. Everything I will never be.

"I can't help you," I say to Ruby, wishing I could disappear. "I'm a writer. That's all."

She rises to go. "You will help him. I've had a clear communication about this, Mr. Worsley. They said you were bound to come into his life soon. Bound to come watch him play. So when you do, I just want you to know a little something about Spear."

"I'm not coming," I say, closing my eyes. "I don't know anything about this so-called communication you've had, but I'm not coming."

"Spear is not some dumb kid, Mr. Worsley. He's a man, full grown, twenty-seven. A father several times. You must come and see him. Promise me?"

"I will not promise," I say, desperate to get rid of her. "But I'll think about it."

"Yes, you will think about it. No question about it. I'll be expecting your call."

Greta rushes in as Ruby leaves, her eyes bright with curiosity. "May I see the picture? Please?"

I push the photo across my desk to her. "It's not possible. He must be jumping off a truck or something. Just outside the frame. Look how high above the rim he is. It's gotta be some sort of trick."

She looks at the picture and puts a hand to her heart. "God, he's exquisite."

"We can meet him," I say, crushed by her admiration of him. "Would that interest you?"

She frowns inquisitively. "Was that an invitation? Almost sounded like one, didn't it? You know I love it when it sounds like you're asking me out."

I take the photo from her and slip it back into the envelope, and I notice that Ruby's hummingbird just touches the end of my name with its beak. "So why *do* hummingbirds represent joy?" I ask, unable to conceal my bitterness. "Because they never stay for long?"

"They don't just represent it, Vic. They are truly bringers of joy." She sits where Ruby sat. "So. I know this may seem a bit forward of me, since we've only known each other for three years, but how about Saturday?"

"To go see this guy Spear?"

"I was thinking more like brunch. Just you and me."

"Saturday," I say, emboldened by the rush of blood to her cheeks. "Pancakes?"

"Your house or mine?"

"Oh, why not mine?" I offer, envisioning the dung heap I call home. "It'll give me an excuse to have someone in to bulldoze."

"I'll be there at nine," she says, beaming at me. "With melons and strawberries."

"I'll make my grandmother's secret sourdough cakes. If I can remember her trick with the starter. Tangy but sweet."

She pauses in the doorway. "You cook? I never would have guessed."

"I used to cook all the time. I'm surprised I've never told you. It used to be one of my favorite things to do."

3

 It is a splendid October afternoon in McKinley Park, the elm leaves glossy yellow, the ducks fat and placid on the blue pond. My great buddy Nolan Smith is sinking jumpers from his favorite distance, eighteen feet. He can get a lock on the basket that only my most zealous defense can break. Nolan is a video artist, two inches my senior. His business card reads:

Nolan Smith
films

we turn chaos into order
(for a reasonable price)

We met in college. He's played me dead even for twenty-five years. Nolan is fair, I am swarthy. His soft gray hair behaves itself, while my unruly brown tends to tangle. He loves his work, where I have come to loathe mine. He is a fount of optimism, in stark contrast to my bitter predictions of the brutal eclipse of civilization as we know it.

Loosening up before we play, I ponder the events of this morning, marveling at the bravery of Ruby and Greta, each in her own way undaunted by my fearful diffidence. I, on the other hand, was terrified to call the housecleaners, my voice trembling as I told them where I hide the key to my front door. They should be there now, the demolition underway. I wonder if Ruby's persistence emboldened Greta to pursue me. And why do I doubt that she likes me, when I know she does? We've *always* liked each other.

I look up from my stretching and moan at what's coming. "Oh, no. The big boys want the court."

Nolan banks one in from the right side and turns to greet the five young black men, each a good head taller than I. "We just got here," he explains to them. "Somebody broke the other rim, and see, we just play one-on-one. He's got a bad back; I've got tricky knees. So it's gonna be a while. That okay?"

"No hurry," says the shortest of the five, a friendly man in shimmering blue sweats, a white headband low on his forehead. "We waitin' on our sixth. You mind we run some tunes?"

"No," says Nolan, smiling hugely. "Not if you don't mind watching a couple midgets go at it."

They laugh, save for the tallest of them, a slender man with carob-brown skin and deeply hooded eyes. Nolan has acknowledged the natural order, paid obeisance, and exonerated his ego, while I must push my old self to the limit, inspiring Nolan to push with me. I know we're just dumpy old farts to these strong, young players, but that does little to blunt my desire to show them what I can do.

They fill the air with syncopated hip-hop and pungent clouds of cannabis, hooting and whistling as we jump and shoot. They applaud loudly for a change I make midair to sneak the ball around Nolan's outstretched arms, and they high-five it when Nolan scores with a left-handed runner off the glass. We can feel their love of nuance, and it inspires us to try some moves we've never used in a game.

As we leave the court, the tallest one, the one who didn't laugh, touches my arm. "Did you play in college, man? Got a sweet release. Like you been shooting over real tall guys all your life."

"I played a little a long time ago. Podunk school. Geeks. We were terrible. I'm sure it was long before you were born."

"You want to play with us?" he asks, unfazed by my disclaimer. "Our sixth ain't showed."

"Me?" I giggle like a little boy. "You gotta be kidding."

"Set you some pics. Your buddy here can sub if you get tired."

"No," I say, feeling cornered. "I can't. Sorry. Bad back."

"Maybe next time," he says, winking at me. "Like to see you pass."

We get on our bikes and pedal homeward, my body humming with excitement at the mere *thought* of playing with those young guys. It's the dream I dream almost every night. Little me shooting rainbow jumpers over leaping giants, making it again and again.

"Why didn't you play, Vic?"

"Come on, Nolan. I'm forty-four. Five-foot-nine and a little. I have a three-inch vertical leap and a three-inch lateral spare tire. I'm too old. The last time I played with anybody but you, I wrenched my back and jammed my thumb and shattered a tooth all in the space of ten minutes. I'm too fragile for the rugby ball of today."

"Thursday?" he says, leaving me in front of my adobe house, its mauve walls festooned with crimson bougainvillea climbing onto the red tile roof—a Mediterranean postcard revealing nothing of the squalor within.

"Thursday," I say, suddenly deflated by the image of Lucas waiting impatiently to complete his section, my column late again, not a word having come to me yet.

I push open my front door and find the Bosley sisters hard at work on seven years of accumulated grunge, the basalt of my bachelorhood, the sordid aftermath of loveless living. Mae, the brains of the outfit, her curly red hair tied back in a fat ponytail, approaches with a solemn frown on her sweaty face. "If my calculations are correct, Mr. Worsley, and they usually are, it'll take about three more days to hack our way through every room. I've met a lot of messes in my time, but this is really something special. Want to pay us for a few more days?"

"Can you have it done by Saturday?"

"With luck and perseverance." She winks at me. "We'll do our very best."

Mae's sister, Karen, approaches with a swollen Hefty bag. She is bald, her biceps bulging. "The Dumpster was a stroke of genius," she proclaims, her voice profoundly deep. "It's nearly full, and that's just with the stuff we *know* you want thrown away."

"The refrigerator is a serious problem," says Mae, grabbing her pink bowling jacket. "Some very scary mold in there, Mr. Worsley."

"Please," I say, liking her style, "call me Vic."

"Okay, Vic." She snaps her gum and winks at me again. "You may just want to give that old thing away and get a new one. Seriously. Oh, and I sent tons of stuff to the cleaners. Curtains, blankets, comforters. Anything we could pry loose. See you early tomorrow. Be good."

"Whatever that means," I say, wishing they'd stay for a drink, but knowing I don't dare invite them with my column looming. "See you in the morning."

•   •   •

Alone amidst my troubled detritus, exhausted from my extraordinary hour of basketball, I am oddly not hungry. I open a cold beer and sit on my sofa, staring at Ruby Carmichael's carefully printed letter.

Dear Mr. Worsley,

I am a devoted reader of yours and I have a vision of you helping my child get a chance to play basketball professionally. He is a great soul with a physical prowess that is truly a miracle to behold. He has never had a coach, but he plays hard every day at Tillsbury Park. I would be very happy to take you there to watch him. If you will do this for me, I will pray for your health and happiness every day of my life. Thank you for your wisdom.

Love,

Ruby Carmichael

I look at the photograph again. It must be a trick. The heels of his shoes are six feet above the concrete, the ball a good seven feet above the rim. I turn the photo over.

Tiny letters announce:

Spear Rashan Benedentes
27 years old
7 foot 3 and ½ inches
302 pounds

The phone rings. I wait for my machine to get it, but the Bosleys must have disconnected it. Reluctantly, I answer. It's Lucas. "Vic, it's after seven. Your column is still a blank. I don't mind staying late once in a while, but this is getting to be a habit with you. I'm not happy about it. I can't go home until the section is full. How much longer do I have to wait?"

"I'm just finishing it," I lie, staring at the picture of Spear, my tired body tingling at the scope of his leap, the strength in his arms and legs. "I'll fax it in no time."

I put the picture back in its envelope and dump it in a trash bag by the front door. There's nothing I can do for the big man, however great he may be. I have a pass to every locker room in the world. I walk among famous men I once dreamed of playing with. But the truth is, I'm not part of the game. I merely write about it. I'm a voyeur, fueled by the energy of formidable youth. I'm a phantom with opinions, nothing more.

I take a shower, change into my blackest clothing, and jog through the deepening gloom down to North Beach, to the steamy clatter and clutter of Cafe Trieste, a cheerful remnant of the fifties, a haven for latter-day hippies and the ghosts of the great Beat poets.

Here, in this time-warped cafe, they care nothing for basketball, so I feel safe to write whatever comes to mind.

> Fifteen years ago, I strode aboard this crazy paper
> ship and warned that we must beware the myth of the
> big man. Look at little Drake University running re-
> lentlessly on huge old UCLA with Lew Alcindor in
> the middle. Drake lost by a shot at the buzzer. Their
> tallest man was six-foot-five. Alcindor was seven-two.

I can't keep this up. I don't even like the game anymore. I gulp my milky java and drift back on the strains of Italian opera to when I was sixteen, five-foot-eight. I failed to make the varsity squad for the third year in a row, and five days after the final cuts, I developed a mysterious paralysis in my lower back that left me bedridden for the better part of a year. When I was finally able to walk again, it was with a pronounced limp and constant pain.

Suddenly, an old man at the next table shouts, "I met Whalen once! Party at Judy's. Fuckin' Philip Whalen. Meltzer was there, Lew Welch, *all* the guys who knew Kerouac." And now I'm seventeen, just getting comfortable with my cane, climbing onto the train with my friend Rico, heading to San Francisco for a monster poetry reading starring Allen Ginsberg, Michael McClure, Philip Whalen, David Meltzer, and Lew Welch.

We sat down in the dark cool of a little church in the Fillmore, and Rico pointed to a pale man with curly black hair sitting two rows in front of us. "It's Robert Duncan himself," he whispered reverently. "My god, my god."

"Who is he?"

"My favorite poet," said Rico, his eyes full of tears. "My numero uno hero."

"What did he write?"

" 'The temple of the animals has fallen into disrepair.' "

The lights dimmed. I took a deep breath and tried to clear my mind. Who was I? What would I become now that I couldn't play basketball? My parents wanted me to be a doctor, or failing that, a lawyer. I was singing in a rock band from hell, my antidote to screaming pain, but I had no illusions about making a living from that. And what about college? Sex? Money?

Michael McClure stepped into the spotlight, looking like Errol Flynn, dressed all in black leather. He leaned close to the microphone and crooned, "I've been hanging out at the zoo, talking to the lions. *Rrrrrr. Rahrr. Roar!*" All the women in the audience started moaning and growling, too. It was my first intimation of the sexual potential of poetry read aloud. I was psychically overwhelmed. And when the house lights came up a few glorious hours later, Ginsberg and Whalen and Meltzer and Welch having set down their drums, spent from their reading and singing and dancing and howling, I knew what I wanted to be. A poet.

I wanted to live in North Beach, to eat my meals at Mike's Pool Hall, to take buses and wear a beret and hitchhike into the wilderness. I wanted to publish six astounding books, each con-

taining seventy-seven truly great poems. I wanted lovers, lots of
lovers. I wanted a Turkish lover and a Swedish lover and a Mexi-
can lover and a young lover and an old lover and a black lover. I
wanted a rich lover. I wanted a lover who worked in a bakery. I
wanted a lover with long arms and a ring in her nose. I wanted to
grow marijuana in my attic under a geodesic skylight from seeds
sent to me by friends in Mexico and Lebanon and Thailand and
Los Angeles. I wanted to drink red wine and read poetry until
three in the morning in a pool hall on Broadway and have every
word be so crisp, so clear and true that all my lovers would cry
for joy, their tears laced with resin from my marijuana. And then
I'd lick their wet faces and get stoned out of my mind and write a
poem so charged with truth that all the poets who ever made
love in San Francisco would be resurrected and given one more
chance to write one last poem.

My reverie collapses in a clatter of dropped dishes, a tired
Italian woman groaning her apologies. The clock above the
espresso machine says midnight. I glance at how little I've written
—a few dozen words on a coffee-smudged page—and all I can
think of is Ruby's photograph of Spear and his masterful flight to
the hoop.

Which leads me to thoughts of Greta and pancakes on Saturday. Or will we call it off? Keep things as they are? We've been
eating lunch together at her desk every Tuesday for the last three
years, fat juicy sandwiches from Max's. She tells me about her
hiking adventures, and about her rambunctious cats, Oliver,
Stiggy, and Cisco. A black, a gray, and a brown, though I'm
never sure which is who or who is which.

I love to watch her talk. I love her face, her voice, her unpre-
dictable variety of expressions. I love following her around the
room with my eyes. She is so at ease in her body. She always
seems to be strolling along, never hurried. I think about her all
the time.

I wish I had more to tell her, but my column precludes nearly
everything but the business of basketball. I write, go to games,
schmooze with players and coaches, give radio interviews, travel,

all the while drinking far too much coffee and red wine. And I shoot hoops every chance I get, in the hope of staying minimally healthy so I can keep writing and drinking.

I fax my sloppy scribbles to Lucas from an all-night copy joint, hoping he'll be able to make some sense of them, and I am so discombobulated from lack of sleep, I get lost, though I've made this walk ten thousand times. I don't arrive home until two in the morning, chilled to the bone, still jittery from so much caffeine. I take a ton of vitamin C and climb into bed. But sleep won't come, so I stumble into the kitchen for a glass of wine, and on my way back to bed I see Ruby's envelope in the trash, and I can't bear to leave it there. So I carry it into my filthy bathroom and tell myself I'll give it one more look in the morning.

On the verge of sleep, I remember when I was four years old, and my nanny, a black woman named Mary who was old and heavy and sweet, would hold me in her arms for our afternoon nap in the rocking chair and I would fall into a delicious dream of walking with her in a forest draped with vines. We would be very quiet. We didn't want to scare the big red birds moving about in the trees. We communicated with secret smiles that only we knew the meaning of. I was black in this dream. Blacker than Mary.

4

 I am straining against a rope around my neck, trying to reach the forest. I look back to see who holds the rope, but it disappears around a hairpin curve. I rush down the road to confront my captor. The rope tightens and—

The front door slams, jarring me from my dream. The Bosley sisters have arrived. I lie on my back, void of energy, overwhelmed by the day ahead of me: A room-by-room consultation with the Bosleys. Three long telephone interviews. Lunch with seven-footer Cosmo Carter, the Warriors' number one draft pick. A Warriors-Phoenix exhibition game in the evening. And somewhere in there, I'll manage to drink several cups of coffee, visit my friendly neighborhood liquor store, and squeeze out another column about God knows what. Declining free-throw percentages as a symptom of moral decay?

I stagger into the bathroom and move Ruby's envelope onto the stack of magazines beside the toilet. I slap my face with cold water and stare into the mirror, not at all enamored of what I see. Time overtaking the last of my youth.

Mae brews a marvelously strong pot of coffee, and I dose

heavily before dialing Dallas, girding myself for twenty minutes of radio fisticuffs with Cody Simms, an extremely popular old sports commentator known for the precision of his insinuations.

"It must be weird to be famous, huh?" asks Mae, pausing on her way out with yet another bulging bag of garbage. "Thousands of people listening to you."

"And don't forget," I sigh, picking up the phone, "that most of them hate my guts."

My connection with Dallas is crystal clear, Cody's drawl particularly annoying to me this morning. "Hey, Vic, how y'all doin'? Lemme just ask you this. Seems like you been after the Warriors' coach fer at least five years now about him not *seerusly* wantin' to make a *seerus* move to get a big man. But yer column today was downright harsh. You got something persnal 'gainst coach Hathaway?"

"Personal?" I snap, barely able to suppress my contempt. "There's nothing the least bit personal about what I do. I'm a theoretician, a strategist. The Warriors are a fabulous collection of players. They win more games than they lose, but fold like picked poppies when they enter the play-offs. Why? They don't have a force in the middle. They lack the heart, if you will, to play the game at its highest level."

"But why be so vicious about it?"

"Vicious? What do you mean?"

"You call him, and I quote, 'a gargantuan fool, a man unable to transcend the fables of childhood into the painful truth of our present reality.' "

I panic. "Today? My column says that today?"

"Yes, indeed." He chuckles. "And that ain't the half of it."

I'm barely conscious through the rest of the program. He quotes my column at length, but I'm oblivious to the separate words, my mind filled with visions of Hathaway hunting me down and smashing me.

Interview over, I sit listlessly while Mae and Karen ransack the ruins around me. What have I done? How dare I preach to others when my own life is such a shambles?

Mae shuts off her vacuum cleaner. "What did you mean by 'a day care center for future geniuses'?"

"A what?"

"In your column today. You said the Warriors organization was 'a day care center for future geniuses who'"—she picks up the sports section—"'must always move elsewhere before making the leap into the artistry of dominance.'"

She frowns at the page. "I like the way it flows, though I'm not really sure what it means."

The phone rings. "Vic. Greta. Get down here. Pronto. Lucas is out of his mind. The phone hasn't stopped ringing since dawn. The boys upstairs are greatly displeased."

"Did you read my column? Was I too tough on him?"

"Tough? You slaughtered him. They should have run it in red ink. And what exactly *is* 'the artistry of dominance'?"

"Listen, I have two more radio shows to do, then I'll be down."

"Sooner the better."

I grab the sports section. There's that ancient photograph of me, my hair obscenely short, my smile pasted on. There's Lucas's stupid headline: Will the Season Be a Re-run? And there are those words I vaguely remember writing nine hours ago in the mocha warmth of Cafe Trieste, Puccini blasting from the jukebox.

> How long, I ask you, must we tolerate a man so inse-
> cure, so frightened of anyone greater than he, that he
> will not allow his team, his family, *our* family, to wed
> the giant who might liberate us from the fragile glitz
> of recurrent mediocrity.

I cancel my other interviews and grab a cab downtown, too crazed to take the bus. The city seems dismal, the clouds low and dirty. What have I done? Who the fuck do I think I am? I couldn't be ball boy to Hathaway.

Greta rises to greet me, her black hair piled high, her breasts uncaged in a silky red blouse, her lips lightly painted. "I still love you," she murmurs, handing me a wad of messages, "even if everyone else hates you."

"Why is that?" I snap, wishing I had the courage to kiss her.

"Because I know why you're unhappy." She moves closer, her voice dropping to a whisper. "And I want to help you."

Lucas barges out of his office before anything good can happen. "Vic. In here. Now."

"How uncharacteristically definitive of you," I quip, following him into an office slightly bigger than mine, with an actual view of the mess down on Mission. "I'm shocked."

"Shut up," he barks, pointing to a chair. "Just sit down and listen."

In all my years of writing for Lucas, he has never spoken to me with so much anger in his voice. He collapses behind his decrepit desk and runs a hand through the scattered remnants of his hair.

"Are you okay, Luke?"

"No, I am not okay. They want me to fire you. Happy?"

Fire me? *The* Vic Worsley? Fired? My heart starts pounding, but I feign bravado. "Who is they? Anybody I know?"

"Them," he says, pointing to the ceiling. "You went over the line this time. You slandered the man. They want you gone."

"And you?"

"I think maybe you need a change."

"To what?"

"Jesus, I don't know. I hate to lose you, Vic, but . . ."

"But what? Tell me. Honestly."

"Honestly?" He looks askance and takes a deep breath. "You don't love it anymore. You don't care about it like you used to. The humor is gone from your writing. Everybody's a villain now, or an idiot. Every player pales next to your hallowed ghosts. Elgin Baylor and Julius Erving and Jerry West are memories. People want to read about *now*. They want to be excited about *now*, about the people playing *now*. That's what we pay you for. To jazz us about *now*. Not to mourn the fairy-tale past, not to con-vince us that life is one big corrupt shithole. We get that from the front section. We don't need it in Sports. We need something to believe in, something tangibly good. Something that gives us hope and makes us itch to turn on a game. It used to be a hoot to read you. Now you just piss people off."

"I'm stunned, Lucas. I had no idea you could be so articulate."

"You never asked," he says, waving away my compliment. "You were too busy."

"Look," I say, hoping the damage isn't too great, "you're abso-lutely right. I went over the line. My life is a little out of control these days. To say the least. I'm sorry. How about if I write a humorous yet sensitive apology?"

"I doubt that'll do it." He shakes his head slowly. "But I'll tell you what. Have that lunch with Cosmo Carter, go to the game tonight, and write a piece that gives Hathaway back his dignity. He offered to resign as coach, you know. After reading your piece."

"Hathaway? Resign? The man's got skin as thick as a rhino."

He lights his half-smoked cigar. "Well, you finally got through. Isn't that what you wanted?"

"I don't know what I wanted. I don't even remember writing it."

"It was vicious," he says, turning away. "I'm ashamed I allowed it to run."

I can barely look at Greta as I emerge from Lucas's office. I feel like a six-year-old, spanked hard and kicked outside without breakfast.

She taps her calendar. "We're on for Saturday? Correct?"

"I'll call you," I mumble, afraid she'll see the fear in my eyes. "Gotta run."

"You won't call me," she says bitterly. "Why'd you say yes in the first place?"

"Look," I say, turning to her. "Why do you want to go out with me? I'm a nasty old sonofabitch. You could have anybody you want. Why waste your time with me?"

Her eyes widen in surprise. "God, Vic, maybe we shouldn't wait until Saturday. That's eons from now. What about tonight?"

"I'm going to the game. The bloody, goddamn, meaningless game."

"I'll come with you." She says it without the slightest question in her voice.

I deflate. "You *want* to?"

"I love basketball," she says, her cheeks flushing. "Always have."

"How could I have not known that?"

"Well, now you do." She scribbles her address on a Post-It and sticks it to my forehead. "See you tonight."

"I'll pick you up at six," I say, my sense of doom giving way to a glimmer of hope. "You may want to bring a pillow. The seats are rather hard."

I jog through the lunch-hungry throngs up Powell to Geary, the air a pungent mix of soy sauce and seafood, fresh-baked bread and sizzling beef and car exhaust. I hurry into Lefty O'Douls, a musty old baseball bar—the quintessential greasy smorgasbord. When I was a boy, my mother and I used to eat lunch at Lefty's before going to matinee musicals at the Curran Theater three doors down. In my teenage years, I switched my allegiance to David's, the Jewish deli across the street, but my subsequent immersion in sports brought me back to Lefty's, a cave of the ancient ballplayers.

Sitting at a table near the bar, the massive Cosmo Carter gorges on a mountain of mashed potatoes and fried chicken, while his tiny agent, Peter Leibowitz, sits beside him, pecking at a bowl of carrot slaw. Cosmo, huge and brown in a bone silk suit, waves me into a chair across from them, while Peter hails the cocktail waitress. The walls around us are festooned with photographs of the San Francisco Giants of my youth. Mays, McCovey, Marichal, Cepeda, Alou. I order a mug of winter wheat wine and wonder what I'll do if they let me go at the *Chron*. I don't have a clue. I have no concept of myself as anything other than a daily writer of sports blabber. It's all I do.

"First up," says Peter, jabbing at his salad, "we want to thank you for this morning's piece. Very pro us, we feel, though the truth is Cosmo would rather go to a team with a less hysterical offense."

"Something a bit easier on the knees?" I venture, amazed at the rapid diminution of Cosmo's food pile. "The Warriors do like to run."

Peter winces. "This has nothing to do with knees."

Cosmo glares. "There ain't nothin' wrong with my knees. I thought you were on *my* side."

"It's a super-fast game today," I say, relaxing into the jargon of our profession. "And even if you *could* find a team that likes more of a half-court set, you'd almost always be playing *against* a fast-break offense. Whoever signs you will need you back on defense to clog the middle. So either way the question is, are you still fast enough?"

"Easily," he says, handing his plate to Peter. "I'd like a bit more chicken, please."

I lean back to get a comprehensive view of the Warriors' great hope, his stomach bulging his shirt, his chin on the verge of doubling. It saddens me to look at him, to sense only injury and failure in his future. "You working out, Cosmo?"

"Every day." He sighs uneasily. "Jogging. Shootin' around at the gym."

"Would you enjoy playing for the Warriors?"

"If they pay me five million, I'll give 'em what they need."

"Who would you rather play for?"

"Look," he says, frowning with impatience. "I'm a bona fide big man. I can shoot, pass, bound, and block shots. I did it two years in Europe, I can do it seven, eight years in the NBA. I come to play. That's my job. But I'm not taking less than somebody worse than me. *That's* the bottom line."

"Do you still love the game?"

He glares at me. "Whoever said you had to love something to be good at it?"

"Of course he still loves the game," says Peter, placing another heaping plate before Cosmo. "And he loves to win."

"What do you love most about it?"

"This," says Cosmo, holding a chicken leg aloft. "And that." He points to a sexy babe in a micro-mini at the bar, applying a fresh coat of hot pink to her grim little lips.

"I can identify," I say, admiring the shape of her legs, the fit of her blouse, "but I mean the game itself."

"What I love about the game itself," says Cosmo, his voice deepening, "is when that buzzer goes off and nobody's pounding on me, nobody's trying to stick his finger in my eye, nobody's ramming my balls with his knee, and I can take a long shower and put on some fine clothes and get to a soft place with some fine women." He fastidiously dabs the corners of his mouth with his napkin. "And now if you'll excuse me, I'm gonna make a date with this lady right here."

Peter swallows anxiously as his first possible multimillion-dollar deal crosses the room and bows to the whore at the bar. "You know her, Vic?" he asks, keeping his eyes on Cosmo. "She a hooker?"

"She's Aphrodite of the sports bar," I reply, watching Cosmo's knees. "But he still better wear a condom."

"I want him signed," says Peter, his voice cracking. "We have to sign soon."

"Or what?"

"Or we'll lose a year."

"A year he might not come back from."

"Don't write that," he says breathlessly. "Please don't write that."

"Why not take the two-point-seven million they offered? Decent chunk of change. It's two-point-six-five more than I make, or made, as the case may be. Your take would be a million at least. Nothing wrong with that."

"Two-point-seven is nothing," he scoffs. "But if you were to write something that made him seem, I don't know, heroic or something, and we sign for something over four, well, I think you'd be nicely surprised by what comes in the mail."

"He *is* heroic." I nod, watching Cosmo slip his huge hand around the tiny woman's waist. "He's a gladiator."

"Yeah," says Peter, gritting his teeth. "I like the sound of that."

I walk home, traversing Chinatown and North Beach, stopping on the edge of Washington Square to listen to a blind violinist play melancholy airs for pigeons and the likes of me. A slender woman with straight brown hair fumbles in her purse for change, and for a moment I think she's Emily, my ex-wife. And though I'm greatly relieved to discover it's *not* Emily, I think about her all the way home.

I had just bought the house, my dream nest on a quiet street high above the bay. I was thirty years old, my confidence growing with every fifteen hundred words I wrote. I was dating a relatively sane woman for the first time in my life and crafting a novel about a Chinese psychiatrist turned detective and his sidekick, an old cartoonist named Grimes. It was that legendary year the Warriors took their first NBA crown, and did so with surprising ease. All the pundits were dumbfounded, save for yours truly, the upstart rookie at the *Chron*.

My dazzling date, Daphne, and I were blissfully drunk in a snazzy Italian joint in North Beach, the place overflowing with local literati, the air dense with the scents of garlic and olive oil and wine. I was waxing eloquent about Charlie Johnson bouncing a pass off the back of Kareem Abdul-Jabbar's head into the hands of Rick Barry for a glass-kissing winner, when I noticed my audi-

ence had grown to include the adjoining table of tall and gregarious women. They were the starters for the Brazen Bombers, a
women's basketball team celebrating their seventy-fifth straight
victory. When Daphne departed for the bathroom, I found myself in a heaven of female jocks, whose passion for basketball was
wildly appealing to me. When they invited me to their next
game, I was doomed.

The Bombers were a stunning team with a shallow bench.
Their starting five were breathtaking to behold. Their passes
were sharp and impeccably timed. Their shot choices were daring yet astute. And their swarming defense was a thing of fright-
ening beauty. They played the game with such obvious joy, I fell
madly in love with all of them.

As the second half commenced, three of the starters sat down
and three bench players entered the game. Two of them could do
little more than run the court and play adequate defense, but the
third was a rare talent, a slender young woman with a preternatu-
ral instinct for rebounding. Her stamina was not great, so she
only played for six or seven minutes, but during that time she
simply *owned* the boards at both ends of the court. She shot six
foul shots with such painful awkwardness it was difficult to
watch, and she ran the court as if mistrustful of her legs. But
when a shot was missed, she was there to vacuum up the
ball. This was Emily, and she was pointedly disinterested in me
until I started dating Jessie, the Bombers' six-foot power forward.

I'll never forget my first one-on-one game with Jessie. I'd
never played with a woman so physically strong and quick. If not
for my long-range jumpers, she would have beaten me with ease.
She was thrilled to discover I could shoot, overjoyed to become
my friend and lover, and if Emily hadn't pursued me with such
deft ferocity, I might have married the tallest woman I've ever
loved.

But I had no defense against Emily. She materialized at my

door one sultry afternoon, just a few days after Jessie and I had broached the subject of marriage. I even remember the dress Emily wore that day, diaphanous and faintly yellow, her lightly freckled skin flushed with a rosy glow, her every joint loose for love. We drank a bottle of wine, and as I poured the last drops into her glass, she smiled sadly and said, "Now I'm gonna make love to you, Vic. Until we both want to die."

5

Late afternoon. I enter my home and freeze in disbelief. Am I in the wrong place? No. I remember it looking something like this when I bought it—spacious and airy and light—and again when Emily moved out. A year after that, I hired Nolan's wife, Esther, to decorate it, and she came up with an English antique scheme that eventually drove me insane with discomfort, which led to the futon and Navajo rug in every room, an epoch culminating with a large poster tacked crudely to my salsa splattered living room wall. It was an exquisite color photograph of a nearly naked Brazilian woman kneeling on the beach in Rio. I stared at her day and night for years and years. Until today, my house was filled to bursting with all the things I haven't been able to throw away for seven years. But now it is nearly empty, and I am awestruck by how huge it is.

I float through my palatial living room into my spotless kitchen. Voluptuous red gladioli erupt from a clear glass vase atop a vast expanse of sparkling turquoise tile. My exhausted refrigerator has been replaced by a gleaming two-door model full of beer and vegetables and neatly organized condiments. My knives glisten on the magnetic rack above the well-scrubbed butcher block. My stove shines like new, daring me to cook again.

"Hello?" I call, wandering into my dining room, the vast walnut table cleared of all but one exquisite jade bowl sitting perfectly alone in the center of it. "Anybody here?"

My bedroom looks like something out of *Architectural Digest*, the bed freshly made, my down comforter all fluffy and white, the windows so clean they're invisible. Prints of two small abstracts by Miró share the wall above the bed, facing a large and mostly blue painting, "Gateway to the Pleasure Bump," by William Yates, a piece I forgot I owned.

There are more flowers in the bathroom, yellow dahlias in a slender black vase, their beauty doubled by the crystal clear mirror. The one little window that's been stuck shut for a decade is now open, admitting the sweet scent of jasmine, and I can't help but say aloud to my perfectly reflected self, "These Bosleys are really something."

I move to the guest room, previously a depository for mountains of old furniture and boxes of never-used stuff. It is now clean and open and welcoming, a framed poster of Picasso's "Three Musicians" centered on the wall above the bed.

Finally, I step into my office, a room I have rarely visited since Emily left, it being the storage dump for the more personal artifacts of my marital and literary catastrophes. But the Bosleys have worked their magic here, too. The clutter has been supplanted by space. My ancient electric typewriter sits alone on its dark teak desk, presiding over a dazzling view down onto the city. The books on my bookshelves have been dusted and alphabetized. And on my once-beloved writing table sits a blue bowl brimming with pink geraniums, a note from Mae beside it.

Dear Vic,

I was going to leave this communiqué for you in the kitchen, but something told me to leave it here. After you rushed off this morning, Karen and I had a conference. We were both feeling depressed and overwhelmed by the mess, not so much for its depth, but for its breadth and depth, and I had the sense that the sooner we were finished, the better it would be for you. (Housecleaning requires more intuition and empathy than most people realize.) So we decided to call in our auxiliary forces and blitz the place, figuring you were paying by the hour anyway, right? (We know oodles of hardworking women looking for extra moolah.)

Given the density of dirt and disarray, we put two people on each room, and two on the outside windows. Karen did the floors and carpets. You will find attached a separate receipt for the dry cleaning of drapes, comforters, and Navajo blankets. As our teams finished cleaning the various rooms (the bathrooms were shocking), we converged on the kitchen. At one point, we had nine people in there, scrubbing and washing and organizing. If you have any trouble locating a particular item, please give a call.

Stuff we weren't sure you wanted to keep or throw away, we put in your garage, which we also cleaned and organized. You have the makings for an outrageously successful garage sale, not to mention a kitchen fit for a gourmet. Such great knives (I sharpened them) and a six-burner stove. Great spice rack! Karen said she didn't peg you as a cook, but I believe you are. Or were.

A word of advice. Deep cleaning like this can totally alter a person's life. Don't panic. Eventually you will come to appreciate how this openness makes you feel. If you can afford it, I'd love to paint your interior walls a soft white, the trim a light gray. I'm in love with your house, and I commend you for throwing off the yoke of

*your junk. Thanks for thinking of the Bosleys. It would be
our pleasure to implement a regular schedule of mainte-
nance for your home and garden. Invoice attached.*

Affectionately,
Mae Bosley

*P.S. Any questions, ideas, or a burning desire to see me
again, please don't hesitate to phone or fax.*

I call her immediately. How could I not? "You're a genius," I
say, delighting in the lyric ambience of the living room. "I love
this Matisse over the fireplace. And the kitchen! My God, it's
amazing. I feel like I've been let out of jail or something. I'm
reeling in all this open space."

"So, *are* you a cook, Vic?" she asks, sounding rather tired.
"Karen says no. I say yes."

"I am, yes," I admit, feeling rather daring to say so. "As a
matter of fact, I'm a good cook."

"I'll bet you are." She yawns. "Listen, Vic, I'd love to talk some
more, but I've gotta go to bed. I'm pretty burnt. I'm glad you
appreciate what we did."

"I'd like to make dinner for you sometime," I blurt. "To thank
you."

"Tomorrow night?" she asks, perking up. "What will you
make?"

"A splendid chicken," I brag, my fingers itching to dice and
slice. "A salad, of course."

"I'll bring wine," she says, warming to the idea. "Having pe-
rused your collection of empty bottles, I know just the kind you
like."

I hang up the phone and wander into my bedroom, dizzy
with joy. After seven years of agonizing aloneness, I'm suddenly
about to date not one, but two delightful women with large vo-

cabularies. "Incredible," I say, flopping down onto the bed. "In one fell swoop, the Bosleys have changed everything."

I take off my shoes and gaze out the French door at more flowers from Mae, purple and yellow chrysanthemums planted in the large Romanesque urns that in the days of Emily overflowed with alyssum and pale blue lobelia, when I was sadder than I have ever been.

We are here on this bed, making love until we are too weary to move. We are here on this bed, and she is confessing her latest betrayal of me. She stands in the doorway to my office, shouting at me, calling me a coward and a fraud. I am lying alone in this bed, waiting for her to come home from yet another rendezvous with yet another lover. We are in the living room. She is weeping as I forgive her again and again. I am in my office, writing with fabulous fury, my novel pouring from my pen, the mystery nearly solved, when Emily cries, "Help me!" and I run down the hallway to the kitchen. She's leaning against the fridge, dark blood dripping from her wrists, an odd little smile on her weary face. As I apply the tourniquets, she murmurs, "You should let me die, Vic. I can't stay true to you. I've slept with so many more men than I've ever told you about. I'm not worthy of you. You deserve someone better than me. You shouldn't have to suffer anymore because of me. You deserve someone who'll love you. Just you."

In my luminous bathroom, the old broken showerhead replaced by a shiny new one, I recall my time in therapy following Emily's recovery and departure, how everything seemed so obvious and clear, the phraseology of addict and codependent so perfectly apt. Yet I was adamant in my refusal to join a support group or use antidepressants. For though Emily was certainly addicted to adultery, to the thrill and shame of illicit sex, I was every bit as addicted to my work and the habits that supported it, none of which was I prepared to give up.

" 'Deep cleaning like this can totally alter a person's life,' " I quote, frowning at myself in the mirror, my face freshly shaven. "Maybe I'll move to Oregon. Write poetry amidst the blackberries. Grow my own garlic."

I don my game disguise of heavy black-rimmed glasses, a

black beret, black T-shirt, old leather jacket, baggy brown pants, gray running shoes. I carry a cane, a vestige of my limping days, now a bit of protection on the streets at night. I am, by my attire at least, the bleak bohemian I always wanted to be. I am rarely recognized when I dress this way, and that's just the way I like it.

The 24 Divisadero carries me along its electric wires into the Fillmore and the Haight, rolling through old neighborhoods I haunted before going off to college, limping along those hippie-clogged streets, living out the last days of the sixties before we fell to the Reaganites, our dreams of communal life choked to death by greed and fear.

Then it was off to college, where I majored in anthropology. I grew a beard and smoked a pipe and wrote anguished poetry and rarely attended classes. I pretended to be Jack Kerouac, cradled by the pastel privilege of college, so safe and unreal. My limp and my scowl kept most people away from me. I was so lonely, I would often type novella-length letters to Rico back home, describing my life as one continuously wild adventure, when in truth, I did little more than read and write.

Then one day at the start of my sophomore year, a goofy-looking young man with extremely short hair and enormous ears stuck his head inside my dorm room and said, "Hi. I'm Nolan. We need a fifth for the dorm team. You play basketball?"

"I'm crippled," I replied, puffing on my pipe. "I have a terrible limp."

"Sorry," he said, shrugging politely. "I thought I saw you shooting free throws at the gym yesterday."

"You probably did. But that's about all I'm good for."

"It's just that we need five guys to show up tonight, or we can't sign up for the league. You don't actually have to play. I can add other players to the team later." He looked at his watch. "It's like in ten minutes at the field house. There's nobody else around. Please?"

So I hobbled down to the gym with Nolan and three other guys, and we signed up for the dorm league. I was on my way out, crossing the court, when a basketball bounced up to me. I caught it and shot in one fluid motion, the ball passing cleanly through the hoop from twenty feet away. And in that moment, the pain I had lived with day and night for three years began to slip away.

"Nice shot," said Nolan, bouncing his eyebrows like Groucho Marx. "You don't look like you have much of a limp to me."

On my way back to the dorm that night, bursting with self-confidence, I boldly flirted with a woman I'd been afraid to approach, and the very next night she took me to bed. She was the first woman I ever made love to, and the first girl I'd kissed since the onset of my paralysis.

Despite my promising introduction to the casual sex of those bygone days, I soon found myself embroiled in a monogamous relationship with a woman who felt that sexual intercourse was, for the most part, a repressive tactic of the patriarchy. Finding little physical outlet there, I became a Frisbee fanatic. When I wasn't shooting hoops or writing cliché-clogged short stories, I was going alone to the windy meadows to bank my platter off the backboard of the sky.

The woman I loved was not, alas, my girlfriend. She taught modern dance in the gym where I played ball. She would hang around after her class, watching us play, and the night I was too stupid to go to bed with her, she confessed in her wonderfully candid way that *I* was the reason she stayed to watch. Why didn't I make love to her? She was so girlish and sexy, it must have been the *idea* of her I couldn't give myself to. She had wrinkles at the corners of her eyes. She was older than I ever imagined being.

Greta lives in a cheerful Victorian on 24th Street, just up from Dolores in a barrio known for its vivid blend of races and sexual proclivities. An enclave of human exotics. I ring the bell and

Greta answers, looking adorable in tight blue jeans and a soft fuchsia sweater, a turquoise beret fit snugly over her thick black hair.

"Yes?" she says tentatively. "May I help you?"

"Hi," I say, smiling nervously. "You look positively edible."

She's incredulous. "Vic? God, I didn't recognize you."

"It's my game disguise. You really didn't know me?"

"No," she says, struggling to smile. "You want to come in?"

"Sure, we've got some time."

Her home is warm and smells of cinnamon. The wallpaper in the hall is a faded pinkish paisley. I follow her into a brightly lit kitchen where two women in white caftans are eating sourdough French bread and drinking red wine.

"Sheila," says Greta, gesturing to an extremely tall brown woman wearing a brilliant pink bandana, "and Lisa," a fine-boned beauty with snow white hair and pale, translucent skin. "This is Vic."

"Hello," says Sheila, raising her glass to me. "You don't look anything like your picture."

"He's in disguise," says Greta, betraying her disappointment. "You want some wine, Vic?"

"Yes, please." I smile curiously at Sheila. "I know you, don't I?"

"Long ago," says Sheila, sipping her wine. "Shall I tell him?"

Greta hands me a brimming glass. "You might as well, or he'll be thinking about it all night."

"Shall I rip you a little bread?" asks Lisa, giving me a most alluring smile. "I made it this morning. Goes fantastically well with this wine."

"I'd love some," I say, frowning at Sheila, trying to place her on one of the great women's teams of the past. "Did you play in the Olympics?"

"Oh, just tell him," says Greta, sounding a bit annoyed. "He'll never guess."

"I'll give you a hint," says Sheila, reaching across the table to clink glasses with me. "You wrote a column about me once."

I freeze. It can't be. My God, it is. Only then she was a he. Lorenzo Considine. One of the greatest college players of all time. "Lorenzo?"

"You got it," she sighs. "But now I'm Sheila, through and through."

"I like your disguise, Vic," says Lisa, handing me a chunk of bread. "The cane is a lovely touch."

"I wish he'd told me," says Greta, gulping her wine. "I'd have worn way more black."

"We've got time," I say, feeling like a cad. "If you'd like to change."

"No, no, you look great together," says Sheila, pouring Greta another glass. "The contrast is brilliant."

"Try trading berets," says Lisa, jumping up to help us make the switch. "I think it'll balance things perfectly."

"This is silly," says Greta, obviously more upset than I'd realized. "It doesn't matter."

"Oh, come on," says Lisa, removing Greta's beret. "Humor me."

Our hats switched, Sheila claps her hands. "Stunning. You look like you've been married for twenty years."

"Don't I wish," I say, putting my arm around Greta.

"God, you look good together," says Lisa, stepping back to appraise us. "Hold on while I get my camera."

"Stop," says Greta, blushing. "I feel like I'm in high school."

"You won't regret it," says Lisa, skipping down the hall. "Years from now, you'll thank me for this."

"To your first date," says Sheila, rising to make a toast. "May it be full of truth."

"They never said that in high school," I say, looking at Greta, loving her more than all my high school crushes put together.

"But take off your glasses, okay?" she whispers, pressing closer. "At least for the picture."

6

We are seventeen rows from courtside, centered, tip-off moments away. Greta gazes around at the dazzle of the Coliseum, the cavernous temple of the Warriors. The plush chairs are filled with rich people and friends of the players dressed to the nines. The blue-collar guys and their babes or their kids crowd the plastic seats high above us. She nudges me. "We are seriously underdressed for this section, Vic. I haven't seen this much flash since my disco days."

"We can move," I say, hoping to please her. "I've never actually cared about what other people were wearing. But if you'd like to sit in the cheap seats, it's no trouble. I watch all my Chicago and Detroit games from up there. The energy is amazing."

"No, these are fine. Just next time I'll want to wear a dress." She leans close, whispering in my ear. "I've seen this woman next to me in the *movies*. Swear to god."

"What fun it is to be here with you." I peer down at my game program, feeling as shy as a boy on his very first date. "What fun to think of this as fun."

"You played on your college team, didn't you?" she asks, sipping her beer. "Wasn't that fun?"

"It was no big deal," I say, embarrassed to be speaking of my puny career within earshot of the pros. "The coach saw me playing in the dorm league, and because I could hit from outside, he asked me to play on the college team. But we were just a tiny school. We weren't part of any official league. We played against Bible schools and junior colleges and teams from the local industrial league. Pretty pathetic stuff, really."

"Were you the star?" She sighs in mock adoration. "Did you score a million points?"

"Not a million," I whisper, enjoying her teasing. "Though I *was* known for my shooting. Occasionally some lesser geeks would seek me out for tips, and I'd always start by telling them that two basketballs can fit side by side through the hoop, but they almost *never* believed me."

She ponders this for a moment, watching the players take their warm-up shots. "From here it looks like *one* barely fits."

"But two can," I say, warming to my subject. "I discovered this when I was twelve years old. My father was putting up a backboard and hoop for me. I had a new ball and a neighbor came by with his old one. The hoop was lying on the ground. Both balls fit."

She shakes her head. "I wish they'd told me that in school. I might have been a better shot."

"Probably," I say, remembering those first few buckets I made on my driveway court, the ball kissing cleanly through. "It can make a huge difference to know the size relationship between the ball and the hoop. For most people, it immediately improves their shooting. But for others the knowledge can be crippling, a retroactive amplification of their ineptitude."

"Sounds like a column, Vic." She leans her shoulder against mine. "Better write that down before you forget it."

I laugh at a sudden memory. "One guy became so furious when I told him, he shoved me and stalked out of the gym. Later that day, I heard he was telling everybody I was a cocky sonofabitch. So that night in the cafeteria I just walked up to him and said, 'Do you have a problem with me?' And he stood up and screamed, 'Listen, everybody! Listen to what this asshole told me!' So with three hundred college kids staring at me, I shouted, 'Two basketballs can fit through a basketball hoop at the same time!' Moments later, a hundred of us were swarming down the hill to the field house, someone brought a ladder and two balls, and I climbed to the rim and revealed the awful truth. I'll never forget that poor guy looking up at me, stuttering his apology."

"Maybe it was the way you told him," she says, nudging me. "The information itself isn't exactly earth shattering."

"You're probably right. I was not a very humble soul."

She sips her beer and studies me for a moment. "I'm glad we finally got to go out, Vic. Or do you use an alias when you're in disguise?"

"Vic is fine," I say, taking her hand.

"Tell me more," she says as the starters come onto the wood. "Tell me more basketball secrets."

"Well," I say, pleased to find her so curious, "it's a little-known fact, but for the first forty years of basketball, *every* time somebody made a basket, they stopped play and had a jump ball at center court. *Every* time. Big yawns. Then some genius decided to eliminate all but the first jump of each half, and the game became infinitely more fluid and exciting. And when the shot clock was introduced, giving each team a mere twenty-four seconds to get off a shot, basketball came into its own as the quintessential athletic metaphor for contemporary culture."

"Which is?"

"A roaring river of change."

She offers me a sip of her beer. "You're a poet, Vic, but I won't tell anybody."

As play begins, I am struck anew by the ferocious power of the game. And as always, I wish I were down there with them, eluding my defender, taking a pass, launching my shot. It's such a magnificent game. Not a metaphor at all.

. . .

"Why so many fouls?" asks Greta, sitting back at the end of the first quarter. "The game never got going."

"Several factors," I say, trying not to be *too* much of a know-it-all. "Exhibition season involves a great deal of testing. Rookies test themselves against the older pros to see how much they can get away with, while the slower players tend to cheat with sneaky fouls. Meanwhile, the officials are busy establishing tolerable levels of brutality. In this particular game, neither team has yet fused into a cohesive whole, so a certain every-man-for-himself tone has dominated so far."

"What happens next?" She sounds slightly disinterested. "More of the same?"

"For the second quarter, yes. Flashes of brilliance in the third. An actual game, of sorts, in the fourth."

She feigns a yawn. "Any surprises?"

"Thurman. This rookie forward for the Warriors, number five. Very strong and confident. Moves well without the ball. But the question remains. Can he shoot?"

"He made those two in close. Remember?"

"But outside? That's the big question."

"Time will tell." She pats my knee. "The season is just beginning."

"I wish I'd known you liked basketball. I would have invited you a hundred times before this."

She stretches her lovely arms. "Don't worry about it. I'm just now starting to understand it, though I am getting a little bit bored with this particular game. You?"

"We could leave," I say, surprising myself. "I've seen enough."

"Good." She grabs her satchel. "Let's go to your house, okay? There's something I've been wanting to talk to you about for a long time now."

"My house is a bit of a mess," I say, relishing the lie. "But then whose house isn't a bit messy now and then?"

· · ·

We jump on a fast train back to the city, my grand apology to coach Hathaway forming itself in my mind. I glance at Greta. Her eyes are closed, tears on her cheeks.

"You okay?"

She nods. "Got grabbed by a bad memory. Be over soon."

"Mind if I do a little writing?"

"No. Go ahead. I'm fine."

I whip out my notebook and the words leap from my pen.

It was absurd and wrong of me to criticize coach Hathaway in the way that I did. I was a blind man feeling the side of an elephant, declaring it a wall. Was it only last night I wrote those angry words about him, those sentences dense with judgment? Yes. But in the intervening hours, my appreciation for Hathaway has risen from the ashes of cynicism. I have supped with the unsigned giant Cosmo Carter and glimpsed the fluid alchemy of Michael Thurman. My love of the game has been rekindled.

How can anyone comprehend the perils of coaching without experiencing those perils firsthand? Hathaway must navigate the treacherous waters of high finance simply to reach the *starting* point of men and balls and hoops, and once there, his every shout, his every choice is scrutinized by men largely un-tested in his field of mastery, myself among them.

It is time for me to return to my beginnings, to those facets of the game I know best, to sing the praises of players improvising brilliantly within the strictures of an ever-evolving ritual, not to wallow in the mire of dollars and cents. I must do all I can to

unearth the magic of the game that captured my
heart so long ago.

I open the door to my castle, astonished anew that it belongs
to me. "Welcome to my humble abode," I proclaim, turning on
the lights. "Such as it is."

"Wow," says Greta, stopping in the doorway. "This is very
nice, Vic. I didn't picture it like this at all. So open."

"Take a peek around," I say, resisting the habit of dropping
my jacket on the floor. "I'll just check my messages."

"May I wander freely?"

"Please. But do forgive the mess."

There is only one call for me. "Vic. It's Lucas. Listen. Don't
send a column. It's official. You're gone. Sorry. I told them you
were going to apologize, but they said 'no dice.' Sorry. Good
luck."

I turn off my machine and I'm sixteen again, walking through
the locker room, tired beyond telling, my scrimmage stats better
than all but a few returning stars. I stop at the coach's door and
scan the names of those who made the team. My name is not
there. My name is missing. How can this be? Boys who cannot
shoot as well, boys who cannot stop me from scoring, boys who
cannot jump as high or run as fast, their names are there. Mine is
not. Where is my name? How can it not be there?

I burn with a sudden fever, reading the list from top to bottom, bottom to top. I am not there. Someone touches my hand. I
turn, expecting the coach to reach over my shoulder and write
my name at the top of the list, but it's Greta.

"Hey good lookin' " she says, touching my cheek. "How about
we get you out of that disguise?"

"They let me go," I say, my throat as dry as a bone. "I'm gone."

She leads me into the living room, the silence deafening. "It's
gonna be okay," she says, releasing me. "You want a glass of wine?
A cup of tea?"

"I'll start a fire," I say, kneeling on the hearth, my eyes aching, my head throbbing. "I'm not sure where anything is. The Bosleys changed everything. In the kitchen probably."

"I'll get us some wine," she says, leaving me to myself. "You make that fire."

I strike the match and hold it beneath the little tepee of twigs. The fire springs to life so quickly I barely pull my hand away in time. I add a few larger sticks, and finally a good log. There. It's going. Now what?

7

 Greta stands in the center of my living room, arms crossed, nodding her approval. "This is a most exquisite pad, Vic. The kitchen is to die for. And that view from your office is stunning. Must have cost you a fortune."

"I wonder how I'll feel not being in the daily news," I say, poking at the fledgling fire. "I was twenty-nine when I landed the job. I've written over five thousand columns. I can't imagine what else I could do."

"You want to smoke a little weed?"

"Pot? I haven't smoked in fifteen years."

She kneels beside me and slips her arm around my waist. "I have some wonderful herb. A good friend grows it in a valley near the coast."

"A valley filled with hummingbirds?" I ask, gripped with nostalgia for the job I've so recently lost. "Is it like heaven? Jammed with joy?"

"Yes," she says, opening a silver locket filled with glistening resin. "There are owls there, too. I'm kind of an owl person. They like to come around me whenever I'm in the woods. And two nights ago, one came into our garden here in the city."

"What did it do?" I ask, admiring how free of conceit she is.

"He sat in the plum tree and screeched up at my window until I leaned out to say hello. Then he circled the garden twice and flew off to the east."

"What do you think that means? That you should take two trips to Nevada?"

"The east is the place of new beginnings," she says, ignoring my jest. "So as he was flying away, I thought to myself, I'm gonna try again with Vic. No matter what he says, I'm gonna trust that he wants to spend more time with me. That's what I think the owl meant."

"How brave of you," I say, ashamed of myself for doubting her. "I thought maybe you were inspired by Ruby. The old lady with the photograph."

Greta retreats to my futon. "Oh, she helped. She showed me how to do it. Just don't take no for an answer."

The fire crackles and pops. I stay on my knees, watching the flames. I want to rejoice with her, but I'm numb with regret. Why? I hated my job. It's good I lost it. Yet I feel empty without it.

As the fire roars into fullness, I join Greta on the futon. "Now, don't laugh," she says, flashing me a smile, "but I'm gonna make a prayer. It's the way my grandmother taught me to use a pipe. No matter what you're smoking."

"Your Indian grandmother?"

"Grandma Tyler," she says, holding the pipe against her heart. "She was half-Wintu, half-Maidu. Funny old gal. You would have liked her. She said to think of the pipe as a telephone to the spirit world, the smoke going both ways. So I give thanks to the Great Spirit for allowing me to be here with you. Getting a chance to know you better." She hands the pipe to me. "Now you add a prayer."

I take the pipe and hold it against my heart, and I see my father's face, his mouth crooked with disdain. I shake my head and hand the pipe back to her. "I'm not big on praying. I was sort of ridiculed for doing it when I was little, though I suppose I could pray to get my job back, couldn't I?"

She strikes a match and holds it over the bud. "Whatever you want. This will definitely help you think about it."

She tokes deeply and passes the pipe to me. I bring it to my lips with some trepidation, recalling why I stopped smoking. Fifteen years ago, I made a vow to myself that if I got the job at the *Chron*, I would never smoke again. What better way to celebrate my termination? The honeyed smoke fills my lungs, and my brain switches lobes immediately.

A long-repressed memory grips me—my mother's spirit appearing in my bedroom at the moment of her death. I can see her so clearly, her eyes full of a fierce determination to live again. And something in her gaze launches me from the futon and down my hallway, chasing a vision of a huge black man flying through the air to the hoop. But Ruby's envelope is no longer in my bathroom where chaos once reigned. The magazine rack holds only a single issue of *Tricycle*, the one I picked up in a used bookstore because it was full of poems by Philip Whalen. The Dalai Lama winks at me from the cover and that sends me rushing to the phone in the kitchen. On the way I notice Greta kneeling by the fire and I'm overwhelmed with shame at how rude I've been to abandon her.

She waves me away before I even begin to apologize. "Don't worry about it, Vic. Make your phone call. Do what you have to do. I'm not offended. Same thing happens to me. The most important idea always rushes to the top."

"I won't be long."

"Take your time. I'm having all sorts of productive thoughts."

I laugh hysterically, the room pulsing as I walk to the phone. The floor is alive, the fire thunderous. Greta rummages in her satchel, sounding like a beast in the bushes.

"Yes," I say into the phone, astounded that such a miraculous apparatus exists. "San Francisco. The Bosley Sisters, House Cleaners Extraordinaire. Would you dial for me, please?"

Seven electronic tones sing a funny little song, followed by three crisp rings, which I inadvertently name Greta, Ruby, and Spear.

"Bosleys'. Mae speaking."

"Mae," I effuse, relieved to hear her voice. "Vic Worsley. Hello."

"Vic. Hi." She yawns. "What's up? Something good I hope."

"Oh, it's just . . . I can't find an envelope. Big one. It was in my bathroom. I wonder where you put it."

"Your office, probably." She sounds quite concerned. "I'm sure we didn't throw anything important out. Did you look in your office? Top right-hand drawer?"

"Thanks," I say, feeling oddly deceitful to be speaking to her with Greta nearby. I know I haven't done anything wrong, yet I feel adulterous. "That must be where it is."

"Are you okay?"

"I'm fine. I'm just a little high. I lost my job today."

"Want me to come over? I'm not doing anything right now. I'd be happy to."

"God, what a sweet offer, but no, I'm . . ."

"With somebody else."

"I really don't think that's any of your business," I snap, surprised by the venom in my voice. "Do you?"

"I'm sorry. That was stupid of me. I feel like an idiot. And now you definitely want to cancel, right? Please don't lie to me. I was *so* looking forward to it."

"Mae, you sound exactly like my ex-wife. Exactly. And you're right. I *do* want to cancel."

"Better this way," she says curtly. "Never a good idea to get emotionally entangled with a client. See ya."

I stay rooted in place, disbelieving the dial tone, expecting her to jump back on the line to drag out the misery. But there's only silence, into which tumbles the saddest of thoughts. *"One down, one to go."*

Greta calls from the sofa, holding aloft a bottle of wine. "Come have some of this pinot noir. It's divine."

"Good idea." I hang up the phone and the weight of Mae lifts from my shoulders. "Throat's so dry."

She pours me a full glass of the dark red wine, saying, "You know, don't you, that I wore dresses just for you? Almost every Tuesday. For three long years. The only day of the week I did. I always felt so daring and regressive at the same time. And I know you liked it. So how come you never called me?"

"I am often a coward," I say, feeling an old pain in my sternum, catching a glimpse of my father's snarling face. "Mostly I didn't think I was good enough for you, if you'll forgive the cliché."

"You're fine, Vic. These things take as long as they take. I know all about that."

"You must have men throwing themselves at you."

"Nope," she says, sitting up straight. "Let's make some food. I'm ravenous."

"Great idea," I say, stirred by thoughts of pasta. "I know just the sauce."

"What if we'd stayed for the whole game?" she asks, following me into the kitchen. "Were you still planning to bring me here? You were, weren't you? You wolf, you."

"I hardly qualify as a wolf," I say, watching her move about the sparkling room, her big eyes full of promise. "I got things only just in case."

"A likely story." She growls sweetly. "Just as you planned it, I'm sure."

I fidget with the dahlias in their blue vase beside my spacious cutting board. "Flowers, flowers. I love flowers," I say, selecting the largest of my freshly sharpened chopping knives.

"I never would have predicted this," she says, perplexed by the jazzy togetherness of my home. "I had you more debauched. Piles of wine bottles in every corner. That sort of thing."

"The secret to happy living is in deep cleaning," I proclaim, my skillet growing hot. "Every seven years, whether the place needs it or not, I hire an army of heavily muscled women to deal with my dirt."

"And the cooking," she says, admiring my finesse with onions. "I had you pegged as a Chinese takeout kinda guy. In front of the tube when you weren't on the road."

"I've never been much of a television watcher," I say, dicing a pile of ginger. "I prefer my basketball live and without advertisements. Besides, I've never really had time for television. Too much to do. Too much to write. Too afraid to call you. Certain you'd say no."

"Vino?" She arches an eyebrow. "How does that poem go? A cup of wine, a loaf of bread, and thou. Ah, wilderness, enough for us now. Until I can get you to go camping with me."

"You'll find wine in most any cupboard," I say, admitting the truth. "I will leave the choice of our second bottle to you."

She bows gracefully. "You like my cowboy boots? They hurt my feet, but I love how they look."

"I love how you look and smell and think. And for all of that, I dedicate this meal to you."

"Which recipe?" she asks, taking down an eight-year-old cabernet with a monster finish. "Or should I say, which noodle? And where's your wine opener?"

"I have no idea. I have yet to acquaint myself with the Bosley sisters' system of organization."

"Women organized this kitchen?" She goes to the drawer closest to the refrigerator. "Then I'll know where everything is."

"Why would the wine opener be by the refrigerator?" I ask, watching her deftly handle the steel screw. "How did you know?"

"White wine," she says, wrinkling her nose. "Keeps forever in the fridge. Easy quick drink. A favorite of women everywhere. Don't ask me why."

"You prefer red."

"I only drink red," she says solemnly. "White wine has no blood." She pours out a glass and holds it up to the light. "Lovely. A bit of history?"

"This cabernet," I begin, quickly chopping the garlic, "is a tempestuous little thing I first tasted five years ago when it was barely three years old. A bit loud at the time, I had hopes she would mellow, and sure enough, I tried her last week, and though her bouquet remains bombastic, she's got a finish that'll keep you smiling for days."

"Nice." She takes a sip. "You could write wine for the *Chron.*"

"Ouch," I cry, nicking my finger, drawing a small drop of blood. "I don't write for them anymore. Remember? I'm a shiftless bum now. I'm my mother's worst nightmare, and you know what? I'm not feeling as bad about it as I thought I would. In fact, I'm not really feeling that bad at all, but then that might have something to do with you."

"You need a drink of this," she says, filling my glass. "I know a little bit about wine myself, and this is about as good as a cabernet gets. A toast to your taste."

"Where are you from, Greta? Your accent defies location."

"Sacramento." She holds her wine up to the light again. "Ninety miles from San Francisco, but I might as well have been born in Arkansas, the backward people I belonged to. Knew how to make babies and grow vegetables and fix things. Simple people. You know, people of the earth. And along comes me, number nine, mama twenty-seven years old. Greta Jeanne, the twig that broke her poor mama's back. She had nothing left. Gave me to Grandma Tyler when I was three, and I grew up with Granny in a cabin on the edge of a tiny town in the foothills with only a hundred people scattered for miles around. Lonely little place. I ran away to San Francisco when I was fifteen."

"How old are you now?" I ask, guessing wildly. "Thirty-three?"

She gulps her wine. "How nice of you. I'm almost forty, my old biological clock ticking wildly away." She swiftly clinks my glass with hers. "To your great work, Vic. To all the beautiful words you've written."

I drink deeply. The wine is magnificent. "Now, that's a great cabernet."

"Vic?" she says, draining her glass. "I lied. I'm forty-two. Just. And you're right, this is a great cabernet."

"I know nothing of wine," I confess, ending my bluff. "I pay fifteen bucks a bottle and hope it's good. But this *is* fabulous, no? It sings in the throat. Not a hitch or a glitch. Gulpable yet potent."

"I love the way you write," she says, drinking fast. "I know this is gonna sound stupid, but I always felt honored to work on your columns. I learned so much about timing. You're so good at that."

"You flatter me." I redden with embarrassment, draining my glass to keep up with her. "But I must warn you of something. I tend toward the grandiose when I'm steeped in red of this quality."

"I like grandiosity," she says, coming close to me. "It turns me on, actually. Especially if it's valid."

I force myself to focus on the mushrooms, delighted and terrified to be speaking so intimately with her. "Mushrooms. Garlic and onions and mushrooms. I always begin with garlic and onions and mushrooms."

"You must," she says, moving into the dining room. "Nice jade bowl." She sniffs the air. "Onions, garlic, and mushrooms simmering in dry sherry with dill, ginger, tarragon, extra-virgin olive oil, and . . . don't tell me. Cumin. I hope I didn't scare you with my baby talk. It's been kind of my obsession lately. I apologize. It may just be a hormonal thing, but I'm checking it out. I went to a psychic, and she said maybe I didn't need a baby. Maybe I just need to create something that *comes* from me. You know what I mean?"

I assess my fledgling sauce. "I know very little about babies, but I do know that you have a remarkable sense of smell. Those are precisely the ingredients I've mixed so far, though I couldn't have listed them myself."

"You don't work from recipes."

"No, I just add things and taste until it suggests spaghetti or linguini or corkscrews, and then I kick the water to a boil and we're there."

"I'll make a salad," she says, going to the fridge. "A mild Caesar. Yes?"

"Why mild?"

She smiles enormously. "I like the way you think, Vic. Why hide a good Parmesan?"

I stare at her in wonder. I can't imagine ever tiring of her unconscious poetry. She is so comfortable in her body. It relaxes me to look at her. "This sauce," I proclaim, "shall be my finest ever."

"Vic?" she says, rinsing big leaves of romaine. "Do you . . . Are you . . . Is that a Gorgonzola?"

"Yes," I say, stirring until the cheese vanishes into the sauce. "You like?"

"So far I love everything you've put in there."

"And now the pesto," I say, bringing forth a small glass jar. "I bought this from a shrewd old Italian woman on Portrero Hill. She's eighty-seven years old and has a big backyard full of basil. Her daughter brings her oil from Italy, and her son sends garlic from the slopes of Mount Athos in Greece. Her pesto is like liquid sunlight."

"This calls for another glass of wine. No?"

"I see no reason to dispute that. What finer way to loosen our tongues?"

"It's so nice to talk to you," she says, filling our glasses. "I'm drunk, I know, but I don't feel scared at all. Do you?"

After dinner, the second bottle history, we sit shoeless on the futon by the fire and compare our pasts. We discover that as children we both loved bows and arrows. She confesses to a teenage addiction to horror novels and erotic science fiction set on other planets. I admit to reading *Superman* and *Archie* comics, as well as memorizing all the songs from *The Roar of the Greasepaint, the Smell of the Crowd*. She graduated from college when she was thirty-five. I left school at twenty, never to return. And to top it all off, we unearth a mutually beloved line from the film *Young Frankenstein:* "But if you didn't make a yummy sound, and *you* didn't make a yummy sound . . . ?" And then the monster would moan from the cellar.

She presses the balls of her feet into the arches of mine. "You know who you remind me of? Sheila Moskowitz, this wild Jewish girl from New York. We got an apartment together in the Mission when I was sixteen. We always got our periods together on exactly the same day. She worked at a bagel shop, I worked in a deli. She taught me how to say 'Fuck you' in Yiddish. Among other things."

"I remind you of her?"

"Maybe it's something about your cooking. The abundance of garlic, perhaps."

"Well, *you* remind me of the best friend I never had but always wanted when I was every age I've ever been."

That knocks us into silence, and I have the strongest sense that we're on the verge of more than talk. Greta floats to my stereo and puts on a disk. Bill Evans on piano, Eddie Gomez on bass. She sways to the melancholy music, beckoning me to come dance with her, and I can't help but think of lines from a poem by William Carpenter.

> *I see the event horizon*
> *through which we fall*
> *into the speed of light*
> *and reverse ourselves in time*

Holding each other, dancing slowly, Greta says, "Why can't people just do this and not worry about what it means or where it's going to lead? Just dance because it feels good."

"Ah, the sixties. The ecstasy of dancing in a happy mob when everybody danced together."

"Yes." She rests her head on my shoulder. "But I mean this,

too. Two friends alone. So what if we don't become lovers? Why shouldn't friends dance together like this? Why isn't this an option?"

"It is," I say, relaxing against her, letting go of my need to make love, wanting only to sway to the sweet sad tunes with her.

"Vic," she whispers, moving away from me. "I have something very important to show you, something about my body. I don't want you to take this as sexual, because it's *way* deeper than that. I mean, there's no doubt you excite me, and I'm pretty sure vice versa, but we need to get through this other thing first, or we shouldn't even bother."

I look into her eyes and allow myself for the first time to acknowledge her deep, perilous sadness. "Whatever you need, Greta, I'm most of all your friend."

"This," she whispers, lifting off her sweater, unbuttoning her blouse, revealing her naked self in the flickering firelight. Slashed across her torso is a dark cord, a jagged scar running diagonally from her right shoulder, across her breasts, all the way to the top of her left hip. She traces the length of it slowly with her left hand.

I stand in mute reverence, waiting for her to speak.

"A man did this to me," she says, her eyes dry. "Twenty years ago. I know you're not that man, Vic, but if we're gonna go anywhere past now with touching each other, we've got to go slower than maybe you've ever gone, or it can't happen. I'm sorry to have to tell you in this way, but it's too basic a part of me to keep hidden." She buttons her blouse. "There."

"I'm so sorry, Greta. So sorry."

"I'll tell you something else. He wasn't a stranger to me. I was married to him. Carrying his child."

"My god, Greta. Why did . . . ?"

"Because I was leaving him. Forever."

"Did he go to jail?"

"No. By the time the police came, he was long dead and they had to pry my little gun out of my hands in the ambulance, though I was completely unconscious."

"You shot him," I say breathlessly.

"Yes, I did. Five times after he got his knife in me." She takes a deep breath. "So that's another thing you need to know."

"You're the bravest person I've ever known," I say, holding out my hand to her. "And I'd love for you to stay the night. Just talking."

"Maybe just talking," she says, coming closer. "And maybe some other stuff, too."

8

 I wake to the thump of the morning paper striking my front door, my heart pounding in anticipation of what Lucas has run in my place. I jump out of bed and race down the hall to my living room, where Greta is just waking up on the futon by the fire. "I like this view," she says, wrapping the Navajo blanket around her. "I like a man in silk pajamas. So soft."

"I rarely wear these," I say, looking down at myself. "I usually sleep naked. But in deference to you, in case we met in the hallway or something, going pee in the middle of the night, I thought . . ."

"That's very kind of you, Vic, but I wouldn't mind seeing you naked. I'm sure it's a lovely sight."

"Well . . . coffee? Pancakes? I'll just get the paper."

I open the door onto a cool and breezy day, the sun beginning to burn away the fog. I turn to watch Greta stretch languidly in bed. What could be better than this? A lovely companion, a beautiful home, a glorious new day. No job, little money, a huge mortgage, and not the slightest inkling about what to do next.

I squat in the doorway, disassembling the paper, feeling sick at the absence of my byline. I've been replaced by a ho-hum pull from *The New York Times*, a little note below the head reading: Vic Worsley—On Vacation.

"A vacation, is it? I wondered what Lucas would call it. I thought he might say 'sabbatical.' But never a vacation. What a bizarre concept."

"I'm in the shower," says Greta, calling to me on her way down the hall. "In case you want to join me. Or just watch."

I pretend not to hear her. My mind is racing with ideas and excuses and apologies. The phone rings. I rush to answer it, hoping it's Lucas calling with a reprieve. Just one more chance.

"Vic? It's Nolan. You're on vacation? Since when?"

"They fired me," I say, his familiar voice breaking the lock on my sorrow. "They fuckin' fired me."

"They'll regret it," he says calmly. "They'll be offering you double to come back. Don't worry. It's their loss, not yours."

"Meanwhile, what do I use for money?"

"You're asking *me*? I can't remember the last time I knew where next month's rent was coming from. But it always comes. As long as I keep doing what I've *got* to do."

"I never should have refinanced," I say, biting my fingernails. "I almost had the place paid off. But now . . ."

"Oops, got a call coming in. This could be that job we've all been waiting for. Hoops later? Don't get too depressed about this. Come on over. Talk to me. You'll be fine."

I'm not alone, I must remember that. I've got friends. And now a wave of relief passes through and leaves me lighter. I don't have to write another goddamn column. I don't have to pretend to care anymore.

Over pancakes, the dining room bright and sunny, Greta and I gawk at Ruby's photograph of Spear, found in the upper right-hand drawer of my desk, just where Mae said it would be. I wish, in retrospect, I had been kinder to her when we broke our date. I was hoping she would go ahead with her plans to resurrect my garden, something she said she'd do for free, just to see how it might look.

Greta shakes her head at the picture. "How could anyone stop this guy?"

"If this isn't a fake, he's the greatest leaper of all time."

"How could he not be a professional?"

"We could find out."

"What you mean 'we'?"

"You said wanted to meet him, didn't you?"

"Yeah." She shrugs and winces slightly. "I guess I do, even if it is kinda scary."

"On the other hand, if I'm not gonna be writing about him, why bother?"

"Oh, you might write about him," she says softly. "You never know. Meeting somebody like this on his home turf could be fascinating. It certainly would be an adventure, wouldn't it?"

"I'm not sure I can handle any more adventures just now. Particularly in that particular part of Oakland. Tillsbury is like ground zero. The Dante's *Inferno* of basketball. Or so I've been told. I mean, don't you think losing my job and spending the night with you are more than enough adventures for one week? Especially if we spend all the rest of them together. For the week, I mean. The nights. No?"

"But what if this is the first step of a major journey for you?" She hands me the photo of Spear. "Maybe Ruby is your guide. How could you pass *that* up? I'd love to study with her. Can you imagine what she must know? Didn't she have the fiercest eyes you've ever seen? With that flame in the center."

"Look, I must tell you, and please don't take this personally, because I do adore you, but I have a very low tolerance for New Age spirituality, mystical quests, and any of that sort of thing. This is especially true when I'm sober. Buddhism is about as close as I get to suspending my disbelief, and that's only because I like their poetry."

"You're such a fake, Vic," she says, finishing her coffee. "Buddhism is nothing *but* mystical. We inhale the universe with every breath we take. Buddha said that."

"So what are you saying? That I'm a coward for not calling Ruby?"

"If I were you, *I* would call her. But I'm not you. I've got black blood in me, so I'm not quite as afraid of Oakland as you are. On the other hand, I'm a woman. And most of the men over there tend to like my looks, and that makes me more vulnerable than you will ever be. But I'd call her in a minute. She's powerful, Vic."

"Okay," I say, going to the phone. "We'll go today."

"I have to work," she says, batting her eyelashes. "For the paper you used to write for?"

"Oh, them," I say, bitterly. "The people who spit me out to die."

"Poor baby," she pouts. "You want violins or cellos? You're breaking my heart."

"There's no need for sarcasm."

"You're right. It's about as useful as self-pity. I gotta go."

"Wait," I say, chasing her to the front door. "Don't go. I'm sorry."

"Don't be sorry," she says, looking deep into my eyes. "Be joyful. Be strong. Be grateful for all you've been given. And if that's too New Age for you, then I must be, too."

"Will you marry me?" I ask, unable to stop the words.

"Sure," she says, laughing uproariously. "But I reserve the right to have as many other spouses as I need."

"Okay," I say, kissing her forehead. "Take the day off, please? Go adventuring with me?"

"Let me just confer with the personnel department," she says, skipping to the phone. "It's been my contingency plan all along."

·   ·   ·   ·   ·

I call Ruby. "Line's busy," I announce with great relief. "Maybe we should just catch a matinee and go to the beach. After all, it says in the paper I'm on vacation."

The phone rings. I snatch it up, hoping it's Lucas.

"Mr. Worsley? Ruby Carmichael."

"I just called you. The line was busy."

"Because I was calling you," she says firmly. "To see if you could come today. The weather couldn't be more perfect, the moon ten days from full, and I had two crows in my almond tree when I woke up this morning. Will you come?"

"*Two* crows?" I say, feigning wonder. "Then I guess we'll *have* to come."

"You will?" she says, stunned to hear it. "Today?"

"Yes. We'll grab a train."

"We? Who is we?"

"Greta. You met her at the *Chron*. The one who knew about hummingbirds."

"Hold on a minute," says Ruby, coughing. "That might not be such a good idea."

She puts down the phone. I can hear her footsteps on a rugless floor. I hear something that sounds like a rattle, followed by a musical clatter, followed by silence. And in this silence, I experience the most lucid sensation that I'm about to fall off a cliff.

"It's okay," says Ruby, back on the line. "Just checked a few things. I'd personally prefer that you didn't bring her, but that's just me. Everybody else says it's okay."

"Everybody else?"

"Spirits," she says simply. "I threw my bones. Please come over any time before one-thirty."

We run down the hill and catch the crosstown Divisadero bus. Greta gazes out the window, smiling like a little girl at the passing sights. I love her so much now, it almost hurts to watch her. She is so precious to me, so open to the wonder of it all. The usually gloomy Fillmore seems positively cheerful. The Haight feels every bit as magical as it did in the sixties; the Castro one vast, jubilant party. I'm in love. The world made new. I might even write a poem about it. Wouldn't that be something?

A big bird wheels in the air over Greta's house. She looks up, shading her eyes. "It's an owl. You see what I mean? They like me." She pauses for effect. "Must be some New Age kinda thing."

"I've never really noticed which birds like to hang out around me," I say, frowning at my lack of data. "Though there are these mockingbirds that sing all night sometimes and keep me from sleeping."

She puts her arms around me. "Mockingbirds are mimics. They sing other birds' songs, though they have their own, too. And they're very brave. They'll attack a hawk to protect their nests."

"So what does it mean that I attract them? Usually in the middle of the night?"

"We'll have to ask Ruby," she says, unlocking her door. "I'm just gonna slip into something a bit less formfitting."

While she changes her clothes, I wander out into her back-yard, a garden dense with ferns and roses. A sunny strip near the northern fence is alive with tomato vines and pygmy corn. All this riotous growth fills me with nostalgia for the gardens I planted with my father. Radishes and corn and sunflowers and zucchini. All the easy stuff so I'd never doubt I could do it.

Lisa and Sheila squat in the gravel path, slowly pulling the stubborn gray weeds. Lisa, tiny and demure, wears a floppy straw hat and a white dress. Sheila, taller than all but a few men on earth, wears a blue bandana and a gray dashiki. They flash electric smiles, Lisa beckoning. "Come weed with us, Victor. Tell us about the game last night."

My knees pop and my joints creak as I squat beside them. Given the weakness of my quadriceps, I am soon on my knees. The weeds are abundant and tenacious, their roots tangled deep in the fertile soil. I fall into a steady rhythm of work, our talk turning to my absence in the *Chron* this morning.

"Didn't realize how addicted I was," says Sheila, squinting at me. "Read you all through college up until today. Still have the piece you did on me when I was you-know-who."

"It feels strange," I say, chilled by a gust of grief, "not knowing what I am now, exactly."

"As if we ever know," says Sheila, wrinkling her nose. "You know what I mean? I had a man's body. I thought I wanted to play under the lights at the highest level. For millions of dollars. I was on my way. On a fast train." She shakes her head and chuckles. "Now I'm in no hurry to get anywhere. Don't care if we ever get all these weeds. Having a good and simple life. A woman. Who would have ever thought?"

"How about me," says Lisa, her eyes widening in wonder. "I was an anorexic, fashion-model speed freak and frigid to boot. When I turned twenty-five and finally stopped looking sixteen, and they didn't want me anymore, I didn't have a clue who I was. Not a clue. That's how come I started wearing disguises."

"Are you disguised now?"

She smiles coquettishly. "No. Only when I go out."

"Tell him about 'Jimmy,'" says Sheila, laughing. "I love Jimmy."

"Yeah, Jimmy's a good one," says Lisa, blushing at me. "I wear a gray suit and a fat red tie, and I put all sorts of goo in my hair."

"Tell him about the shoes," says Sheila, cracking up. "The shoes are the best part."

"Spats," says Lisa, licking her lips. "Black and white. The quintessential greasy fag."

"So you become a man?"

"I try," she laughs. "But I don't think I fool too many people. My boobs are too big and my face still looks like a woman's."

"So what does 'Jimmy' do?"

"He *shops* for me," she says, sounding rather prissy. "I have a hard time actually going out into the world, but Jimmy *loves* to shop. Groceries, wine, the bank. Nobody ever hassles him because he's so . . . fussy."

"Snippy and strange," says Sheila, rising to stretch. "Nobody likes to mess with a snippy fag. Male or female."

"How tall are you?" I ask, amazed at how far away her head is.

"Six-nine. Grew three inches after my sex change. They said that might happen, and it did."

"You still play?"

"No, I'm a dancer now." She turns slowly in a graceful circle. "Got a whole new vocabulary."

"Do you ever long to play again?"

"I dream about it now and then," she says, squatting again to find her place in the weeds. "But they're not very good dreams."

"I'm ready," says Greta, calling from the back porch, her hair hidden under a faded brown scarf, her face obscured by enormous dark glasses. "Oakland here we come."

"Nice disguise," says Lisa, waving good-bye. "Our theme for the day."

"Bon voyage," says Sheila, winking at me. "Give my regards to Tillsbury. Say hi to the boys."

Streaking under the bay, our BART train humming, Greta leans comfortably against me, her oversized jumpsuit revealing almost nothing of her true figure. I am deeply doubting the wisdom of our impulsive departure to a place I know only in nightmares. The blackest of ghettos where no white man can ever be safe for long.

"How did Ruby sound?" asks Greta, gazing up at me. "Glad we're coming?"

"She sounded incredibly serious," I say, beginning to wish I wasn't doing this. "Not happy at all."

"You seem so tense. You okay?"

"Well, the thing is, Tillsbury Park is . . . totally black," I say, swallowing hard. "*You'll* be white in Tillsbury Park, so I will be . . ."

"A little polar bear." She grins at me. "A polar bear in a sea of black sharks."

"Reassuring image."

"Let's hope Ruby knows what she's doing," she says, kissing my cheek. "But just in case, I have a gun."

"A what?" I whisper, breaking a fine sweat. "A gun?"

"We come from different places, you and I," she says, without a trace of fear in her voice. "Trust me on this, okay?"

"But the statistics show . . ."

"Fuck the statistics. *I'm* a statistic that's been saved because of this gun. Okay? There's no way I'm going into Tillsbury Park with a white man and an old black lady, unarmed. You can go without me. I'll pray for you. But if you want me to come along, I bring my gun."

"It's funny," I say, giggling anxiously, "but I had a whole different vision of this. More of a genteel stroll in the park to watch some hoops."

"Different," she says, patting her trusty satchel. "Nothing like a stroll."

"Maybe we should just forget this," I mumble, chewing hard on my lower lip. "Before I throw up."

"It's your call, Vic." She kisses my chin. "If we don't like it, we can always leave."

"I'm being overly paranoid, aren't I?"

"Probably not. You're probably being exactly the right amount of paranoid."

"So you agree that this is a bad idea? You think we should forget this?"

"That's up to you, Vic. It's your gig. I'm just coming along for the ride."

We detrain in the heart of Oakland, and I am a puff of white in a seething festival of blacks and browns—Africans, Asians, Hispanics—the tunes from the boom boxes meshing in a complex crush, the ground awash in garbage, the walls and sidewalks dense with gang graffiti. We hold hands and weave our way up the stairs, running a gauntlet of desperate men.

"Dope. Right here. Come with me. Get you so high. *Here.* Right here."

"Crank. Got me some fresh tabs. Do what you need to do. The best. *Clean.* Very very clean."

"Animals. These girls won't let you down. Anything you want. No taboos. Come on. Both of you. Sexy sexy. What you say *goes.* Gorgeous. Guaranteed."

As we emerge into daylight, an old taxi slides close, its back door opening automatically. We jump in, the driver blurry through green bulletproof glass, his voice rumbling from a speaker on the ceiling. "Welcome to beautiful downtown Oakland. Where may I take you? Hotel? Sightseeing? Jack London Square?"

"We're picking someone up on Landfort Drive," I say, straining to sound cheerful. "Then we're going to Tillsbury Park."

"Not in my cab," he says, shaking his head. "I wouldn't go to Tillsbury for double my usual fare."

"Triple?" I ask, liking his sense of precaution.

"Not if I have to wait there."

"Maybe we should just forget this. I mean if the place is too dangerous for a cab to wait, what's gonna happen to *us?*"

"My meter is running," says the driver. "Just wanted you to know. Cost you two dollars so far."

"It's probably not that bad," says Greta, exasperated with me. "Ruby wouldn't ask us to go there if it was *that* bad."

"It's bad," says the driver. "You won't find anybody who'll park there, except on weekends when the families go. Rest of the time, forget it."

"Maybe this Spear guy could come over to San Francisco and play at a park near my house," I suggest, my heart racing. "That shouldn't be too hard to arrange."

"Up to you," says Greta, sitting back and folding her arms. "Like I said, this is your thing, not mine."

"It's not that I don't *want* to go. It's just that . . . I'm afraid."

"What would make you less afraid?"

"Talking to Ruby. Getting some sort of assurance from her."

"Take us to Landfort Drive," she says to our driver. "We'll make our next decision there."

Landfort Drive is aptly named. Every yard has a chain-link fence around it, and many of these fences are topped with vicious loops of barbed wire. The windows of each boxy little house are protected with heavy iron bars. The rooftops bristle with antennae. Huge Dobermans and Rottweilers stand guard at the gates, barking at anything that moves.

Ruby's house is the only one on her street with no fence around it, no bars over the windows, no metal cage enclosing the front door. In place of the usual ragged lawn, a field of tall silver sage waves in a light breeze. And behind her house stands a larger home, three stories high, a pleasant hodgepodge of additions.

"Oh, *this* Ruby," says the driver, peering out at the sage. "Call her the herb lady. My sister went to her for headaches one time. Old lady gave her some kind of tea. Worked like a charm. She swears by it. You want me to honk my horn?"

"I'll go to the door," I say, feeling suddenly chivalrous. "Just be a minute."

Greta grabs my wrist. "Honking will be fine."

He beeps twice, but no one comes out. I check my watch. If anything, we're early. He beeps again. The front door opens and a giant man in a bright pink bathrobe, his bald head glinting in the sun, jogs over to us and signals for me to roll down my window.

"You can't do that," says the driver, shaking his head. "I control the windows. You know this guy?"

"No, but I'm sure . . ."

"Yes?" says our driver, barely cracking his window to communicate with the giant. "What's happening?"

The man leans close to my window, blotting out the sun with his enormity. His voice is soft and distant through the dense glass. "Ruby says go to the park. Ewing Drive entrance. Says she'll meet you there. At the turnaround."

"Why the change of plans?" I ask, my stomach knotting up.

"Why the change?" translates our driver.

"She wanted to go a little early to talk to Spear, 'cause he was kinda nervous about your coming. But don't you worry. I'll be there shortly to put his mind at ease. I'm Godfrey, Spear's big brother. Even if he *does* have a good three inches on me now."

"Great," I say, biting my thumb. "He doesn't even want us to come. Terrific. Wonderful."

"Thanks," says Greta, waving to Godfrey.

"Thank you," says our driver, giving Godfrey thumbs up.

"To go or not to go," I gasp. "That is the question."

"Oh, let's go," says Greta, nudging me. "We can do this. Could be fun. With Godfrey on our side, what could happen?"

"You're right," I say, tapping the bulletproof glass. "To the park."

"Looks like where I lived when I was married," says Greta, frowning out at the ruined stores. "They even have palm trees, just like Los Angeles. Dying in the smog."

"How long were you married?"

"Three years," she says gruffly. "Three years I don't like to think about."

We stop at a light. Seven big men in matching silver jackets enter the crosswalk, each with a different Arabic letter carved into his close-cropped hair. Greta pulls her hand from mine and reaches into her satchel for her gun.

The light changes, but the men linger in front of us, challenging our driver to hit his horn. He waits a courteous moment, then another, until the last of them moves slowly out of our way. A wild thought comes to me. What would happen if I jumped out of the cab and shouted, "Hey, can I come?" Would they kill me?

"That was some of the Muslim team," says our driver. "You ever seen them play?"

"No. Are they good?"

"Oh, yeah. They play all over. You like basketball?"

"Actually," says Greta, letting go of her gun and taking my hand, "we're devotees of the Great Basketball Spirit, which is why we have nothing to fear."

"Devotees, huh?" says the driver, laughing dryly. "Well, you're going to the right place, that's for sure. If nobody shoots you."

9

Tillsbury Park. I'm prepared for gangstas, and we do spot a few, but mostly there are children, swarming the swings and slides. A few old ducks share the big muddy pond with floating islands of fast-food Styrofoam and congealed garbage. Young girls with babies in plastic strollers sit together in the shade, shouting warnings to their older children and flirting aggressively with the young men passing by.

Ruby is decidedly pensive in a short black dress, her white hair streaked with fresh red paint. "Mr. Worsley," she says, offering me her hand. "How kind of you to come. This is a good sign you came so quickly. Spirits like a decisive soul." She turns to Greta and sighs heavily. "You're even prettier than I remembered. Gonna cause some commotion. Which is why I didn't want you to come. It's nothing personal. I just didn't want to make this any more complicated than it already is."

"I won't be any trouble," says Greta, moving quickly to kiss Ruby's cheek. "You won't even know I'm here."

"It's not me I'm worried about," says Ruby, squinting into Greta's eyes. "You got Indian blood in you?"

"Wintu and Maidu," says Greta, bowing slightly. "You?"

"All sorts," says Ruby, turning to me again. "We'll go over the hill now. To where the men are playing."

We traverse a muddy soccer field and surmount a small rise topped by a single oak, its trunk gouged with thousands of names and initials and dates. Below us lies that hallowed run I've heard described by countless pros. Tillsbury. The asphalt proving ground of Oakland. A level rectangle, roughly two-thirds the size of an official court, the rims true, the nets new.

As we draw closer, Ruby points to the orange rings. "Spear does all the repairs around here. Keeps the backboards painted and the nets fresh. You see any frays up there? No frays. He respects this game. It's his discipline. You'll know what I'm talking about when you see him play. Understanding, as Rashan says, will be yours."

Nearing the court, we make our way through a throng of teenaged men. I am barely noticed, but Greta draws a chorus of raves.

"What choo got under them baggy clothes, mama?"

"Shed some skins, give us chilluns a thrill."

"You got my vote, honey. Whatever you running for."

"You got a license to look that good? *Hmm?*"

The older players nod deferentially to Ruby as we take our seats on metal bleachers along the southern edge of the court. Ruby and Greta are the only women in the audience of twenty or so. I am the only white male for miles around. I can feel the men looking at me, and it is all I can do not to panic and run. Relax. Take a deep breath. Everything is going to be okay. These guys are just like the guys I've played with my whole life, except they are more ferocious than any pro team I've ever seen. The desire to win is so strong here, the game in progress is like a war, constantly slowed by flagrant fouls and violent arguments over every point. Ruby touches my knee. "Won't be like this when

Spear plays. He won't tolerate it. They're just fighting for the right to play him."

Greta whispers to me. "What does she mean? The right to play him'?"

"Court protocol is roughly universal," I say, hoping I know what I'm talking about. "The victorious team plays the next game against a team assembled by the first person to challenge them. They call it Winners, and I assume Spear must have that honor. Yes?"

"He begins his play at two," says Ruby, nodding regally. "You might say he has two o'clock winners. Perpetually."

"Where is he?" I ask, scanning the park, seeing somebody six-foot-seven or -eight, but nobody taller. "Not here yet?"

"He's praying," says the man to my right, an older fellow with white hair, a briar pipe clamped between his teeth. "He ran his seven miles, did his shooting drill, his jumping drill, his blocking drill, and now he's praying. You ask Ruby."

"Spear seems to be rather famous around here," says Greta, breathing a sigh of relief. "I think we're gonna be just fine."

"Who does he pray to?" I ask, expecting Ruby to say Allah. She folds her arms. "I don't really know. Don't think it has a name. He prays over there by that big old redwood, sits quiet like a stone, him and his teacher, Rashan de Witt."

"He has a teacher?" I say, not liking the sound of this.

"Sort of a guru," says the older man, removing his pipe, squinting at me. "Hey, aren't you Vic Worsley? Writes for the *Chron*?"

"Wrote," I say, feeling a twinge of regret. "They let me go as of yesterday."

"That's a shame," he says, replacing his pipe. "You really know the game, even when I don't agree, I can say that."

"Well, thank you."

"Name's Carl," he says, extending a well-worn hand. "I wrote to you a couple times. You get my letters?"

"Carl McKay," says Greta, prompting me. "You remember?"

"Oh. Carl McKay."

"McCelvey," he says, looking away. "Close enough, I guess. Wrote you about Spear. Told Ruby I would. Figured you were swamped."

"Doesn't *read* his mail," says Ruby, grimacing at another argument on the court. "Quit crying and get playing!" She taps her wristwatch. "It's almost two!"

"Yes, Ruby," says a muscular little man with a freshly shaved head. "Next bucket takes it."

And a splendid bucket it is. A bronze Adonis rises into the air twenty feet from the hoop, arching his shot over a defender. The ball tumbles down and strikes iron, the rebound snatched by a massively muscled jumper. He flicks a pass to a sleek young man who catches it in full stride, takes a giant step, and feeds cross-court to the little bald man who pogos into the lane, where he's forced by defenders to make a behind-the-back pass into the hands of the massively muscled jumper whose rebound began it all. He launches himself over two leaping defenders and jams the ball home.

"Jesus," I whisper to Greta. "Twenty years ago, *any* of these guys could have played in the pros."

"Yes, Juanishi," says Carl, clapping his hands. "Now for the real game."

"The real game?" I ask, perplexed. "In what sense?"

Carl clears his throat. "After you see Spear play, you won't need to ask that question."

The winners stow their jive and look to the east where Spear emerges from the trees. I shake my head in disbelief, for even at a hundred yards he seems impossibly huge, his hair clipped short, his dreadlocks gone. And though I have seen seven-footers night after night for fifteen years, he eclipses any man I have ever known. He is so enormous, yet so exquisitely graceful, he might be a god incarnated as human.

Trotting beside this astounding colossus is a skinny man about my size, his dreadlocks gray, a neatly pressed cotton shirt tucked into sharply creased trousers, his feet in sandals, an open smile on his wrinkled face. He bows to Ruby, bows to Greta, and extends his hand to me. "Mr. Worsley," he says, with a trace of Philadelphia. "I am Rashan de Witt. Welcome to Tillsbury."

"Pleased to meet you," I say, his touch reminding me of an old poet I camped with in the mountains behind Big Sur the summer after I dropped out of college. Each morning, the old man would wake up crying, overcome with joy to be alive for another day.

"It is my honor," he replies. "Please allow me to introduce my friend Spear Rashan Benedentes."

Spear bows to Ruby and bows to Greta, locking eyes with each of them. And now he is reaching out to me. If I stood on this bleacher, I still wouldn't be as tall as he. He takes my hand gently, as if I were a child.

"Hello," I say, my voice cracking. "You've cut your hair since Ruby's photograph."

"It was getting in my way," he says, his voice incredibly deep and warm. "When I'd be in the air, you know, I would think of it, feel it on my neck, and it impinged on my concentration, so I cut it off. You know what I'm talking about?"

"Yes," I joke, touching my unruly tangle. "I keep mine short for the same reason."

He lets go of my hand and steps back. "You play?"

"With an old friend," I squeak. "Just goofing around."

"Play now," he says, gazing at Greta. "Show your lover what you can do."

"Bad back. I'm forty-four. Besides, I've got the wrong shoes." I shrug red-faced at Carl. "No shorts."

"Don't worry," says Spear, raising two fingers to summon someone. "We have everything you need."

"Oh, no, please. I'm really not in your league at all."

"I'm not in *any* league," he says, grinning hugely at me. "I just come to play."

"Don't be teasing him, Spear," says Ruby, standing up on the bleacher. "If he doesn't want to play, don't make him play. That was the rule when you were little, and it's the rule right now. Don't force a person to do what they don't wish to do. It comes back to haunt you. I'm warning you."

"But he *does* want to play," says Spear, holding Ruby's hand. "That's why he writes the way he does. That's why he's here." He turns to me. "That's what you dream of, isn't it?"

"I'll get killed," I say, glancing out at the blur of black men, too terrified to see them clearly. "I can't take the physical contact."

"No one will touch you," he says, shaking his head to reassure me. "My man Thomas will trade you his shorts for your pants. What size shoe you wear?"

"Ten," I say, "but . . ."

"Go on," says Greta, nodding to me. "Relax. You'll do fine."

In a stupor of disbelief, I find myself behind the bleachers, putting on some other guy's jockstrap, some other guy's shiny yellow shorts, and some other guy's shoes. I return to the court, awaiting further instructions, shivering with fright. As I watch the men warm up, each of them dunking the ball with absurd ease, I remember sitting on the B team bench in high school with Jim Shaw, itching to play, and Jimmy saying, "First time you touch the ball, gun it. Might be your only chance."

I step onto the asphalt and a ball appears in my hand, a gift from Spear. I ease up a ten-footer before I can worry about missing, and miracle of miracles, it goes in. I flip up a lazy hook from eight, a clean swish. I scoop an underhand from seven and it knocks in nicely off the backboard. I jog to the corner and sink a twenty-footer, on and on like this, fourteen without a miss, the brothers frowning as Spear feeds me in perfect rhythm with my release.

"White man can shoot," says the bald, browless man who made the winning assist in the last game. "But if I ever guard you, expect a bit of traffic."

"I'm Vic." I offer my hand. "This is very nice of you guys to let me play."

He won't shake at first, but something happens, some subtle command arrives from Spear, and he grabs my hand. "I'm Pogo. Tight with Spear. Glad to know you. I was just makin' noise."

Spear comes close and I tremble at the edifice of his body, his biceps as big as my torso, or so it seems. "Give to the open man," he whispers thunderously. "Somebody always gonna be open. Nobody will touch you unless you go inside. If they do, they answer to me. And that's the last thing they want to do."

"I don't feel right about this," I say, my body growing numb. "Are you sure this is necessary?"

"I don't know about necessary," he says, grinning down at me. "But it might be a gas. I love how you write about the game. Be fun to see you play."

So we begin. We begin and never stop for fifteen of the most glorious minutes of my life, though I never once touch the ball. I run back and forth, delirious to be playing with them, despite the fact that the man I'm supposed to guard is so swift, I can't stay on him. He scores all but one of their eleven buckets, shooting bankers unencumbered for the entire game until Spear leaps impossibly high to snag a shot before it can start down, and fires a long pass to Pogo who wins with an effortless dunk.

"Same fives," says Spear, freezing the players. "Double time."

"Twice as fast?" I gasp, grimacing at Greta. "I'll have a heart attack."

"No, no," says Spear, resting his hand on my shoulder. "Double time is two times twelve. We play to twenty-four. One point a basket, same as before. Takes it to another level."

"I'm kinda tired. I haven't played full court in years. Make that decades. Maybe this isn't such a good idea."

"You want to stop? Stop. Don't hurt yourself."

"On the other hand, I'd love to."

"You want to shoot?"

"Only if it's utterly convenient. I'm just happy to be running with you guys."

Spear smiles. "I like you, man. Gonna get you involved, set some double pics. Be looking."

"You know," I say, grimacing at the ground, "I'm not writing for the *Chron* anymore, in case you're doing this because you thought . . ."

He frowns curiously at me. "You think I'm doing this to get something from you?"

"Well, it just seems odd that you would want *me* to play. I mean, I *love* it, but I hardly deserve to be on the same court with . . ."

"If you love it, that's all that matters," he says, signaling the others that we're ready to resume play. "Doesn't matter who wins. It's just something great to do."

Pogo starts things off by zinging the ball to me, stinging my fingers. Spear sets a pic on two men, and I dribble into the clear twenty-five feet out, a bit beyond my usual range, but it's worth a try, so I fire away, missing hideously. No matter. Spear rises above the others to tap it in with two fingers.

He is simply beyond anything in my experience. His timing is clairvoyant, his elevations astounding, his passes unerring. I keep waiting for him to do something wrong, but his only fault seems to be his desire for *me* to shoot. I miss and miss and miss again, my shame growing hotter with every failure. We are falling behind, and it's my fault. Spear passes to me once more and sets another pic, freeing me from eighteen, but I don't feel worthy to try again, so I pass it back to him.

"Shoot the damn ball!" cries Ruby, jumping to her feet. "You're wide open."

The ball comes back to me, and I fire before I can think to question the wisdom of my attempt. The ball sneaks over my defender's fingers, climbs high into the blue sky and tumbles down rattling through the hoop, electrifying my heart and erasing my fatigue.

Godfrey, the leader of the other team, makes a long set shot and seems primed to make four more. We're down twenty to nineteen. We'd have won by now without all my misses. I don't want to handle the ball so late in the game, but the pass comes to me again. My teammates block for me, and I am about to shoot, when I see Pogo breaking for the hoop, and the ball leaps from me to him and he slams it home, sending me dancing back on defense, exultant.

I take only one more shot, the last of the game on a return pass from Spear, a defender rising to block me. But I'm quick enough to get it off, and I walk from the court feeling tall and strong and momentarily unafraid. I know the game was rigged in my favor. I know these men were told to go easy on me. I know that the worst of them could destroy me one-on-one, yet I'm ecstatic, as if I've just won the championship of the whole world.

I watch the next game sitting close to Greta. I put my lips to her ear. "I did it. I actually did it."

"You were fine," she says, patting my knee. "You made that great pass and you made the winner."

"Nice release," says Carl, winking at me. "Smooth."

"Stop," I say, blushing to my bones. "They let me shoot."

"I had no idea," says Ruby, frowning quizzically. "Thought you just *wrote* about it. Shows you how little we know, doesn't it?"

A fight breaks out on the court. Spear pulls the two combatants apart, growling his disapproval. They glare at each other, shaking with rage. Ruby nods her approval. "Spear won't let them play until they touch hands and forgive each other. That's his rule. He won't stand for violence on his court."

"He is fierce today," says Rashan de Witt, sitting alone two rows above us. "I think you've inspired him, Mr. Worsley."

"Mind if I watch with you?" I ask, moving up beside Rashan, leaving Greta with Ruby.

"Not at all," he says, bowing. "I am honored."

"I hope you don't mind my asking, but are you and Spear Muslim?"

"No," he says, bowing again. "Buddhist."

"As in Zen?"

"As in the daily practice of meditation," he says, bringing my attention back to the game with a subtle nod. "The fundamental belief being that all people and all things are part of the same miraculous whole."

We watch in wonder as Spear leaves the ground and lifts the ball above his head, flying toward the rim, his brother rising to block him, the ball leaving his hands to kiss high off the backboard and fall cleanly through the hoop, Spear catching his brother and tumbling off the court with him, laughing.

10

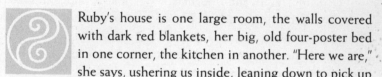Ruby's house is one large room, the walls covered with dark red blankets, her big, old four-poster bed in one corner, the kitchen in another. "Here we are," she says, ushering us inside, leaning down to pick up a young gray cat. "Take a chair by the fireplace. I'll get my new tea going. I just mixed it up this morning. Every bit as good as coffee. Takes only three or four twigs to boil a kettle of water. What could be better than that? Sycamores drop twigs all year long around here, and after a big wind we get enough wood for a month. That way my utility bill stays *down*."

Greta sticks her nose in Ruby's tea jar. "I smell peppermint and rose hips and chamomile."

"That's my base," says Ruby, nodding. "What else?"

"Ginseng?"

"You got a good nose, but you still haven't guessed the main ingredient. You'll know it when you taste it."

Rashan bows to each of us. "I'm sorry to leave you, but it's my turn to prepare supper tonight, and I'm running short of time.

Our house is the one just behind this one. Please come and visit when you're over this way again."

"It was nice to meet you," says Greta, waving good-bye. "I'm sure we'll be seeing you."

"Yes," he says, nodding to her. "It has been a distinct pleasure to meet both of you."

"Save me something," says Spear, smiling fondly at Rashan. "I'll be home soon."

"Here," says Ruby, handing Rashan a loaf of freshly baked bread. "Make sure that little girl Miranda gets some of this. Don't let all the other kids push her out of the way. And tell her not to be afraid to hit back if she needs to."

"I will encourage her to be strong," he says, kissing Ruby's forehead. "Will you come over tonight and tell us one of your stories? The children wondered why you didn't come over last night."

"Oh, I guess I'll come," she says gruffly. "After a while."

The kettle hums and she makes our tea, a pungent green brew, bitter and invigorating. The secret ingredient is seaweed. We drink in silence. Greta curls up in a rocking chair with a big white cat in her lap. I'm too excited to sit. Spear kneels on the floor, watching the steam rise from his cup.

Ruby takes off her apron and folds her arms. "Now, I know what you're thinking, Mr. Worsley. He's no kid. He's a man. Fully formed. So why hasn't he tried out for the pros? What's wrong with this guy? Am I right?"

"Well, I can see there's nothing wrong with him." I smile anxiously at Spear. "You're a phenomenal talent. But she's right, I am curious as to why you haven't turned professional."

"It's a long story," he says, sipping his tea. "I don't mind telling it, but I don't want to bore you."

"I couldn't be less bored. I'm still zooming from that run at Tillsbury. And I have endless time, now that I'm out of a job."

"We're never out of a job," says Ruby, seating herself in a well-cushioned rocker. "There's always plenty of work to do."

Greta takes off her dark glasses and the room seems to brighten. She gazes at me with ironic tenderness. "You can always get a job as a cook. I'll hire you. Then you can be *my* assistant for a change."

Spear breathes deeply to collect himself. Even on his knees, his every movement seems momentous to me, the small house rendered even tinier by his hugeness. "I quit going to school when I was ten." He closes his eyes. "I didn't know how to read, so it was useless to stay."

"I tried to teach him," says Ruby, pursing her lips. "But he was just too wild. Played ball all day long. Ran with his pack of boys. Didn't come home for two or three days at a time."

"I was definitely a wild child," he says, opening his eyes. "Six-foot-three when I turned twelve. And I'll tell you, Vic, there's absolutely no doubt in my mind that playing ball is all that kept me from killing somebody or getting killed. As it was, I started selling dope when I was fourteen, sleeping with the girls who came to watch us play, making babies. Drove poor Ruby crazy. Didn't I?"

She nods, staring steadily at him. "We lived through it, and we were strengthened by it. Now tell him how you met Rashan."

"Well, one day a friend of mine brought this college scout to watch me play at Tillsbury. I put on a good show against a couple old semi-pros, and he said if I'd give him twenty-five percent of my first year's salary, he'd get me on a junior college team in New Jersey or somewhere, and from there to a big school. After a year he said I'd be drafted by the pros for my size alone."

"You were how old?" I ask, nodding my thanks to Ruby as she fills my cup. "And how tall?"

"Seventeen. Seven feet tall. But see, I could hardly comprehend what he was talking about. I barely knew where I was gonna sleep from one night to the next, or with which woman. I was almost always stoned. I owed too many people too much money. I had three kids I knew of, enemies all over town. I had a gun, and I knew a guy who needed a big man for muscle in his coke trade. He said if I'd work for him for six months he'd pay off everybody I owed, get me a nice apartment, and buy me a big car." He bows his head, his memories weighing on him. "I didn't know what to do. I could leave my friends and move across the country and try to play college ball without knowing how to read, or stay home and make some big money quick with my size."

"I threw my bones for him," says Ruby, folding her arms. "And the spirits said to leave him alone. They said he would find his own way."

"So," says Spear, his eyes brimming with tears, "I'd just heard from somebody that my best friend, Pogo, the guy running point today, was sleeping with one of my women. That's how ignorant I was. I actually thought they belonged to me. And I was on my way downtown to beat him up, when I see these three hoods waiting for me at the corner, guys I owed some big money to. So I ducked down an alley, and here's this old milk truck and this goofy-looking Rasta man bowing to these two old ladies holding hands like sweethearts. Now, everybody in town knew they'd been fighting and clawing at each other for years. It didn't make any sense to me that people could change so dramatically, after being so hateful to each other. So I go over to him and say, 'How'd you do that, man?' And he smiles at me, that secret little smile he has, and says, 'I just helped them talk to each other. I helped them get past their anger so they could hear each other, and then they found out they didn't really hate each other, they had just misunderstood.' "

"Is that what he does for a living?" asks Greta, hanging on his every word. "Is he a therapist?"

"He's a counselor," says Spear, smiling proudly at her. "And so am I."

"They have their office in Rashan's milk truck," says Ruby, clearing her throat. "I'll never forget that night when Spear came home and said he was going to work for a man who needed an apprentice. I thought he meant a plumber or an electrician. A trade, you know? But it was Rashan."

Greta frowns in fascination. "So what's his background? Does he have a psychology degree?"

"He was a Baptist minister," says Spear, obviously delighted by his mentor's history. "Then he became a Buddhist. But I'll let him tell you all about that. About his wild days at the zendo."

"It's a great story," I say, unable to shake the feeling he's telling me all this because he wants me to help him. "I wish I could put it in my column, but I don't have a column anymore, so I don't know what I can do for you, though I *do* know some agents, and I could make a call or two and see about getting you a tryout with a semi-pro team. Does that sound feasible?"

"What I'd like," he says calmly, "is for us to get to know each other. See what happens."

"You mean you'd like *me* to be your agent?" I say, inadvertently calculating twenty percent of nine million.

He shakes his head. "No, I mean we'll just play together and go from there."

"Play? Come on, Spear. I'm two feet tall. I'm a hundred and seventy-five years old. Get real."

"Slow down now, Vic," he says, surprised at my vehemence. "When we start playing every day, we'll find out what's real."

"Every day? What would be the point of that? I don't understand."

Greta sits up, spilling the cat from her lap. "He's inviting you to come play with him. What's so hard to understand about that?"

"To what end?" I squeak, the face of my mother looming in my mind, her mouth forming the words, *"Money. What about money?"*

"To fulfill his destiny," says Ruby, punctuating every syllable. "The time is now. Spirits are very clear about this."

"I don't know about destiny," says Spear, picking up the white cat and kissing its nose. "I'd just like to run with you some more. There was magic out there today, Vic. Didn't you think so?"

"We need a commitment," says Ruby, pacing angrily around the room. *"Now."*

"Why so soon?" I say, wishing we could go back to telling stories. "Why so definite?"

"We can't wait another year." She looks out her window and shakes her head. "His time has come. There's no question about it. Surely you can give us a month, Mr. Worsley. A month goes by in no time."

"A *month*," I gasp, the span of days enormous. "A month is a *long* time. Especially when you don't have a job."

"A month is nothing," says Ruby, scowling at me. "Yes or no?"

"We'll just play together," says Spear, nodding hopefully. "We'll start you on Monday. That'll give you the weekend to get used to the idea. What do you say?"

Time hangs suspended. The only poem I ever finished writing comes to me.

> *How could I not know the answer?*
> *How could I not know*
> *how to jitterbug?*
> *Shall I live my life*
> *as a goodly tramp*
> *or as the pawn of fear?*

I look at Greta, my new best friend, perhaps one day my lover. Her eyes are closed, and I know she's praying for me. I look at Ruby. Her head is tilted back, her eyelids fluttering, her lips moving silently. But I'm afraid to look at Spear. That's it, isn't it? I'm terrified of the very men I worship. I've made good money writing about them. How could I possibly turn him down? I force myself to look at him, and to my amazement, he has assumed the full lotus position, the palms of his enormous hands open to receive whatever this life may bring, the fire crackling behind him, his face radiant. So I close my eyes, and *I'm standing on the edge of the court at Tillsbury, Spear whispering, "Give to the open man. Somebody always gonna be open."*

"Yes!" I cry, opening my eyes. "I'll be here on Monday."

"Yay," says Greta, jumping up and waltzing Ruby around the room. "You did it. You got old Vic to say yes."

"Now, don't be silly," says Ruby, breaking away from her, smiling in spite of herself. "I didn't do anything but ask."

And as we laugh and shake hands to seal our pact, I look into Spear's eyes and we're boys again. Boys who like to run and jump. Boys who like to win. Boys who love to play the greatest game since running down the deer.

11

Sunday afternoon, McKinley Park, the blustery wind a definite factor in our shot selection. Nolan stands at the top of the key, catching his breath before we play the final point of our fifth game. We've been going an extra hour every day to prepare me for Tillsbury. Sleep has not come easily these last few nights. Tomorrow, I'll take the morning train to Oakland, where Spear will be waiting for me.

"So are you and Greta lovers?" he asks, smiling hopefully. "Must be exciting. Someone new."

"We aren't, actually, yet. Or . . . we don't know. We're mostly kissing now. We took our first bath together last night."

"Sounds promising." He shoots, banking it in off the backboard. "Sounds great! Even just naked must be a thrill, huh? Don't get me wrong, Esther is still a very sexy woman, it's just that after twenty years, you can't help wondering what it would be like with someone new."

"Hence, you go to movies with me featuring athletic sex with impossibly gorgeous babes."

"And she goes to those soft-focus romances where innuendo is everything and sex is indicated by a messy bed in the morning." He flops down on the grass. "So you're sure you want to do this Oakland thing? Sounds scary. I don't know if I could enjoy myself being so scared. I like the way *we* do it. A great workout without fear of injury. I bet they bang like shit over there."

"Maybe not," I say, remembering how clean the play was with Spear on the court. "Mostly fast breaks to set up dunks and circus shots. It's better than I ever imagined. They have the most complex vocabulary of moves, to quote Sheila, Greta's housemate."

He grins. "Greta. Tell me about her."

"And Spear is their leader," I say, ignoring his inquiry into my love life. "He's just incredible. Light-years better than anyone I've ever seen."

"Playground ball," says Nolan, picking at the grass. "Kid stuff. That's what my dad would say when I'd come home from the gym. Kid stuff."

"My mother called it 'that damn bouncing thing you do.' "

"And your father?" he asks, arching his eyebrow. "The human encyclopedia? What was his diagnosis?"

"He shot around with me a few times. He could have been pretty good. But like you say, it didn't qualify as work, so why do it?"

"But now we call it aerobic exercise. Doctor's orders." He slaps me. "You wanna go for a beer?"

"I thought you weren't drinking anymore."

"Only on special occasions. It's not every day my best friend goes off to war."

We stop in at Defarge's, our local brew pub featuring a bevy of comely waitresses. Mimi of the enormous eyes and the partially observable breasts takes our order, snapping her gum, her hips swaying hypnotically as she snakes her way back to the bar, guaranteeing an enormous tip from Nolan.

"In my mind," says Nolan, nodding in Mimi's direction.

"Many times. Esther forgives me. She likes her cuties in *Esquire*, I like my cuties wherever they find me. It all balances out. The main thing is to be friends, or it won't last two years. That's how I'd write the wedding vow. We promise to be best friends, and treat each other with utmost respect and patience. For as long as we can."

"I've always envied your relationship with Esther. It seems so solid. So comfortable. So warm."

"Not always." He forces a smile. "It's like Esther's mother says. The most important thing you need for a successful relationship is the ability to forgive each other. *If* the sex is pretty good."

Two pints down, the ache in my lower back finally subsiding, Nolan looks me in the eyes. "But see, I always envied the way *you* gave yourself to the game. Even if we were just geeks on a po-dunk team, as you are so fond of saying, you ended up eating lunch with the best. You sat around talking to Dr. J. and Magic Johnson. Jesus Christ, Vic, you've *lived* it. At the highest level."

"But I need to play, Nolan. I need to go as far as I can before I get any older. It's like Greta wondering about having a baby. I'll never be able to do this again, if I can even do it now. Did I tell you she dreams she's pregnant? Every night?"

"No. But tell me," he says, a faraway look in his eyes. "I'm beginning my parallel voyeuristic experience with her. So tell me as much as you feel okay about telling me. If you don't mind."

"What about Mimi?"

"I still love her, too. Now tell me more. Do you sleep to-gether?"

"Last night was the first time we slept in the same bed." I flag Mimi. "Two more, please."

"So I take it we're getting drunk." He smiles. "I haven't been drunk in two years. I guess it's okay, huh?"

"It's too late now, Nolan. Because here she comes."

"Naked?" he asks, taking the brimming glasses from her. "You sleep naked with her?"

Mimi smiles at me expectantly. "I don't know the rest of the story, Vic, but I can't wait to hear your answer."

"Silk pajamas," I say, smirking. "We're taking things slow."

"That's the best way nowadays," she says, winking as she slinks away.

"I love her more with every beer I drink," says Nolan, watching her go. "Her voice, her body. Mostly her body."

"Oh, I'll tell you something about Greta," I say, gulping the froth. "You'll like this, Nolan. This is right up your alley."

"I should videotape the entire romance," he says, waving imperiously to the room. "Interviews cut into action segments. *Greta and Vic.* Go on."

"Well, it's about her hair. She has this fantastic tumble of thick black hair, and sometimes she braids it quite severely, and sometimes she just lets it go. But in the evening by the fire, every night we've spent together so far, she braids it loose, and it stays that way without any rubber band or ribbon. An untied braid. I find it devastatingly sexy."

"I could videotape her making this braid. I could make an entire short film. *Greta's Braid.* It's genius. And this is the best beer and the best bar in the world."

We walk our bikes to my house, the world galvanized into dramatic harshness by the receding effects of Defarge's dark brew. We arrive home at the precise moment Greta comes pumping up the other side of the hill on her old three-speed Schwinn. She's wearing an ankle-length baggy brown skirt, clodhoppers, a pink dress shirt, a fat red tie, and an old leather aviator helmet with a hawk feather jammed into one of its seams. Her lips are painted dark red, the only sign of makeup. And her hair, soon to be a Nolan Smith production, is a windblown tangle of epic proportions, as wild as a storm-tossed sea.

"Hi," she says, flashing one of her more incisive smiles. "I'm Greta. You must be Nolan."

He turns to me. "You said she was beautiful, Vic, but you said nothing about her being the woman of my dreams."

"Flatterer," she says, leaning over her handlebars to kiss me. "Bring him in, Vic. We like him."

"I can't," says Nolan, extending his hand to her. "My dear wife and I are celebrating our twenty-second wedding anniversary this evening, and if I were to come in, I doubt very much that even such a momentous occasion would suffice to drag me away from you. But even this, this passing of strangers on a sidewalk, has been a distinct pleasure. I am deeply smitten, and not merely because I am a debauched drunkard, but because you're *you*. There's no doubt about it."

She takes his hand and looks into his eyes. "I *knew* he'd have a sweet best friend. The cynical guys almost always do."

"Oh, and she's honest," he says, relishing her touch. "And just a little bit cruel, too. That's good, Vic. We like the razor's edge."

At dusk, Greta and I stand on the bedroom veranda, sipping a somewhat bitter zinfandel. "Not so good," I say, frowning at my glass. "Sorry."

"Scared about going tomorrow?"

"Feverish, actually. Haven't been sleeping well."

"I'm proud of you for taking a chance like this. You're being incredibly brave."

"I don't feel brave. I feel completely out of control."

"Oh, that." She laughs and clinks my glass with hers. "Welcome to the club."

We migrate to the living room and she puts on some good old Rickie Lee Jones. "Come on, Vic," she says, unlacing her boots. "Let's dance for a while, huh?"

"I'm not much in the mood," I say, feeling out of sorts, Defarge's beer no longer a pleasure. "I'm very very tired."

"Then you can just sit and watch me," she says, dancing over to the fire, giving herself to the gorgeous music, shaking out the tension in her body.

As I watch her making wild shadows on the ceiling, I imagine her with a baby in her arms. And it seems wonderful, though try as I may, I can't see myself in the picture.

On our walk to the top of the hill, the brightest stars centered around Orion, we kiss for the longest time, she promising divine and extraordinary ministrations of love, I echoing her as we rush back down to my decadent cave.

But our passion subsides as we barge through the door, as if something in the air were an antidote to lust. So we sit apart on the futon by the fire, neither of us capable of speaking. A deep sense of gloom descends on me, and I brace myself for her to say good-bye. But instead, she slides over beside me and gives me a long shoulder massage, her fingers strong and sure, and I fall asleep in her arms dreaming we make love, and her scar opens and a child emerges. A boy of three or four, fully clothed.

My little snooze over, I tell her my dream and we kiss each other right to the edge of complete surrender. Except we don't give in, both of us certain the time is still not right.

We busy ourselves apart from each other. I do the dishes and listen to Bonnie Raitt's most heart-wrenching hits, while Greta takes a bath, after which she bundles up and rushes out, barely saying good-bye. I feel abandoned, my life a pointless waste. I don't know if she's angry or sad or if I'll ever see her again. There was such great terror for both of us at the brink.

I wait a miserable hour before calling Nolan. I get his machine with Miles Davis blowing cool jazz in the background. "This is Nolan Smith. Films. We turn chaos into comprehendible order for a reasonable price. And if this is Vic, I can't wait for the next installment. Please leave as long a message as you'd like."

"Nolan. Things have not gone so well. Things . . ."

My front door opens. Greta stands on the threshold with three full shopping bags. "Hi. It's me."

"Never mind, Nolan. She came back."

"I *really* want to cook something for you. Okay?"

"May I help you?"

"You may cut things up, but leave the sauce to me."

Our tummies full of her righteous spaghetti, the allspice dominant, I can't fall asleep beside her. My body is too much in love with her body to stay unaroused. So I sneak out of bed and retire to the trusty futon by the fallen fire, and when the buzz in my brain finally gives way to sleep, I dream that Nolan and I are playing together at Tillsbury, the two of us against everyone else.

Part Two

Mulch Cloud

Ah a poet makes a boat

to take us off on seas of time

where nothing but vision

allows us fusion with the Almighty

wheel whose center is a ring

of mirrors, a well of clouds

Am I free of fear?

DAVID MELTZER

12

Today is Thursday, the fourth day of my sojourn in Oakland, my apprenticeship well underway. I have stepped onto this path, and I am determined to stay on it, though there are times when I deeply doubt my sanity. I met Spear one week ago today, though it sometimes seems an eternity.

Yesterday, I caught a glimpse of my face in the mirror. I barely recognized myself. I seemed younger. Focused. There was no question about what I had to do. Play with every ounce of strength in my body, or be overwhelmed and humiliated.

I have stopped drinking wine and beer and coffee. The afternoon headaches have been murderous. I rarely think about writing. When I do, the concept seems foreign to me. What good would words do me on the court? If it doesn't keep the man I'm guarding from getting the ball, it has no value. If it doesn't enhance my jump shot, who needs it? I can do things with a basketball I haven't been able to do in twenty years. And late this afternoon, when I return to my hilltop villa across the bay, I will not rush to the machine wishing for a call from Lucas. Instead, I will take a hot bath, eat an early dinner, and go to bed, there to rest my weary bones and dream of Tillsbury until my alarm clock or Greta rouses me for a late-evening snack and a long walk to keep me loose for tomorrow.

Spear is still huge to my senses, huge in my dreams, though I no longer quake when he comes near. I know him as a human being now, capable of great anger and disdain, yet always striving to be rigorously fair. He is quick to praise any player who handles the ball with artistry, opponents included. On my second day here, Thomas capped a breathtaking drive against us with a dandy little scoop shot over Juanishi. It was an utterly brilliant combination of power and delicacy. Spear stopped play to marvel at the beauty of it all. "That's it! Right there! Pure genius, Mister T. God, you fly so high, it makes me wanta cry."

He is a pilgrim on an unmarked path. Basketball is the foundation of his spiritual practice, his dedication contagious. Every move he makes, with or without the ball, is imbued with the sublime energy of his devotion.

So here I am, standing on the court, breathless with fear, nearly paralyzed by the growing sensation that every ounce of my strength may not be enough to sustain this odyssey much longer. I am smack dab in the middle of a ferocious showdown with my own teammates. Why? Because I've made several idiotic goofs that may cost us the game. The opposing team is a gang of trash-talking teenagers eager to knock off the reigning champions. We are down nine to five, and for the first time in my brief career here, Spear is not inclined to back me up. A most unpleasant development, to say the least.

Juanishi, a massively muscular Chinese Hispanic black guy known for his fearless crashing of the boards, shakes a menacing finger at me. "Listen, you little white shit, you couldn't walk on the same court with us if you weren't Spear's boy."

Pogo, our stupendous point, the physical being I most wish to be, snarls at Spear. "I've known dead guys faster than him. Why you want him to run with us?"

Wild, the wide-chassis forward with a great underhand move,

scrunches up his face at me. "You his little whore? Bet he don't hardly fit."

"Heaven forbid!" I cry, aghast at the thought of it. "Don't be ridiculous."

My girlish disclaimer transforms Juanishi. He bats his eyelids and sashays around, squealing, "Heaven forbid! *Heaven* forbid!"

The guys all laugh, the tension breaks, and the game resumes. I focus completely on playing defense. My last three flubs are weighing heavily on me, so I don't even want to *think* about touching the ball again. I want to stay out of this as much as possible. But my man keeps leaving me open, and Pogo keeps dishing to me, until finally I can't resist a shot from twenty feet away, the ball rippling through the net. And seven more times in blissful succession the bodies shift to the right as I slip away to the left, taking Pogo's pass and stroking it down, breaking the backs of our youthful opponents.

"Vix," says Wild, bumping fists with me as we walk off the court, "I take back what I said. You are one deadly shot. Blew those boys away."

Juanishi nods to me, his upper body heavily muscled from years of weight lifting at San Quentin. "Way to knock it, Tiny. Gettin' automatic out there."

Spear winks at me and touches my arm. "Quite a groove. Feeling pretty good now, huh?"

Thomas descends from the bleachers and shakes my hand. "Looked like me out there, man. Gettin' more leg into it now."

Pogo wipes his bald head with his red bandana and gives Thomas a thoroughly disgusted look. "That's such bullshit. Who can't make a few twenty-footers with nobody guarding him? You guys proud of beatin' a bunch of fuckin' teenagers we shoulda beat twelve zip if this little shit hadn't fucked up so much?"

Spear frowns at his friend. "Hey, Pogo. You guys were grooving out there. No need for that kind of talk."

"Yes there is," says Pogo, standing up to him. "I've taken this bullshit long enough. You said give the man a chance, we did. Monday, Tuesday, Wednesday, and now it's fuckin' Thursday, man, and the midget can't play. He can't play, Spear. Simple. No can do. And you got Thomas coming off the bench for this dog meat? It's a fuckin' insult, man. Not just to him, but to me. Makes me sick having to pass to him."

"Hey, Po," says Wild, wiping his brow. "Vix workin' hard to get open. Knockin' down most every shot he takes. Makin' some good passes, too."

Pogo sticks a finger in his mouth, pretending to vomit. "Why you talkin' such bullshit, Wild? You don't really think he can play? Do you?"

Juanishi shrugs and gives Spear a goofy little smile. "He hits when he's open. He ain't Thomas, but we're still winning."

Pogo scowls at all of them. "You pussies. You fuckin' pussies. This man is a joke, and you're all just too scared of Spear to say so."

"Hold on," I say, tiring of his abuse. "I'm not as bad as you think, Pogo."

"No, you're worse," he mutters, walking away. "You couldn't score a bucket off me one-on-one in a million years."

"You're wrong," I say, calling after him. "I could score off you."

He freezes in his tracks. "Fifty dollars says you can't."

"I don't play for money. Let's just play to play."

He turns and points at my face. "No, Vickie. If I'm gonna waste my time with shit like you, I want something for it."

"Okay," I say, looking at Spear. "If I can't score off of you at least once playing to fifteen by ones, I'll never come back here. You'll never have to play with me again. That should be incentive enough for you, huh?"

He snaps the ball to me. "My pleasure. My extreme pleasure."

"Wait a minute here," says Spear, coming onto the court. "This is not the way to resolve this. Let's talk about . . ."

"Butt out," says Pogo, clenching his fists. "He challenged me, man. He made the bet, not me."

"Come on, Pogo," says Wild, sighing heavily. "What's the point? We all know you can shut him down. So what? Spear can shut *you* down. That's not what the game's about."

Thomas looks away, embarrassed. "Let it go, Pogo. I can deal with this. Okay?"

Pogo squints at me. He's a beautiful man, his features accentuated by his baldness, his skin dark honey brown. "You want to let it go, Vickie? Wanna keep on pretending you can play? When we all know you're bullshit."

"Let's play," I say, eager to have things out with him—the champion of their collective doubt. "Shall I shoot for outs?"

He laughs dryly. "No, honey, you take it out. Ain't gonna make no difference."

"I don't know about that," I say, quickly launching the ball from twenty-eight feet, arching it high over Pogo's outstretched arms, holding my breath as it falls through the cloudy sky and splashes cleanly through the net.

"Yeah!" says Wild, clapping his hands. "That Vix can *shoot*."

Pogo pounds the ball with his fist. "That's bullshit! You didn't even bring it in."

I'm stunned by his denial of my score. "What are you talking about? You were all over me."

He slams the ball to the ground. "Bullshit. No point playin' with you if all you're gonna do is cheat."

A silence falls. I glance over at Spear and Wild and Juanishi and Thomas. They are frozen in anticipation, waiting for me to respond. And for some inexplicable reason, I'm not angry. Nor do I doubt that I can score again. Somehow, over the last four days, I've gained a confidence in my ability that I haven't felt since my college days, and Pogo, ironically, has been the prime architect of my rebuilding.

I smile at the ball in my hand. "You know what? I honestly didn't know I had to dribble before shooting. You seemed to be guarding me. But I'll let you make the call. If you think I broke the rules, let's run it again."

"You have to dribble in," says Pogo, nodding rapidly. "Otherwise you could shoot from out of bounds, couldn't you?"

"That's true," I say, taking the ball from him and dribbling to my left. He presses close, his hands flicking all around me, and with no particular shot in mind, I leave the ground and put up an awkward left-handed runner from fifteen feet away on the side. He doesn't expect it, but he's such a magnificent leaper that he still manages to touch it, redirecting it against the backboard from where it clanks through anyway.

"Can't call that one back," says Wild, clapping his hands. "Wasn't pretty, but it sure went in, didn't it?"

Pogo slams the ball to the ground. "Sonofabitch! That was pure luck. You gonna say that proves you can play? You gonna count that?"

"What do *you* think I should do?" I ask him, fascinated by his unwillingness to accept what I've done. "I don't really care if we count it or not, although they do count those in the NBA."

"Oh, now you gonna play in the NBA?" He grimaces at me. "I blocked that shit. Pure luck it went in, and you know it."

"So you're saying it doesn't count?"

"I'm saying if you're a man, Vickie, you don't count it."

"Okay." I take the ball from him. "Let's not count it. But if it goes in this time, no matter how it happens to do that, we count it. Agreed?"

"Ain't gonna go in," he whispers, his eyes locked on the ball. "No way."

"Why not?" I ask, flushed with the heat of my newfound faith. "Why don't you think it'll go in?"

"Because three in a row against Pogo Malone can't be luck."

"So my first shot was luck, too? I thought you said I cheated."

He says nothing, his hatred tangible, and I realize that this moment embodies my favorite part of basketball. One man against another. His instincts against mine. Our bodies the vehicles for our intentions, the outcome unknowable.

I bring it in, dribbling to my left. My first impulse is to shoot quickly again, but I can sense that he's set for that, so I circle back to my right, his body cloaking mine, the force of his concentration inspiring my most crippling doubts. There's no way I can shoot. He can jump five feet straight up. Maybe he's right.

Maybe the first two were luck. But as we rush toward the baseline, his reflex to stay in bounds slows him ever so slightly and I
leave the ground, launching my shot over his fingertips as I fall
away out of bounds, the ball climbing over the corner of the
backboard and dropping cleanly through the net.

Pogo doesn't curse this time. He retrieves the ball and brings
it to me, placing it firmly in my hands and striking it three times
with his fist. "That was more than luck," he says, looking me in
the eye. "We'll see you tomorrow."

At a pizza place ten blocks from the park, I stand at the
sidewalk window lost in self-congratulations until five big boys
close in around me, and one of them says, "Hey, motherfucker,
somebody got on the wrong side of town, and it ain't us."

I turn to look for Spear, my heart in my throat. The biggest
kid punches me in the shoulder. "Can't you talk, motherfucker?"

I don't move. I don't say a word. My every instinct tells me
that to run or fight would be suicide.

"I asked you a question, motherfucker," says the boy, rearing
back to hit me again.

I bow my head and clench my teeth, bracing myself for the
blow, but it never falls. The boys back away from me, frowning
uncertainly as Spear emerges from the alley where he went to
pee. The little Asian man behind the bulletproof window shouts,
"Pizza ready. Extra garlic and mushrooms."

"Gimme two large combinations," I stutter, shoving him a
precious twenty. "You guys like combinations?"

An awkward silence falls, broken finally by a kid with watery
eyes. "Make one just vegetables," he says, shrugging. "I'm kind of
allergic to cheese."

"Can you say thank you?" asks Spear, looking at each of the
young men. "Let the man pass with our lunch. We just played
some serious ball. This man has an outside shot put all of you to
shame. Let him pass. Unless you want to deal with me."

The boys are stunned that I'm with Spear. "This for real?" asks their leader, squinting at me. "He really buy us two pizzas?"

"It better be real." Spear raps the glass and glowers at the little man with the wilted chef's hat. "Got that, Sammie? Give the boys good food, or I'll hear about it."

"Not bad," says a skinny kid, sneering at me. "White motherfucker oughta pay."

The boys giggle, but their leader silences them. "You heard the brother. Say thank you to the motherfucker."

So they chorus happily, "Thank you, motherfucker!"

Eating our pizza while we wait for the F Bus to San Francisco, Spear smiles at me. "Remember that play you made in the first game today? You were staying away from the fracas in the key, bouncing around on the left wing, and Juanishi powered one off the iron and it deflected to you, and you put it back in before anybody could think to stop you. And Wild shouted, *Too* quick, Vixer. Might just make the team.'"

"When will I know?" I ask, embarrassed to have my minimal exploits recounted by such a great master. "Will you carve a list on the oak tree?"

"Already did," he says, nudging me. "You've been at it four days. Not such easy work, is it? But you got over a big hump today, Vic. No question about it."

"Because I scored off Pogo?"

"Partly that. But mostly because you finally came to play, not just to see if you could. You were totally into it. Seemed like you knew how you wanted to use yourself. You know what I mean? It was a pleasure to watch you, even when you blew it."

"You're too kind. So now what?"

"So tomorrow's Friday. Then Saturday we run the zoo, and Sunday we have the play-offs."

"I've heard the guys talking about the zoo. What exactly goes on?"

"We call it the zoo because *all* the animals come to play. The older guys with daytime gigs, the used-to-be college players, big guns from out of town. They all come on Saturday." He appraises me critically. "I don't know if you're quite ready to play a zoo, Vic. Maybe not this week. But I want you to come and watch if you can. Ruby comes on Saturday. Everybody does. It's a big party."

"And the play-offs?"

"Sunday," he says, dreamy-eyed. "Cream of the cream. Sky high, my friend. Blow your mind. Not to be missed."

"Ruby come on Sunday, too?"

He solemnly shakes his head. "No women on Sunday."

"Any white men?"

"Not until *you* came along." He winks at me. "Won't that be fun for you?"

"Hey, Spear?" I say, smarting from the blow at the pizza parlor. "No bullshit. I don't want to come if it's not okay. I'm not doing this to scare myself."

"Then why *are* you doing it?" he asks with unmistakable contempt.

"What do you mean? Because I agreed to."

"Yeah, but why did you agree, Vic? So you could experience *black* culture? Have a little sociological adventure and run your love handles off?"

"Of course not," I say, deeply dismayed. "I like you, Spear. I like what's going on with us."

He grimaces in pain. "Yeah? Then how come you never ask me over to your house? Because you don't want your friends knowing you're spending time with me?"

"No, Spear. Not at all. I've just been so tired, I . . . ."

"Don't lie to me, Vic. Tell me the truth. Are you ashamed to be my friend?"

I'm crushed by his question. "Look," I say, my heart aching, "you want a tryout? I'll make some calls. Will that do it?"

"No, no." He waves my words away. "You don't get it, do you?

I just want to visit you at your house. I'd like to get to know you,
Vic, and I don't understand why you don't want to get to know
me. Besides, we're not ready for a tryout yet."

"What do you mean? You're great. You'll make it easily. I
know you will."

"Make what?"

"The pros."

"Who said I wanted to make the pros?"

"Isn't that why Ruby came to see me in the first place? Because
you wanted to be the Warriors' big man?"

"No, my friend." He puts his huge hand on my shoulder.
"*Ruby* wants me to be the Warriors' big man."

"So what are you saying? You want to play point?"

He laughs. "I want to be your friend, Vic. From the minute I
saw you. That hasn't happened to me but two or three times in
my life. I thought you wanted to be my friend, too. That's why I
asked you to play with me. Because whether you believe it or not,
I *know* this game will lead us where we need to go."

"So," I say, locking eyes with him, "what are you doing tonight? Want to come over for dinner?"

"Can't tonight," he says, smiling as he flags the approaching
bus. "My boy Isaac turns nine today. Big birthday party. I'd be
honored if you could come. Seven o'clock?"

"I'll be there," I say, deeply relieved to be friends again. "May I
bring Greta?"

"She would be most welcome," he says, giving my shoulder a
squeeze as I climb on the bus. "Ruby talks about her all the time.
Loves that her name is Eagleheart. She's still calling you Mr. Worsley. It always takes her some time to loosen up, but when she
does, she can be sweet."

On the bus, awaiting the loading of two people in wheel-
chairs, I open my window and call out to Spear. "Hey, I'm proud
to be your friend. I'm sorry I didn't let you know. I'm kind of a
social klutz. Always have been. Forgive me?"

He bows, bending from the waist. "I should have asked you
about it sooner instead of letting the anger build up. It's like

Rashan says. It's never a matter of right or wrong. It's always a misunderstanding."

The bus ride home is uneventful, save for a blind man's dog growling at a man with a badly fitting wig. I gaze out at the railyards of Oakland, the warehouses ringed with barbed wire, the overweening billboards selling beer and cars and impossible lives, and I hear Spear saying, "Whether you believe it or not, I *know* this game will lead us where we need to go." I wish *I* were so trusting. But I can't help wondering for the thousandth time if I've made a mistake by agreeing to play with him. My savings are evaporating, my mortgage is growling, and every time I leave Oakland and head for home, whether I ride the train or the bus or the ferry, I fall into doubt and despair. Maybe the best thing I can do is get him an agent, return to reality, and find some sort of paying gig.

I stumble off the bus at the bottom of my hill, too tired to climb, so I flag a cab, despite the extravagance. The driver is familiar to me, a gray-bearded Haitian, his eyes brimming with light. "Hello, again," he sings in his raspy way. "You live just up the hill here, yah? With the bougainvillea like back home on the island."

"Yes," I say, sighing heavily. "The one with the tile roof and the dying lawn."

"You sound tired out. Better take care. Body needs to rest."

By the time I reach my front door, I'm wracked with chills. Greta emerges from the kitchen, her hands oily from tossing salad, her lovely smile fading at the sight of me. "God, Vic, you look like death."

"I'm so weak, I can barely stand up."

She takes my hand. "You're like ice. You need a hot shower."

"I need to lie down before I fall down."

She helps me into bed and covers me with three thick blankets, and I shiver for a long time before I break a sweat and fall into a delirious sleep, my dreams a jumble of frantic scrambles for the ball.

I wake in darkness, drained of strength, my fever raging. Greta touches my forehead, her hand shockingly cool. "You're burning up, Vic. I'm gonna get you some aspirin."

"I'm so weak. So incredibly weak. What time is it?"

"Seven."

"Oh, no." I throw back the covers. "I have to call Spear."

"Stay where you are," she says, covering me again. "I'll bring you the phone."

He answers on the second ring. "Where are you, friend? We're holding the show for you."

"I'm ill, Spear. Terrible fever. I overslept. I'm sorry I didn't call sooner."

He says nothing, but his anguish is palpable.

"I guess I just pushed my body too hard. I'm weak as a kitten."

I hear a child calling him from the distance. "Come on, Papa! Time for my ceremony. Ruby dyed her hair all green, and everything."

"I'm sorry, Spear. I was really looking forward to it."

"I believe you," he says, his voice full of kindness. "I'm disappointed, but I know you've been working hard. Making a great effort. Can I bring you some soup or something tomorrow?"

"Sure, if you want to."

"Tell me how to get there."

As I give him directions, my fever breaks. "Or who knows? Maybe I'll wake up cured."

"Take a day off," he says calmly. "Be good to hear what the men have to say without you listening."

"Which, of course, you will repeat to me in great detail."

"When I bring the soup. How about four o'clock? Is that a good time for you?"

"Four. Perfect."

Greta comes in and helps me take three aspirin. She feels my forehead. "You need to rest, sweetheart. I'm gonna go home. I left you some salad and tofu burgers in the fridge. Call me when you feel better."

"Did we have a date?" I ask, feeling rotten for forgetting.

"No, I just dropped by. Let myself in. Thought I'd surprise you with dinner. Is that okay?"

"Fine," I say, kissing her lips, feeling the dryness of mine. "I want you to come over whenever you want. That's why I gave you the key."

"I've just been thinking about all sorts of things I want to talk to you about. But they can wait."

"Tell me now," I say, holding her hand. "I miss you."

"I miss you, too." She kisses my cheek. "You should sleep. I'll be over for breakfast. After I pick up my results. Remember?"

"That was fast," I say, my fever returning. "I thought it took much longer."

"Tests are faster now," she says, tucking me in. "Yours are probably ready, too."

I fall asleep, and *I'm floating a few feet above the floor of the lobby at the* Chron. *I'm telling Greta and Lucas all about a game I played today, and as I speak, the game materializes around us.*

Thomas, rakishly handsome, rises into the air with the ball. "You got a sweet touch from nineteen, Vic. Put more leg in it you could go to twenty-three."

Godfrey releases a shot from long range. "Uh oh, it's the Vixter. Beware."

Juanishi flies by, dunking rapaciously, shaking a finger at me. "You hesitate, you don't get no breakaway."

Billy Wild, his dexterity astounding, launches a running hook. "Use what you got any chance you get."

And Pogo vaults sideways through the lane, his eyes fixed on the hoop as he dishes to me for a wide-open jumper.

But his pass never reaches me. I'm not really in the game. The ball cannot penetrate the invisible shell that separates me from them.

13

Waking from my healing hibernation, I take a long shower and sing "Oh, What a Beautiful Morning" with great gusto, deeply relieved not to be going to Oakland today. I don my plush purple bathrobe and wander through my spacious home to the kitchen, where a letter awaits me on the refrigerator.

Dear Vic,

It occurs to me that one essential component of our relationship is missing, aside from wild and uninhibited sex (soon?) and that is the writing of love letters. So here is one from me to you.

I do remember the very first time I saw you. I'd only been working at the paper for a few weeks. We were all staying late to get out a big baseball issue, and you came wandering in—handsome and unshaven—with a column about Danny Ainge, full of your theories as to why he had eschewed the easy life of baseball for the glorious dangers of basketball. Lucas introduced us, and as you devoured me with your beautiful brown eyes (don't try to deny it) you said, "At last. A good reason to come down here."

I was, at that time, not the least bit interested in starting a romantic relationship with a man, and I was relieved when you didn't ask me out right away. Then about three months later, when my relief was turning to frustration, you dropped off a column at my desk and said to me, "I'm gonna get a sandwich at Max's. Want one?"

I blushed from head to toe, nodded dumbly, and grabbed my purse, thinking we were going out, only to have you say, "No, that's okay. You stay here. I'll bring them back for us. What kind would you like?"

I think I said, "Tuna," and then you left. I was so turned on I had to go to the ladies' room and take care of myself, which is when I knew my disinterest was officially over. At least regarding you.

So. The years have somehow passed, and here we are. On the verge of the verge. Lisa says being in love makes me seem taller, but it's just 'cause I'm floating.

Call me.

Greta

Or call me Ishmael. Whatever you do, call me.

Fueled by her words, most specifically the phrase "wild and uninhibited sex," I dress quickly and splurge once again on a cab to my doctor's office. Cabs may be my most difficult habit to break, but then poverty should take care of that. The driver is a big woman with curly brown hair squished under a Giants baseball cap, the stub of a cigar hanging from her mouth. "If you wanna talk," she says, checking me in her rearview mirror, "say so. Otherwise, I don't talk. But I will. If you want."

"I'll daydream," I say, staring out at the foggy morning, drifting away to the last moments I spent with Emily, the moving van rolling away down the hill, pretty Emily standing by her red Mustang, gazing past me at the house, waiting for me to say something. But no words would come to me. I was glad she was going away. I looked forward to my empty house, my empty life, for at least now there would be a chance to fill it with something other than dishonesty and pain.

"I left a list," she said, her dimples deepening in that way I once found irresistible. "Just in case. I put it in your medical file."

"A list of what?" I asked numbly, chanting to myself, "*Go. Go. Go.*"

"In case, you know, something comes up." She forced a false little smile. "It probably won't. If it hasn't by now."

"What are you talking about?" "*Just go away. Please. Get in your car and go.*"

"Remember that one infection we got a few years ago?" She stared down at the sidewalk. "Just in case you get another one. I left their numbers. The other men . . ."

"I don't want to hear this," I said, cutting her off. "Just go. Just get the fuck out of my life."

"I didn't do it to make you mad," she said, walking around the nose of her car. "I did it to be considerate."

And with that, she left me precisely where she wanted me. Hating everything about her.

My thoughts drift to Tillsbury, and I wonder what the guys would think if they knew I hadn't had sex with a woman in a decade, my forties as barren as my teens. What would they think if I hadn't first appeared to them with Greta hanging on to me for all of them to see? There is no question that she endows me with power in their eyes. I may be middle-aged and slow, but a gorgeous woman loves me, and Spear, their great leader, has chosen

me to be his friend. So despite all physical evidence to the con-
trary, I must be a formidable man.

My doctor's office is on the seventeenth floor with a pan-
oramic view of the Golden Gate to the north, the Bay Bridge and
Berkeley to the east, the great city revealed to be an impossible
geography of hills and waterways and skyscrapers, the ground
blanketed with curving roads and bridges and houses and swarms
of cars and buses and boats. The miraculous result of little or no
planning.

The nurse waves me into the corridor of my doctor's inner
sanctum. Dr. Shragg, not yet forty years old, his hair as white as
snow, his right eye twitching, pauses in the hallway between
examining rooms. "Congratulations, Vic. No bad guys. Cecilia
will give you a dated certificate." He frowns. "Are you still on
vacation? Miss your column. I hardly know how to start my day
without it."

I want to tell him the truth, but there doesn't seem to be time.
"Yes, I'm still on vacation."

Outside, the wind at my back, I flirt briefly with the idea of
walking the fifty blocks home, but a wave of fatigue washes over
me and I hail a cab. Once again, it's the old Checker driven by
my favorite Haitian.

He grins at me as I get in. "Two days in a row. What are the
odds of that in this big place?"

"Oh, I'm a very lucky guy. Very very lucky."

"Good for you," he says, pulling into traffic. "Maybe some of
that gonna rub off on me. Could be *my* lucky day, too. You like
to hear some tunes? I'll run some very nice reggae. Keep us nice
and cheered up."

Restless in my sparkling kitchen, I gorge on tangelos and
watch the clock. Nearly eleven. Five hours until Spear arrives. I

desperately want a triple *latte,* but I drink Postum instead, sitting on my bedroom veranda, looking out over the jungle of weeds and vines conquering my backyard. Little yellow birds dart around me, snatching lacy-winged bugs from the air. A blue jay lands atop a skinny tree I don't remember planting. I haven't written a single word in a week. Perhaps I'll never write again. But what else will people pay me for?

I read Greta's letter again, and it propels me to my office, where I sit down at my old typewriter and gawk at the fantastic view I've denied myself for so long. This is how I used to deal with loneliness. Banging out words to numb my sorrow. Or was it something else I was numbing? The vision of myself as a failure?

I pick up a fast black pen, the ink loose in the cannon.

Dear Greta,

> *I loved finding your letter this morning. It made me feel rich and strong. What a week. So many highs and so many lows crammed into such a short span of time. I wish I were more open to the magic of it all, but my cynical self has such a powerful hold on my brain, I keep dismissing the onrush of miracles as nothing more than a chaotic prelude to poverty—a last childish fling before the ava-lanche of unpaid bills drives me from my home and onto the mean streets I now walk with Spear.*

> *A week without writing and my sentences sprawl like uncaged tomatoes.*

> *You see the bent of my thoughts, my fears sabotaging what might otherwise be a grand adventure. If only I weren't so neurotically fixated on the getting and having of money. It was not always thus. I lived out of a backpack for three years after quitting college, proving to myself that as long as I lived fearlessly, I would always find enough of what I needed along the way. And I always did.*

That all seems like someone else's past, because now
when I think of losing this house . . .

Some love letter. Let's get that job back first, then we'll write
love letters. I leap up and dash down the hall to the kitchen. I've
never had a phone in my office, having learned as a fledgling
novelist that phone calls are the primary impediment to unbro-
ken concentration. I punch in Lucas's number and try to imagine
him smiling.

"Sports. Eagleheart."

"*Greta* Eagleheart, love of my life?"

"You're there," she says, her voice rich with lust. "I'll be right
over."

"Could you see if Lucas is available?"

"I'll patch you through, baby, but I'm on my way. Got my
good news." She pauses. "You?"

"I'll chill the champagne."

"And start a fire," she says, kissing the receiver. "Get that
house nice and warm."

I listen to Muzak while I wait for Lucas to answer. A pair of
chirping electric violins masticate and finally kill "Your Cheatin'
Heart." What am I going to say? Do I really want my job back?
Maybe I should call later. I used to think I was such a sly fox, my
access to the biggest stars the envy of every other writer. Now I
feel like an unpracticed kid looking for my first job.

"Vic? How are you?"

"Great, Luke. How are you?"

"Oh, mildly interested in this thing you're doing over in Oakland. Greta says you're actually playing with some pretty good
black guys? You gonna write about it?"

"I don't know. What do you think? Would you run it?"

"Probably not, but maybe. I'd have to see it first."

"No possibility of an advance?"

He hesitates. "Look, Vic, the wound is still too fresh here. Sorry. But do keep us in mind. I'd be happy to take a look at whatever you write. And if *I* can't do something with it, I'm sure you'll find somebody who will. Keep me posted. Gotta run."

I collapse on the futon, too depressed to start a fire, and I'm twenty-three again, sitting in Beatnik's Vegan Juice Bar with Tosca Soryano, the angry young editor of *Alphabet Threat*, the anarchist rag I sent my very first columns to. "More swear words," says Tosca, picking his nose. "Write it down just the way these guys really talk. Every other word is 'cocksucker,' right? Then try me again. These show promise. They're different. You definitely have your own style. Made me want to shoot some hoops, and I hate basketball. If your sentences weren't so clean, I'd print you every week. We don't pay in actual money, of course, but I'll buy you lunch any time we run something. Deal?"

Greta bursts in and yanks me back to the present, her raven black hair all tousled and windblown, her schoolgirl skirt kissing her sweet thighs, her flimsy blouse clinging to her breasts. She kicks off her shoes and wraps her arms around me. "Nothing to stop us now, huh?"

"Not a thing," I say, my ennui evaporating in the heat of lust. "If only I can remember what it is I'm supposed to do."

"Don't worry," she says, dizzying me with a kiss. "Come to bed. I'll give you a little refresher course."

But still we do not make love. We hesitate as I am about to enter her. There is something else to be said first. We are both still afraid. So I lie beside her, trying to think of something tender to say, but blurting instead, "I sometimes think about that man you killed, and it frightens me."

"I would never kill you," she says simply. "It's not a possibility. I only want to love you. It's like Ruby says, 'A man well-loved makes a good hunter.'"

"When did she say that? Have you been going to see her?"

"Just twice," says Greta, kissing my throat. "She's very wise, and she can be very cranky, too, but she helps me. And she reminds me of my granny, though she's much more talkative."

"How does she help you?"

"Gives me magic potions," she says, straddling me. "Didn't you wonder why you were falling more and more in love with me? I spiked your food, Vic. You're *doomed* to love me."

My body buzzing, I unconsciously brew myself a cup of coffee, only to throw it down the drain in horror at what Spear would think of such a habit, not that he's ever said anything about coffee. It's just a feeling I have. He's not a man in need of such a drug. In deference to him, I eat three apples and a tuna sandwich instead, while reading a story in *The New Yorker* about a man in love with his sister's daughter's girlfriend, told from the point of view of a puppy recently born to a dog living under the house of their next-door neighbor, a blind Apache seer named Gottlieb.

Four o'clock is fast approaching. Greta has returned to the *Chron*, where she will resume her chasing of the writer jocks, cajoling them to finish their columns, rewriting half of them before they go to press, doing most of Lucas's job.

We're lovers now. My entire body is tingling with new life. I can see through walls. I can see all the way to Oregon. It was the most divine release at the end of a long, hot holding and speaking without words as we moved and waited, locked deeply in every good way, until the wells within us loosed their liquids and glued us for life.

I wander through my palazzo, and I imagine selling it. I let it go and survive on whatever it brings me. Find another way to make money. I wonder if I could be happy living somewhere else? Or do I need this particular house? I love the light here, the relatively safe streets. But, yes, I could live somewhere else. People do it all the time.

Greta Greta Greta Greta Greta Greta Greta Greta Greta Greta Greta Greta.

I call the *Chron*, my heart pounding. I'm obscenely in love with her, greedy for every morsel of contact.

"Sports. Eagleheart."

"Hi. It's me."

"Can't talk right now. But I'll be over tonight. If you promise to ravish me again."

"I promise because all the molecules in the universe have been reconfigured by what happened today."

"Watch out, Vic. Sounds kinda New Age, doesn't it?"

"It *is* a new age," I say, growing hard at the thought of her. "I call it the New Age of Wild and Uninhibited Sex."

"Endorphins," she says, matter-of-factly. "I gotta go."

Spear and his son, Isaac, an extremely tall nine-year-old, arrive precisely at four. Isaac's yellow jumpsuit is intentionally too large. Advance planning for rampant growth. His floppy sandals reveal carefully painted red toenails. His face is a tender miniature of Spear's, his hair tangled and quite blond. Spear seems elegantly comfortable in a bright turquoise shirt, a burgundy tie, baggy black slacks, and red leather sandals. His toenails are painted dark blue.

We sit in the living room and wait for Ruby's special soup to warm slowly on the stove. I'm drinking ginseng tea, Spear and Isaac have peppermint. Isaac catches me looking at his toenails. "We painted them 'cause we're studying Egypt, and the men there used to do this, the pharaohs." He smiles mischievously at Spear. "Pharaohs were black people, huh, Papa?"

"We went to the De Young a couple weeks ago," says Spear, nodding. "African art show. Did you see it?"

"No, but I've heard it's wonderful."

"I liked the masks best of all," says Isaac, frowning at me. "Excuse me, but are those big books over there by the fireplace maybe art books?"

"As a matter of fact, they are. Please, help yourself."

Spear watches his son cross the room. "He loves to draw. He's got a good little jump shot starting to fall, but he'd much rather draw. Wouldn't you, Isaac?"

"Paint, draw, clay," he says, kneeling at my bookcase, pulling out a fat volume of Van Gogh. "Who is this?"

"A painter," I say, jumping up to check the soup. "One of the first guys to put his paint on real thick. You can have that book if you'd like."

"I can?" Isaac looks to his father, his eyes wide with wonder. "Can I?"

"Yes, you may. Now what do you say when someone gives you a gift?"

"Thank you very much," says Isaac, leafing through the book. "Hey, are these black people in here? Picture called 'The Potato Eaters.' "

"All kinds of different kinds of people," says Spear, rising to follow me. "That's one of Ruby's favorite expressions, and she also says not to boil that soup or you'll kill the power of the garlic. Says you need to flush your system."

"I can't tell you how exhausted I was. I haven't played half this hard since high school. And that, as you know, was a million years ago."

Spear watches Isaac turning the pages. "I don't know what I would have been like if I'd played in school. We teach our kids at home. My wife Chaka has her teaching certificate, so it's legal. Public school over where we are is way too dangerous."

"How many kids do you have?"

"In the house, five. Four are mine." He looks around at my commodious home, his eyes sparkling. "I think you're gonna find our house very interesting, Vic, seeing how different you live. This is quite a place for just one man. Must be nice to have all this space, huh?"

"Yeah," I say, inhaling the scent of garlic and sage and thyme. "Hey, I appreciate your bringing this. Thanks."

Spear looks away. "You know, Vic, you don't have to play

at Tillsbury anymore. You can just come and watch if you want."

"Wow," I murmur, crestfallen. "I've been waiting for this. Every day for a week. The short old white guy gone as far as he can."

He shakes his head. "No, man. Not at all. You've barely started. But it doesn't seem like something you want to keep doing."

"I love it. I love running with you guys, but I'm sure you'll all be happier without me there."

"That's not my truth," he says simply. "I think you could be great."

"Bullshit," I snap, wishing I'd never met him. "I'm not seventy-three. I'm not twenty-seven years old. I'm forty-four, okay? I'm five-nine and a little. Pogo was right. I got lucky, that's all."

He calls to his son. "Isaac, you be careful turning those pages. That's not a comic book."

"Look," I say, turning off the soup, "I'll sit down with you and tell you how the business side works, hook you up with a decent agent, get you a tryout, and we'll leave it at that. Okay?"

Spear takes a deep breath. "I'd rather we play some more together. Take you through the zoo at least once. See what happens."

I want to throw him out of my house, but I'm afraid he'll hurt me, and I realize I've *never* stopped being afraid of him and Oakland, of the hatred that waits for me there. I'm sick from fear.

"Why do you want me to play?" I cry. "Do you enjoy watching me humiliate myself? Is that it? You get some secret delight out of watching the little white man make a fool of himself?"

"Is that what you think you're doing?"

"You *know* it is," I say, trembling with rage. "You know they all think I'm pathetic."

Spear shakes his head slowly. "Not so."

"Oh yeah? I suppose they missed me today. Sent their wishes for my speedy recovery?"

"Yeah, as a matter of fact they did. Juanishi and Wild especially."

"Don't lie to me, Spear. Please."

"I don't lie, Vic. Gave it up a long time ago."

"So . . . they actually mentioned me?"

"Yeah," he says, nodding as he remembers. "Juanishi drove the lane, last point of the game, Godfrey in his face. He dished to Thomas, and T. missed a twenty-footer, and after I tapped it in, the guys jumped all over him saying, 'Vixter don't miss that shit. He's automatic from there.' "

The tears spring to my eyes. I see myself going up for the shot, the swarm of jumpers between me and the net. "Really? They actually said that?"

"Truly," he says, pointing at the soup. "You drink that down and we'll go for a walk to keep your legs stretched out. You'll be fine come Monday. Don't forget the zoo tomorrow, play-offs Sunday, and a big barbecue Sunday night at the house. Maybe you'll bring Greta for some of that, yeah?"

Isaac joins us in the kitchen with his summation of Van Gogh. "A very good painter," he says gravely. "A *very* good painter. Made sunlight out of big yellow blobs. Almost seems like if you touch them, they'd be hot."

The soup is dense with garlic, laced with blazing cayenne. Isaac makes a face, but dutifully drinks his down. I break a powerful sweat, my eyes bulging, my throat screaming for a beer.

"Have another bowl, Vic. I can see by your eyes that you need it. You see his eyes, Isaac? That's the cure trying to break through. The heat from inside makes them bug out like that."

"Mine doing that?" asks Isaac, pulling at the corners of his eyes.

"No, you're clean," says Spear, mussing his son's hair. "Clean as a whistle."

"How come you're not clean?" asks Isaac, frowning at me. "You *look* clean?"

"Well, maybe 'clean' isn't the right word," says Spear, touching his son's hand. "Maybe a better way to say it is that when you get older and you don't always eat what you should, your body gets clogged up, and the heat from Ruby's soup is trying to burn those clogs out and let everything flow better inside him."

The phone rings. I answer languidly, the soup a divine soporific. "Worsley's Garlic Works, Vic speaking."

"Change of plans," says Greta, sounding far away. "I need my womens tonight. Gonna stay home. But I want to see you soon."

"That's fine," I say, sending my love through the phone to her. "Would you like to watch some basketball at Tillsbury tomorrow? Spear says it's quite a show on Saturday. Lots of women come."

"Ruby be there?"

"Yeah, I think she's refereeing."

"Then yes. I'll take us to breakfast before."

"I love you," I say, grinning idiotically. "Madly."

"Emotions abound," she says softly. "See ya."

I suppose wherever he goes, a man of Spear's size attracts attention, but he absolutely stops traffic in my genteel neighborhood. People come out of stores and cafes to get a better look. Second-floor windows open and people lean out to gawk. And at the peak of our little mountain, three gawky white kids charge up to us with pens and paper, eager for Spear's autograph.

He smiles sweetly down at the boys. "Just who do you think I am?"

"I don't know," says one with thick black glasses, "but you must be *some*body."

"I must be, huh?" he says, winking at me. "You heard him, Vic. I must be."

"Are you on the Warriors? Which one are you?"

"I'm a Buddhist," says Spear, bowing low to them. "My name is Spear Rashan Benedentes, and this is my son Isaac, and my good friend Victor Worsley. Who are you guys?"

"We're just kids," says the smallest of the three. "Just regular kids."

"What are your names?" asks Spear, looking at each of them. "You have names, don't you?"

"I'm Vance Thompson," says the one with thick glasses. "Or you could just call me Vance."

"Okay, Vance. And you?"

"I'm Colin Cohn," says the smallest, grinning wildly at his friends and dancing in place. "I'm more of a baseball player."

"I'm Derek," says the last. "But I don't really like my name."

Spear nods with great understanding. "I didn't like mine either. But do you want to know something? It's okay to change it. You can call yourself whatever you want, and nobody can tell you otherwise."

"What was the name you didn't like?" asks Derek, staring up at Spear.

"Mike Jones," says Spear, looking at me. "Just didn't feel right. Then my friend Pogo named me Spear, and so for a couple years I went by Spear Jobijana. Then I gave up Spear for a while and everybody just called me Cruise Control. And then I met my master Rashan de Witt, a very wise man, and after a year or two with him I had an amazing dream."

"And *I* know what happened in the dream," says Isaac, his eyes round with wonder. "A beautiful woman with flowers in her hair came floating down out of the sky on a black stallion and told him his name was Spear Rashan Benedentes."

"Wow," says Derek, shaking his head in wonder. "That's the coolest story I've ever heard."

"And it's totally true," says Isaac, nodding at the boys. "Even if it *was* a dream. Huh, Papa? That dream was real."

"As real as anything," says Spear, picking up his son and kissing his cheek. "As real as all these wonderful new friends we just made."

14

 After Spear and Isaac have descended the hill to catch their train back to Oakland, Van Gogh wrapped in a Gonzo Records bag, I try to nap, but my brain won't shut down. So I drink another bowl of Ruby's salutary concoction, break another malodorous sweat, and find myself in my dining room, continuing my letter of this morning.

Dear Greta, Part II

> *What a rare mood I'm in. How odd to be writing again, to be doing what I used to do every day, and how appropriate that my first scribblings since The Great Firing should be to you, O fountain of love. I am deeply desirous to see you and hear you and hold you, to tell you of the most inspired shot I've made so far, a fallaway from out-of-bounds, Pogo forcing me to arch it higher than I ever have, the ball tumbling down through the net to*

shouts of approval from even my most grudging team-mates.

I've been thinking about Ruby and how wonderful it is that you visit her. I find her rather intimidating, to tell you the truth. She seems to have the clearest notion of what I'm supposed to be doing, while I, as you know, can barely see past tomorrow, and even tomorrow is largely a mystery. My befuddlement seems a source of exasperation to Ruby, but then she doesn't have a two-thousand-dollar mortgage payment to worry about.

Which leads me to thoughts of Spear and how much money a man of his size and talent could make in the NBA today. I know it's crass to think in those terms, but . . .

I drop my pen and call Nolan. He answers on the first ring. "Personal Projections. Nolan Smith speaking."

"I've entered another dimension. The basketball is *way* beyond anything I've ever imagined."

"I assume we're speaking of Oakland," he says, his voice full of laughter. "Or have you actually left the planet?"

"It's *like* another planet. You've *got* to see Spear play. He's incredible."

"So you're having fun," he says, sounding almost fatherly. "That's great, Vic."

"Sometimes it feels like I've gone to heaven, and sometimes I'm scared to death. I was too sick to go today, so you wanna shoot some hoops? Not too cold. Couple hours of light left."

"I thought you just said you were sick."

"I was, but I've apparently been cured by Ruby's garlic soup and the escalation, shall we say, of things with Greta."

"I want lavish details," he whispers emphatically. "See you at McKinley in twenty minutes."

I coast down to our safe little park on my trusty old bike, my latest fantasy for Spear assuming epic proportions. I'm on excellent terms with Alexi Stepanaiovitch, the biggest man in all of basketball, the seven-five Lithuanian center for the Clippers, due to arrive in San Francisco next week. I wrote seventeen columns about Alexi's adjustment to America, on and off the court, some of the best stuff I've ever done, so now he sends me gifts from Paris in the off-season and takes me to lunch whenever he comes to town. Wouldn't a film of Alexi playing against Spear be the most superlative way to open any coach's door? And who better to make such a film than Nolan?

We find our court occupied by tall guys finishing a four-on-four. Nolan wrinkles his nose at their body-banging play. "Ouch. Maybe they'll quit after this one."

"If not, we'll take winners," I say, feeling about six-foot-seven. "These guys are slow as snails."

He smiles wryly. "What about your bad back? The forty-four years? Ruby's soup take care of that, too? Or was it the acrobatic sex? Or hasn't it happened yet?"

"We'll stay outside." I put my sweatband next to the pole, claiming the next game. "They don't defend outside."

"Are you sure?" he asks, starting to stretch. "Lotsa contact out there."

"First sign of violence, we quit."

Six of their eight stick around. Nolan and I grab two six-footers with fabulous hands, and a lively game ensues. I am much improved by my four days of training with Spear. In the company of these softer San Francisco folk, I am simply unstoppable, hitting every shot I take. I thread passes through thickets of arms. I draw two and three defenders, dishing again and again to Nolan, and we walk away winners at dusk.

Our legs give out on the steep uphill, and we have to walk our bikes the last few blocks to my house. "Great game," says Nolan, giving me a sidelong glance. "You were something out there today."

"Isn't it amazing how we only do what we *think* we can do? But when our *thinking* changes, so does everything else."

"Please," he says drolly. "Let us not make too much of this. You got hot. Big fuckin' deal."

"You're right," I say, flushing with embarrassment. "I guess I'm a little full of myself. Sorry."

"Hey, don't get me wrong. You were great. Just try to stay humble, okay?"

"Sorry. I was being a pompous asshole."

"No," he says, softening. "You're fine, Vic. It's just . . . things are not so good with me lately. My ego is not so pumped, so it's a little hard to see you so high. No big deal."

"What's going on?" I ask, putting my hand on his shoulder as Spear would put his hand on mine. "Something with Esther? She wants to remodel again?"

"No, Esther is fine," he says, unaccustomed to such a show of affection from me. "It's just that I'm bustin' my butt night and day and not gettin' much for it."

"It'll come, Nolan. It always does."

"Since when are you such an optimist?" He frowns quizzically. "Wasn't it you who said the world was coming to an end?"

"We've got at least another month," I say, feeling the strongest urge to write him a big fat check. "Maybe two."

"You slept with her, didn't you? In the biblical sense. You knew her and it was good. Am I right?" He slaps me on the back. "It's been such a long time I almost didn't recognize the symptoms. But you did, didn't you?"

"Yes, there's that," I say, miming a shot, "but I've also got my jumper fallin' from twenty-two, too."

"I want to film you playing with these guys! Interviews, action sequences, group discussions, local scenery, gangstas, gorgeous women. *Vic and the Guys.* You never know what's marketable these days. It's a brave new world. What do you say?"

"Once again, my friend, our great minds are about to converge, though I'll want to focus mostly on Spear."

"Fine. But I still want those lavish details. When the time is right, of course."

.   .   .

I am melancholy as evening falls, waves of doubt battering my fragile ego. Am I a boastful narcissist or a proud warrior? Am I a selfish worm? Or am I reaping the rewards of—dare I say it— karma accumulated over years of struggle? Or is this nothing more than dumb luck? Why does it all have to make logical, linear sense? Why am I so mistrustful when things go well? Why can't I just enjoy it?

I think of all the men and women I've resented for their noto- riety and prosperity. I recall my mother's oft-repeated explana- tions for why anyone succeeds at the highest levels. "He must have dirt on somebody important," she would announce with great authority. "And she must have slept her way to the top." Stated as fact.

It occurs to me that in basketball, you might sleep with the queen of the universe, but if you flop on the court, you're done for. Statistics are merciless. Shooting Percentage. Rebounds. As- sists. Steals. Blocked Shots. The numbers don't lie and the crowd knows the truth.

I wander into the living room and click on KJAZ just as Cannonball Adderley finishes "I Can't Get Started." I light a little fire and stare at the flames, musing about what to do next, won- dering why I so rarely listen to music anymore. I go to my stereo and put on an actual record, one of those old things you play with a needle, and Roland Hanna's "Roses Not Mums" carries me back to this afternoon's game with Nolan.

I drove the right edge of the lane, leaving the ground some ten feet from the hoop, holding the ball with both hands. My defender leapt with me, another rising against me on my left. I knew that any shot I tried would be blocked, yet I didn't panic. I shifted the ball to my right hand and hooked it around the body of my inside defender, barely touching him as I loosed the ball parallel to the end line, where Nolan caught it and laid it in.

I learned to do this at Tillsbury. It doesn't always work. Some- times a man on the opposing team picks off the pass. Sometimes there is no one there to receive it. Sometimes it catches someone unaware, bouncing off their shoulder. But this time it worked, Nolan shouting his triumph.

Has it been only ten days since I wandered down to the *Chron* in my habitually gloomy way, hungry for my weekly glimpse of Greta? It seems like *years* ago that Ruby stood in my office proclaiming the greatness of her child to my disbelieving ears.

But *is* Spear great enough? It's one thing to be a dominant force on a playground, quite another to do battle with the very best, night after night before screaming millions. I still find it difficult to understand why he wants *me* to play with him, and why he's so eager for me to go through the zoo. He can't possibly expect me to do well.

The fire licks the well-aged pine. I wish Greta were here. I'd love to share this spacious moment with her, to hold her in my arms and let Hanna's rhapsody wash us into easy talk. I long to thank her for knowing what I needed.

I wander into the kitchen and heat up the last of Ruby's soup, the sage in its scent inspiring me to call her. I imagine her in a rocker by her own fire, savoring her latest concoction of herbs, the white cat snoozing in her lap.

She answers on the second ring. "Glad you called, Mr. Worsley. Missed you at Isaac's birthday last night. Wanted to tell you I've been seeing all sorts of things about you. Usually right before I go to sleep. Big letters floating all around you, and I hear a voice saying, 'There's a line between love and fascination.' "

"Anything about new sources of income?"

"Not yet. But I'll take a look. Hold on."

I hear her rummaging in a drawer. And now the bones rattle in her hand and clatter onto the table. "There's not much here about money. But there's definitely something in your way. Something to do with basketball. Something you're afraid to do. What do you think that could be?"

I laugh, seeing myself in the thick of things around the hoop. "Oh, I'd love to drive the lane. I'm tempted all the time, though I know I'll get killed if I try."

"You mean going inside?"

"That's the primary thing I'm *not* supposed to do. One good body bump from some two-hundred-and-fifty-pound guy and I'm finished. Maybe for life. I could break my back. But I think about it all the time because they leave it open for me. To taunt me, I'm sure. Because they know I don't dare."

"That's it, Victor," she says with great conviction. "Do you mind my calling you Victor, Mr. Worsley?"

"No, I prefer it."

"Well, Victor. If you ask me, I'd say that's the key. You've got to drive that lane. Be like living in a house and never going in the living room. You have to see these things clearly and then trust that the higher powers will help you. I'm talking about the spirits that truly rule the world."

"Spirits? Like ghosts?"

She laughs. "You think I'm a crazy old lady, don't you? Then how come my soup is making you feel so much better?"

"Do the spirits have names?"

"Thousands of names," she says reverently. "All living things have a spirit. That time you went into the desert and the stones spoke to you? That was not a hallucination, Victor. The stone people do speak. All you have to do is listen."

"How did you know I went into the desert?" I freeze in disbelief, my throat constricted by sudden fear. "I've never told anyone about that."

"Spirits showed me," she says softly. "You were very brave to go out there, Victor. All by yourself. Not many people have the courage to do that."

"I was lost," I reply, staggered that she knows of my secret past. "There was nothing brave about it."

"You went alone into the wilderness. No teacher told you to go. No one drove you there against your will. You followed the urging of your heart. Looking for God. And yes, you were scared, and you ran from there, but before you did, you heard the voices, didn't you? And having heard them, you can never say the earth does not have a soul."

"Ruby . . . I'm blown away."

"Aren't we all," she chuckles. "Is Miss Eagleheart there?"

"No, she's at her house. You want her number?"

"I have it, thank you. She's quite a fine woman, Victor. I'm glad you brought her along that first day. Shows you what I don't know, doesn't it?"

"Well, you can't know everything, I suppose."

"Who would want to? Where would be the mystery?"

"By the way, your soup truly has cured me. Thank you so much."

"That's an old Indian soup," she says gruffly. "Thought it might do the trick."

In my office closet, at the bottom of an old cardboard box filled with failed fiction, I find a dog-eared sketchbook containing the only proof of my trek into the desert north of Santa Fe. I was twenty years old, recently fled from college, my body strong and tan from working as a landscaper. I'd hitched a ride from Santa Cruz to Santa Fe with Laurie, the moody sister of a fellow communard. My stated mission was to check out the Southwest scene and try to score some decent mescaline for a bash on Panther Beach to celebrate the spring equinox.

We pulled into the outskirts of Santa Fe, the sky on fire with sunset, a party raging at the ranch house where Laurie lived with the other members of her art band Black Chair. I fell into easy conversation with a dazzling diva named Dianne, the embodiment of all my romantic fantasies, a lovely witch with hungry eyes and restless hands. She said she was leaving on a quest the next day to a secret spring several miles from their ranch. She said it was a magical place where visions abounded and where the silence was so complete, there was nothing to obscure your dreams.

So early the next morning, I followed her into the desert, my heart full of hope, my body eager to meet hers in the cool oasis I believed we would reach in a few hours' time. The air was crisp and clean, the vistas breathtaking. The delicate cactus blooms were opening to the sun, the hummingbirds darting from flower to flower.

We'd only gone a mile or so when Dianne took my hand and smiled sadly at me. "You know what? I've changed my mind. Something tells me I'm not ready for this. It's still a long way to the spring, and I'm already kind of scared."

I felt a keen disappointment, and I realized that beyond whatever sex we might have enjoyed, I had already given myself to the idea of sitting quietly to await a vision. This yearning was so strong in me that I decided to go on without her. She gave me a tender kiss, pointed to the east, and left me alone before I could change my mind.

My journal tells me that I walked to the base of Red Monk, a red rock butte about seven or eight miles from Laurie's ranch. There were no trees there, only a few large shrubs and cactuses. I located a spring at the base of a huge black boulder in a small arroyo that cut into the wall of the butte. All kinds of birds and wasps came there for the water. I saw one big snake, not a rattler. Black with yellow stripes. Two horned toads. A hawk flew quite low to take a look at me, and there were buzzards floating high in the blue above. I could hear crows, but I couldn't see them. I was glad I came, though I wished Dianne were with me. Or someone. It was *so* quiet. When I sat down to rest, I heard loud drumming, and then I realized it was my heart.

I barely slept that first night. I was warm enough, but I was worried about snakes or scorpions getting into my sleeping bag with me. Still, I had good energy and I decided to do some exploring and stay another night.

I climbed partway up the butte. There was almost no plant life there, though I saw hundreds of lizards. I could see my camp below me in the arroyo. It all seemed so primitive. I wondered if I'd come to a different spring than the one Dianne had talked about. My sense of direction was off. I looked back the way I thought I'd come, but I saw no sign of Santa Fe. I remember kicking myself for not bringing a compass.

At dusk, I was almost to the top of the butte, and I could see Santa Fe to the west, so I stopped worrying about finding my way back. And then a very strange thing happened. I heard voices and a woman laughing, so I climbed the last few yards to the top expecting to meet other people. But the butte was empty. I was absolutely certain I'd heard voices, not the wind. Then coming down, I thought I heard a rattlesnake and I jumped away from the sound and landed wrong, spraining my right ankle. It turned out to be one of those clacking grasshoppers. By the time I made it back to my camp, my foot was all puffed up and aching terribly.

In the morning, my ankle was so swollen I could barely walk. I soaked it in the spring, which was quite cold, and that helped ease the pain. I had enough food for a couple more days. Thank God I'd brought along that jar of peanut butter. I remember how the quail became quite bold, drinking at the spring a mere arm's length away, as if they knew I couldn't possibly catch them.

That night, I heard a screech owl, and then a few moments later I could have sworn I heard someone talking. I called out, but no one answered. I hadn't slept well for three days, so maybe I was just hearing things.

I thought about my mom and dad, how disappointed they were in me. And then I had the profound realization that I didn't feel any lonelier out there than I did back in civilization. Nobody really knew me.

I fell asleep for a little while, waking to someone calling me. This happened three times, until I was wide-awake and heard the voice again. It was an old man's voice, speaking in unintelligible singsong. Then I fell asleep and dreamed I was walking across the desert, following a white tiger. I had a bow and arrows, but I wasn't hunting the tiger. We were traveling together. When I awoke, I realized that my dream was a story the old man was telling.

I brew some tea and sit by the fire, hoping to remember more about my time in the desert, but now a much earlier memory comes to me. I am five, standing beneath the enormous oak tree that shades the kindergarten playground. Wendy Boatman is teaching me how to pray. She shows me how to kneel down and hold my hands together and look up at the sky, where God lives. "Ask him to bless people you love," she whispers. "And if you want, you can ask him for things you want and he might give them to you. Or he might not."

It seemed a wonderful thing to do, so I prayed every night for a long time, until my mother caught me doing it and told my father, after which he took it upon himself to prove to me that God was a lie invented by dishonest men to keep us enslaved to them. I endured his lectures throughout my childhood, eventually accepting scientific atheism as my personal religion.

I do some stretching to counter the fierce tightening of my muscles. I lie on my back and hold my knees to my chest until a divine drowsiness comes over me and . . .

I drive the lane and rise over my defender until I'm flying high above the treetops. After a long time in the air, I come down onto the back of a gray stallion. I am an Indian, riding bareback, my hair in a long ponytail. I dismount in a forest and send my horse away to wait in hiding. I move silently through the trees until I have a view onto a lush meadow below me where sheep are grazing, and now the people come, thousands of them, filling the meadow. They stand in orderly silence until they begin to fall, their bodies shattered under a rain of silent bullets, not a single one surviving.

My horse comes for me and I ride away from the meadow, climbing higher into the mountains until the trees disappear and there is only granite. My horse can climb no farther, so I go on without him until I find myself on a sheer cliff, hanging on for dear life, the city lights far below me.

Why did all those people have to die? Why have I brought myself so near to death again? I look up. Greta is sitting on the peak above me, her legs dangling over the edge. I'm about to ask her to throw me a rope, when she simply reaches down and pulls me up beside her, as if I am weightless.

15

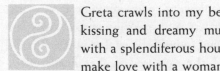Greta crawls into my bed at dawn, and after much kissing and dreamy murmurings, she rewards me with a splendiferous hour of sex. What a joy it is to make love with a woman of such strength and sureness. Perhaps the Buddhists are right to suggest that human incarnation may be, under the best of circumstances, preferable even to nirvana. And truly, nothing could be better than looking up at Greta, my hands cradling her breasts as she cries for joy.

Over French toast and waffles at Chez Ben, the place packed with jabbering vegans, I write a poem for her on my napkin.

> *your black hair*
> *your flashing eyes*
> *your red-brown skin*
> *the divine heat of your*
> *unpremeditated tenderness*
> *your supple strength*
> *your keen clairvoyance*

the song of your voice,
my gratitude
my joy
my astonishing good luck

I hand it to her with my usual disclaimer. "This is very rough. Forgive me. Way too many 'my's.' Sorry."

She reads it to herself several times, her eyes widening in delight. "Sounds fine to me. I'll just have this enlarged and framed and hang it over my bed. If you don't mind."

We skip to the station, the sky full of rain clouds, our train pulling in the moment we arrive. I'm wearing slacks and a dress shirt, but I've brought my shorts and high-tops along just in case. My legs are aching to run, my eyes keen to shoot. As we take our seats, I shiver at the thought of driving the lane, flying into that forbidden territory where anything might happen.

Greta's outfit is demure, a flowery yellow summer dress with a button-down collar, black loafers, and sparkling purple socks, her hair in a ponytail, a loaded gun in her little wicker purse. "I could go back to bed right now," she says, resting her head on my shoulder. "Maybe we oughta just go back to your place. *Hmm?*"

"But I promised Spear I'd come."

"Oh, you'll come," she whispers, kissing my throat. "That's no problem."

"Shall we?" I ask, desperate to please her. "Go home? Forget the zoo?"

"No, let's go," she says warmly. "We'll make love tonight."

She says it without the slightest innuendo, and I realize that I've never experienced anything like this before. Love as a given, not as a means of control. Not a promise, not a lie, not a tease, but the simple, lovely truth of our mutual desire. "Being with you is a continuous revelation," I say, kissing her hand.

"Revolution," she says, taking off her sunglasses to show me the depths of her eyes. "Reconfiguration. Resuscitation. Renovation. Re-creation. Revelation."

· · ·

Rashan meets us in his milk truck at the Oakland station. I point to the lowering sky and suggest it might rain, but he assures us that the clouds will blow away and leave us a lovely afternoon for watching basketball. "Your dress is most appropriate," he says to Greta. "You're a very beautiful woman, if you don't mind my saying so. May I know your age?"

"Forty-two," she says, glancing at me. "I'm a Leo with Scorpio rising, if that's of any interest to you."

"I know nothing of astrology." He shrugs apologetically. "But my wife Rachel studies it. She'll be at the game. I think you'll enjoy her."

I barely recognize Tillsbury on this last Saturday of October, the park filled to bursting with big families and gangs of friends gathered for barbecues and basketball. Greta draws few stares, beauties abounding, but *I* am the focus of intense scrutiny, being the only white man in the park. And just as I begin to question the wisdom of my being here at *all*, Thomas and Wild swoop down on us, bumping fists with me and bowing to Rashan.

"Missed your outside stuff, Vix," says Wild, his eyes all over Greta. "Missed your automatic."

"Forgive me for staring, mama," says Thomas, salaaming to Greta, "but it's impossible not to look at you. I guess you knew that."

"This is Thomas," I say, introducing him to Greta. "And Wild. Two of the great ones here."

"You're too kind," says Thomas, bumping fists with me again. "You gonna play today, Vixter?"

"Spear said I should just watch. He said he didn't think I was ready."

Wild glowers at me. "Oh, come on. I got winners. T. just had breakfast, he ain't digested yet. Come on, Vixter, you play two guard for me. Set you some awesome pics."

"Wild, you know I'm only allowed on the court with Spear. Don't do this to me, okay?"

His glower deepens. "What? You his little puppy dog?"

"No, but . . ."

"Then do your thing. Use what you got. And what you got is cream from twenty-three. Spear don't *shoot* for you, does he?"

"But everyone knows I could never have played here without Spear."

"Maybe you *got* here because of him," says Thomas, bumping shoulders with me, "but you're here now, and if those aren't your game shoes in that bag, what are they? Christmas presents? For me? Oh, you shouldn't have."

"Ruby here?" asks Greta, eager to move along.

"Since the crack of dawn," says Wild, laughing. "Saved the best seats in the house. Old gal talkin' about Vix like he's famous or something. Says you write about basketball. I might like to read some of that shit sometime, except I got bad close-up vision, so I might ask you to read some out loud to me."

"Speaking of seats and being saved," says Thomas, nodding hopefully at me, "you mind if I sit with your woman while you play?"

Greta squints at Thomas. "Excuse me? If you want to sit with me, you better talk to me. You dig?"

"I certainly do," says Thomas, savoring her style. "May I? Sit with you?"

Rashan touches my arm. "Come along. Ruby's been waiting all morning to see you. She dyed her hair black in your honor."

As we thread our way through the huge throng of people gathered around the court, a little girl on her father's shoulders gapes at me. "Why that white man here, Papa? He a policeman?"

"Rashan," I whisper, tapping him on the shoulder, "do you think I should play?"

"If you want to, yes. I would enjoy watching you."

"Do you think Spear will be angry with me?"

"Why should he be angry?"

"He didn't think I was ready."

"Do you think you're ready?"

"I don't know. I'm not sure."

"Perhaps you should take a moment to meditate."

"Here?" I look around at the sea of unfamiliar faces. "Now?"

"When else?" He stops in front of the bleachers. "Ah, here's Ruby."

She sits at the heart of a conflagration of colorfully garbed women, her frizzy hair shiny black, her dress a tapestry of old silk scarves. "Welcome, Victor," she shouts, waving to us. "Carl's got a seat up top for you. Greta, come sit by me."

"See you later, darlin'," says Greta, squeezing in beside Ruby. "Have a good time."

Rashan touches my arm. "Up there, you see? Carl is saving it for you."

"I'll sit with Carl," says Thomas, stepping up into the bleachers. "You play, Vix."

I change quickly behind the bleachers and hand my clothes up to Thomas, returning to the court just as Juanishi, our unstoppable forward, takes a jumper from eighteen, only to have it swatted away by a hovering phantom fully four feet off the ground. He directs his block to a streaking teammate who snaps a pass to a little boy, so small I hadn't noticed him at first, standing in the far corner of the court twenty-five feet from the basket.

He catches and shoots in one fluid motion, sending the ball so high in the air that even the raucous women fall silent as it tumbles down through the hoop and wins the game.

Wild urges me onto the court. "He's beyond automatic. Just don't leave him open, okay? Not even a tiny little bit."

"He's *my* man?" I say, feeling the heat of a thousand eyes upon me. "I have to guard that little guy?"

"If you can," says Wild, shaking his head. "It's not as easy as you think."

As I begin my stretching, my heart in my throat, Juanishi charges up to Wild, demanding to play again. Wild frowns curiously at him. "Aren't you tired, Juanja? Thought you had that boy out of your system. Don't you want to save yourself for Spear?"

"I want to play *now*," he says, glaring at me. "If Vix gonna play, I'm gonna play."

"Cool," says Wild, knowing better than to argue with him. "Love to have you."

Juanishi turns to me with fire in his eyes. "Little fucker so small he vanishes. You can't let him out of your sight. Hides behind big guys. Pops out. You *can't* let him alone. You hear me? *Drape* your body over him or he'll get free and score."

"I'll try," I say, wiggling in place to loosen my back, causing a wave of laughter to ripple around the court. I swing my arms and kick my legs, a warm-up dance I learned from Spear, and the women laugh uproariously.

Juanishi stays beside me, oblivious to the crowd, glaring at the little boy. "Watch him, Vix. Won't miss one."

The boy shoots rainbows from all over, and he not only never misses, he swishes every shot, finishing his show by turning his back on the hoop and flinging the ball over his head from twenty-five feet away, the crowd gasping as the ball splashes through.

Juanishi shakes his head. "I hate that little shit. Never misses. Never."

I take a few practice shots. The ball feels heavy, my legs leaden. Maybe this isn't such a good idea. I knock in a few short hooks and play a bit of easy one-on-one with Wild, but I can't shake the feeling it's wrong for me to play without Spear. He said I wasn't ready. He should know, shouldn't he?

My team is composed of Juanishi, six-eight, Wild, six-two in every direction, Tower, a slender stranger to me, six-nine, and Pogo, who reiterates Juanishi's advice. "Got to be glue on the boy. That's the only way. He gets a step on you, he'll score."

I survey our opponents as they complete their warm-ups. They are a relatively short team, save for their center, a lumbering seven-foot albino with short white hair, sporting an old Knicks jersey, green with gold trim, number seven. "That's Tupelo," says Juanishi, nodding as the big man dunks without a jump. "And that's Slap." He nods in the direction of a hyper six-foot teenager who seems to be growing even as we speak.

Pogo points to the astounding leaper who blocked Juanishi's shot. "That's Lundy. Motherfucker can sky."

"Pretty boy is Jessie," says Wild, gesturing affectedly at a slender man with coal black skin, six-one, wearing a shimmering blue leotard and pink high-tops, his ears studded with earrings, his long black hair tied back with a blazing pink ribbon. "Don't let those fag clothes fool you. He can jump to the fuckin' moon."

"You just worry about the boy," says Pogo, nodding slowly. " 'Cause if you think about anything else, he'll burn your ass so bad you won't be able to sit down for a week."

"But he's so tiny," I say, watching the child loft a perfect pass into Tupelo. "I just won't let him get it."

"You do that," says Pogo, winking at Wild. "You just do that."

I take one last practice shot, my stomach in knots, the ball going virtually nowhere. I'm about to give up, to declare myself too weak, when I feel that huge warm hand on my shoulder, Spear's hand, and I turn to face him, expecting his disapproval. But he's smiling.

"Couldn't resist, huh? Got you hooked. Listen." He draws me into a warm embrace. "Victor, my man, these guys got nothing to lose. You know what I'm saying? All they want to do is win. First thing they're gonna do is test you. Slap's gonna slap you, or they'll leave you all alone, or they'll block you out to free the boy, and he doesn't miss, see. He *must* be denied the ball. You can do this. Believe me."

"No problem," I say, hearing the crowd murmur at Spear's show of intimacy. "He's so little, and he doesn't seem all that fast."

"Forget about how little he is," says Spear, releasing me. "Just stay with him."

"So you're not mad at me for playing today?"

He steps off the court. "Who am I to say if you should play or not?"

The game begins, and they test me immediately. The boy double-teams Pogo, everybody else tight on his man, leaving me all alone with the ball twenty feet out on the left wing. There's no one to blame but myself for a miss, so I'm greatly relieved as my shot rattles through.

Now they attack, Jessie zipping a back-spinning bouncer to the boy, and though I'm close to him, he launches the ball before I can think to jump. The net barely ripples. The boy disappears. He is so small I feel foolish guarding him.

Wild runs by me grumbling. "Glue yourself to him. Glue."

Juanishi hits a banker from fifteen, and we are barely back on defense as the boy shoots again, my hand in his face long after his release, the net snickering behind me as he slips away to harass Pogo. I look to the sidelines. Spear shrugs.

I cross the mid-court line and the ball skips to me from Wild. I release it in rhythm and watch it swish through, but now the boy is shooting again, Pogo too late to block him. We are tied at three. The boy is some sort of fantastic protégé, Mozart with a basketball, shooting symphonies at ten.

As Pogo goes up for a spectacular dunk, the boy glides away, readying himself to receive and release. It's true, he isn't particularly fast, but his actions are so void of hesitation, even the slightest uncertainty on my part is all he needs to get open. Realizing this, I leap to block what I only *hope* will be his shot, and even at that I'm barely in time to touch the ball as it leaves his tiny hands. But touch it I do, though I have no logical sense of how I did it.

"Yes!" shouts Juanishi, grabbing the rebound. "Now go!"

I rush down the court, still unguarded, and Juanishi hurls the ball to me. I release from twenty-three, scoring cleanly. But now the boy is shooting again before I can think to stop him.

Spear nods to affirm my thoughts. I must give up the shooter's role and guard the boy even when *we* have the ball. I can't take my eyes off him. I can't even blink or he'll beat me.

Pogo feeds me cleanly. I zing it back to him and set a pic,

saying as he slides by, "Leave me out this time. I gotta learn the boy."

He nods in agreement, and I rush to hover near the child as he gnats around Wild. I peer down at him, straining to match my movements to his. He is oblivious to me, his concentration unbreakable.

Tower takes the ball to the hole, and as Tupelo moves to block it, the boy slips away to the other end of the court. I follow swiftly, acting as Juanishi instructed, draping myself over the boy, though I feel obscene in doing so.

Jessie wants the boy to have it, but I am too close, so he goes up himself. Tower and Pogo climb with him, and in the split second I take my eyes off him to watch their triple ascent, Jessie makes his pass and the ball is flowing through the boy's hands to the basket.

Juanishi jogs by me. "Game tied," he says wearily. "Do something."

Pogo comes close. "You wanna switch around? Try Slap?"

"One more point," I reply, watching the boy run to hide behind Wild.

Juanishi misses a hook. Jessie snags the rebound and hurls it to Slap who fires to the boy as I leap into the future, finally grasping the truth of his timing as I swat his shot away.

We lose the game, though the boy manages only one more bucket. I leave the court profoundly weary, my legs so tired I can barely walk to the bleachers.

"You okay?" asks Greta, handing me a dry shirt as I climb past her on my way to a seat beside Carl. "Need to lie down?"

"He's fine," says Ruby, glaring at her. "What's he want to lie down for?"

Greta glares right back. "Because he was sick as a dog yesterday. And he looks a bit beat."

"Sorry," says Ruby, clearing her throat. "None of my business. Just seems like a man wouldn't want to lie down after running like that. Not such a good thing for the heart."

"I'm okay," I say, kissing the top of Greta's head. "Thanks for asking."

I take my seat between Rashan and Carl, deeply gratified to know I won't be touching another basketball today. "Now *this*," I proclaim, "is a good place to be."

Carl shakes my hand. "Quite a show, Vic. No easy feat."

Rashan beams at me. "Most fascinating performance of the day."

"The boy was incredible," I say, dizzy from my game with him. "How old is he? Ten? Can you imagine him at seventeen?"

"He is well past seventeen," says Rashan, straight-faced.

"He'll never get any bigger either," says Carl, frowning at the court. "Wish Spear would hurry up and play."

"Past seventeen? You're joking."

Rashan lowers his voice. "His pituitary gland stopped working when he was nine. He is now, I believe, around forty-five. Name is Lonny Lewis, though everybody calls him 'the boy.'"

"God," I say, wincing at the thought of his life. "What does he do? For a living?"

Rashan raises an eyebrow at Carl. "Shall we tell him?"

"Why not? Did better than most against him."

"He's a basketball hustler. Plays for big money they say."

"True," says Carl, lighting his pipe. "Travels all over the country in a big old school bus. Him and Tupelo. Very nice people. I had lunch over there one time. They park it over near the estuary. That's where I fish for bass. They both like to fish, too. Had that bus done up inside like a hotel room. A nice hotel room. They make a pretty good living shooting hoops, I'll tell you."

"Wild and Thomas knew, of course," I say, feeling suckered. "I hope they were amused. No wonder everyone was laughing."

"Some people laughed a little before the game," says Rashan, nodding slowly. "But I didn't hear anybody laughing when you blocked his shot."

"You blocked *two* of the boy's shots," says Carl, staring gravely at me. "Only Spear ever did that before you."

"You're not just saying that, are you?"

Carl shakes his head. "I don't just say things. And you can mark my words. People gonna talk about what you did for a long time."

Greta signals me to join her, which I gladly do. Ruby glares at me in greeting, and at first I think she's displeased to have me here amidst the women. But as I hold my ground, I realize that her glare is not one of anger, but of confusion.

"Did well against the boy," she says gruffly. "Not many do."

"My legs are shot. *So* tired."

"I had no idea," she says, squinting up at the sky. "Shows you what I don't know. Couldn't believe it when you blocked his shot. Nobody could."

Her words take me back to a college game against the best team in our league, a gang of semi-pros paid to play for Sylvania, the outcome never in question, their lead nineteen at the half. Then something happened, someone smacked me in the nose as I fought for a rebound, and I woke into a dream in which the ball belonged only to me, and no one could stop me from scoring. Fourteen buckets in a row they told me after. And at the pizza parlor, celebrating our valiant effort, the star of Sylvania came up to me and said, "I couldn't believe you, man. Nobody could."

Ruby serves us salmon sandwiches on homemade rye, the fish as tender as a perfectly ripe peach, the prize of Godfrey's last trip to Oregon.

"Wild flesh," says Ruby, chewing thoughtfully. "Give you strength in your sinews."

"Good for the stomach, too," says Greta, savoring the succulent meat. "Good for your dreams."

"You know why?" asks Ruby, squinting at Greta.

"Tell me, please."

"Because the salmon leaves her place of birth and goes out into the deepest ocean, and doesn't return until she's full of dreams from the underwater spirits." She nudges me. "At least that's what *I* believe, Victor. Have as much as you like."

Greta introduces me to Rachel, Rashan's beguiling wife, a round-faced woman in a white dress, her black hair captured in a long braid, her skin yellow-brown. "You played the boy like a demon," she says, her green eyes sparkling. "Nobody's wondering why you're here now."

"And this is Chaka," says Greta, touching the hand of a tall, heavily muscled woman with dark brown skin, her head shaved, her right cheek scarred with a crude X. "Spear's wife."

"Pleased to meet you," I say, shaking her hand. "I've met your son, Isaac. He's a wonderful child."

"He *is* wonderful," says Chaka, her grip firm, "but he's not my child. Belongs to Camille. My child with Spear is named Rama. He's five, Isaac's nine."

I blush. "Sorry."

"Not a problem." She winks at Rachel. "Everybody is somebody's child. Isn't that right, Ruby?"

"Children don't ask to be born," says Ruby, nodding. "They don't get to choose who they're born to, and if they don't get love when they're little, it's a sad life ahead."

Greta leans close. "I've got *so* much to tell you."

"You have children, Vic?" asks Rachel, looking from me to Greta and back again to me. "Something tells me you do."

"No," I say, recalling the months of sorrow that followed Emily's first abortion. "Not that I know of."

"You would know," says Ruby, glancing furtively at me. "Even if you couldn't admit it. Part of you would know."

Chaka stretches her long arms to the sky. "Almost never too late for a man to make a baby. Unless you snip that little tube."

Ruby stands up. "Save my seat, please. Nature calls."

Greta and Chaka join Ruby on her trek to the bathroom, leaving me alone with Rachel. I'm mistrustful of how familiar she seems to me, so I focus on the players warming up. Spear is all in black, shooting soft jumpers from fifteen and twenty, rarely missing. He has Pogo running point, Juanishi at forward, but his other mates are new to me. "I know Pogo and Juanishi," I say, smiling shyly at Rachel, "but who are the others?"

Rachel moves closer, her shoulder touching mine. "The tall one is Chandler, Carl's grandson. Chan played in the CBA a couple years ago, but he gets real nervous in close games. Had to take a break. The other guard is Larry Diamond, but everyone calls him Rat." She laughs melodiously. "I don't know why, except he steals the ball all the time. Sneaky hands. Maybe that's why."

"You know the game."

"I love it. I love everything about it."

"Your husband is a wonderful man," I say, looking back at Rashan.

"He's very wise," she says quietly. "Very kind."

"The boy is gone," I say, watching the game begin. "The giant, too."

"When one goes, the other goes," she says, studying my face. "Besides, they don't like to play against Spear. He knows how to beat them, and they like to win."

The game begins with Rat stealing the ball from Jessie and firing to Spear at the top of the key, the crowd roaring and rising with him as he leaves the ground and spins full circle in the air, cradling the ball against his heart until his opponents descend to earth, leaving him all alone to give the ball into the hoop.

"Isn't he the most amazing man?" says Rachel, her eyes brimming with tears. "The most impossible man."

"As great as there has ever been," I say, grinning at the sight of Ruby leading Greta through the cheering throng. "Or so it seems to me."

Spear's team reigns supreme for three breathtaking games, each consortium of opponents more formidable than the last, until finally a team is assembled that even by professional standards would be considered gargantuan. Two seven-foot forwards, a seven-one center, a six-seven point guard, and a six-nine shooting guard.

Spear substitutes Godfrey for a limping Juanishi, while Thomas comes in for Pogo. Chandler and Rat both seem very tired, but they stay in. Brilliant as they all have been, I can't imagine them prevailing over this fresh and gigantic fivesome.

We put on sweaters and sweatshirts, the air growing chill. This will be the last contest of the day. I am weary and excited, strangely moved by my game against the boy. I put my arms around Greta and hold her tight to keep myself from floating away.

Spear begins by lofting a high arching shot from thirty feet, a seemingly desperate start, though there is nothing desperate in his attitude, nor vague about the result. The ball snaps through the net, and the crowd reacts with a vibrant hum.

Chaka shimmies in her seat and circles her fist in the air. "Show time. Bring it on home, daddy."

The giants lumber down the court, their faces set in grim determination. Their center pump-fakes twice and starts to go up, but Rat slaps the ball away and zips it to Chandler who hurls it the length of the court, where Spear springs high to catch it and score with a delicate floater from fifteen, the crowd gasping at the magnitude of his flight.

The looming guard backs in on Thomas, looking to shoot, but Chandler doubles him, so he hooks a pass to one of his seven-foot forwards who goes up for a jam, only to have the ball cleanly snatched by Spear. He rifles the ball to Rat for an uncontested layup, and just like that it's three, nothing.

The giants work the ball into their center, and he jams it home without resistance.

Now Thomas brings the ball up and lofts it high to the right of the hoop, where Spear ascends far above his twin defenders, catching the ball with his left hand and tossing it lightly down through the net.

The crowd roars. Rachel and Chaka and Greta high-five back and forth, and Ruby touches my knee, saying, "You see what I mean? The man levitates himself."

There is no way to stop him, short of grabbing him and holding him, which they do, but even that fails, for whenever they release him, he flies to the ball, shooting from far and high, the hoop inhaling his every release.

16

On the slow train home from Tillsbury, Greta and I hold hands in silence, our faces tilted away from each other. It is a dreamy transit for me, my body humming with exhaustion and exhilaration. All I can think about is playing against the boy. Everything I thought I knew about the game is in question now. For once in my life, I was the giant. But what good did it do me? Stopping him had nothing to do with size. He's a specialist, the purest of pure shooters. Never thinks about rebounding. Almost never passes. To stop him, I had to become his mirror opposite. To deny him the ball, I had to deny myself the ball.

"The boy," I say aloud, seeing my hand closing on his shot. "There was no room for self-deception. None."

"I wish you could have seen it," she says, closing her eyes. "It was like a dream, you in the middle of it all trying to stop his incredible flow."

"You could write a column." I wince as I say it. "Though it's not as easy as it seems."

"I *do* write." She opens her eyes. "I've been writing since I was a little girl, you know? My granny started me. I try to write for an hour every morning, and another hour somewhere else in the day. For forty years. With occasional lapses, of course."

I tingle at the thought of such devotion. "Have you ever tried to publish?"

"I *knew* you were gonna ask me that." She nudges me playfully. "And I'm not gonna tell you."

"Sorry. I always hated it when people asked me that, too, before I sold anything."

"Who said I hadn't sold anything?"

I hold up my hands. "This is obviously a sensitive area for both of us. I'm sorry I asked."

"I'm glad you did," she says, taking my hand. "I *am* too sensitive about it. So I'm sorry, too. You want to come over for dinner? Sheila's cooking. It's bound to be good. She said there'd be plenty for you."

"I should go home and shower first. Change my clothes. I smell like a herd of goats."

"We have a shower," she says, rising as the train slows. "You'll be amazed at how civilized we are."

The sky above Greta's house is sharply divided, dusk to the east, still a blue day to the west, a vast flock of starlings wheeling back and forth from one color to the other, the sunlight glinting off their wings. The wild glamour of it all reminds me of childhood evenings at the beach, when I would watch the shadowy gulls drifting in the wind, wishing I could be so free.

The house is redolent of garlic and cayenne, the opening salvos of a no-nonsense curry. "Thai," I say, suddenly starving. "If I'm not mistaken."

"Sheila mostly cooks Thai," says Greta, stopping at the bottom of the stairs. "I'm gonna change into something a bit less prim."

"May I watch?" I ask, kissing her.

"Go say hi to Sheila," she says. "I'll be down in a little while."

The aroma has altered dramatically by the time I enter the kitchen. "Cumin?" I ask, glancing quizzically at Sheila. "Did you just add cumin?"

"Good nose," she says, slowly stirring her sauce. "You cook Thai?"

"I had a brief flirtation a few years ago," I say, laughing at the memory of my crazed quest for the finest coconut milk, the freshest lemon grass. "I quasi-mastered one dish and then gave up in despair."

"It's a way of life," she says, winking at me. "Have a taste. See what you think."

Standing beside her, dipping my spoon in the reddish brown mélange, I am struck anew by her size. She is nearly as large as Spear, and I can't help recalling a play she made as a man. An end-to-end dazzle of power. Two shot blocks and a steal leading to a race against three other giants, Lorenzo dribbling the ball like some circus showstopper, finishing his run with a picture-perfect sweeping hook from the extreme right corner, clinching the regional championship. "Stunning sauce! You're a genius."

She laughs in delight. "You're too kind. Nothing it needs?"

"Rice and chopsticks," I say, laughing with her. "Though the Thai themselves prefer to eat it with a big spoon."

She dips her finger into the dense nectar of herbs and spices and coconut milk. "I'm gonna fluff it with zucchini and mushrooms and tofu. But I'm happy with this base. You up for a little red wine?"

I shake my head self-consciously. "Can't. I'm in training."

She arches her eyebrow. "Got a fine dry red I'm sure you'll enjoy. Sunday tomorrow. Glass won't hurt you."

"And Bill Evans playing on the stereo," I say, nodding acquiescence. "What could be better?"

"Bill, Bill, Bill," she says, pulling the cork. "The soundtrack of my transformation."

"Mine, too," I murmur, recalling the countless times I lowered the needle to his records, as a junkie puts the needle to his arm. "Or part of it anyway."

She fills our glasses. "Did Greta tell you about the room? Nice little pad."

"The room?" I say, bewildered. "No."

"I guess I jumped the gun," she says, clinking glasses with me. "We've got a room for rent. I thought she'd have mentioned it to you by now."

The audacity of the concept floors me. "Me? Live here?"

"Just a thought." She savors the red. "Is this not divine?"

Greta appears in shorts and sweatshirt, her hair tumbling down. Sheila pours her a fat glass of red, and Greta smiles approvingly as I propose a toast. "To Spear and his fabulous band of warriors."

Sheila clinks Greta's glass. "Did you tell him my Spear story already?"

"No," she replies, touching her glass to mine. "I thought he'd like to hear it directly from you."

"I played against him one time, the year before I quit. He must have been fourteen. Already about six-six. Bunch of us college boys went over to Tillsbury to fool around with the locals, and we ended up getting our butts kicked. Mostly because of Spear."

I try to picture him as a fast-sprouting teen. "Was he a good shot even then?"

"Never shot at all," she says, shaking her head. "But he ate *every* rebound, and he could blocks shots like nobody I've ever seen. Uncanny anticipation. I told him he could play college ball easy, and he laughed in my face and said, 'If all they got in college is pussies like you, I ain't even gonna waste my time.' " She laughs uproariously and claps her hands. "If only he knew how prescient he was."

"You were one of the greatest ballplayers of your generation,"

I say, marveling at her transformation. "I'll never forget your senior year. That last-second shot against Duke in the quarter-finals."

"You wrote about it," she says, her eyes shining. "I remember reading that column over my morning coffee and thinking how sad it was I didn't want to be what you said I was. Not so much that it was sad for *me*, but for everybody else who was in love with whatever they thought I was supposed to be."

"He was just doing his job," says Greta, taking my hand. "Want a little tour before dinner?"

"Be about half an hour," says Sheila, rising to check her rice. "We've got to give this curry the time it needs. You know there's nothing sadder than a hurried curry."

Lisa, her head recently shaved, shares a huge table with another tiny woman in an otherwise empty room, the walls crowded with freshly completed finger paintings. They work swiftly, each of them making a picture every minute or so. They both have headphones on, listening to separate tunes.

Lisa looks up from her newest smear of colors, her brow beaded with sweat. "Can't talk now," she says, flashing me a devilish smile. "We've got to finish another couple hundred of these by tomorrow. We're doing a booth in the Haight. People from the burbs snatch these up so fast it makes your head spin."

"I'm Jan," says her partner, a sweetly smiling woman of indeterminate age. Her long fiery red hair is braided ornately, like a fancy loaf of bread. "We've both got rent due. This usually works. But one time . . ."

"You'll like the room," says Lisa, bending to her task. "Great view of the garden."

"Oh," I say, surprised anew by the idea of moving here. "The room for rent. I'd love to see it."

Jan sizes me up with a practiced eye. "If you like any of these, we'll give you a good price, since maybe you're gonna be living here."

"It's just a thought," says Greta, blushing at me. "Came to us the other night when we were dancing. Sheila suggested it, actually."

Lisa pins up her latest creation, a breeze of yellow bisecting a rollicking sea of blue. "We dance all the time. I guess you probably should know about that before you decide. You'd be welcome to join us, of course. Or not."

"I actually do dance," I say, sheepishly admitting it. "Though I'm almost always alone when I do."

"You can dance however you want," says Jan, removing her headphones and holding them up to my ear, blasting me with a hiss of drums. "There aren't any rules or anything."

"This is the room," says Greta, standing in the middle of a vast chamber on the second floor, two enormous picture windows looking out on a verdant garden, framed by the leaves of a towering sycamore. "Good indirect light all day with sunshine in the late afternoon."

"It's crazy," I say, intoxicated by the space. "I can't live here. With you. Could I? Maybe I could. A desk right here at this window, my bed in front of the other."

"For when you're not sleeping upstairs with me," she says, swallowing me in her embrace. "Like how about now?"

Greta's attic resembles the inside of a Bedouin tent, the walls draped with colorful blankets. Her bed is vast. Her snow white comforter leaps off a background of purples and reds. She has a teak piano standing to the left of the bed, a dark chest of drawers to the right.

"My stereo stuff and books are under the bed, and my writing space is in the little room above this one. Kind of a loft. You could use it when I'm not here during the day."

I touch her shoulder. "Are you serious about this? Me living here?"

"Then you won't have to worry about money," she says, afraid to look at me. "We could carry you until you got a new gig. Sell your house. Move in here. Start over somewhere new."

"May I kiss you?" I ask, moving closer. "To thank you for offering. I mean, I've lived alone for so long. Completely alone. It's hard to imagine living here. But now that you've planted the seed, I . . ."

"Speaking of which," she says, holding me tight. "Could I interest you in testing the texture of this particular bed?"

"Tasting the texture of you."

"We'll have to wait," she says, guiding my hands to her breasts as she kisses me. "Dinner's any minute."

"Thai gets better the longer it sits," I say, lifting off her sweat-shirt. "We'll be fine."

"Got that right."

Dinner demolished, we play *Scrabble* in the living room, a driftwood fire flickering in the hearth, Jan snoozing on the sofa, the four of us in huge armchairs around a big coffee table. Sheila wears old-fashioned reading glasses perched on the tip of her magnificent nose. Lisa keeps her left hand on her forehead for the entire game. Greta comments on the poetic value of every word we spell, while I feel irrationally driven to win.

Sheila spells EXIT with her x on a triple-letter score. "That should wrap it up," she yawns, looking at me. "You guys surren-der?"

"Not so fast," says Greta, spelling SQUID on a triple-word score. "I believe this keeps me within striking distance."

"I hate this game," says Lisa, tossing her letters into the box. "I'm more visual. When we play *Pictionary*, I rule supreme. I'm making tea. Who wants some?"

Sheila places the three-minute timer beside my rack of letters. "You in or out, Vic?"

"I will spell one last word," I say, using all seven of my letters to spell EQUITIES across Greta's SQUID.

Sheila hums to herself as she tallies our scores. "It's gonna be close. But I'm afraid you both made your runs a little too late. And Sheila wins by a hair."

Lisa calls from the kitchen. "Phone for you, Vic."

"For me?" I ask, jumping up to take it. "But who knows I'm here?"

"It's me," says Ruby, sounding very close. "Got a minute?"

"For you? Always."

"Too kind," she chuckles. "But listen, what you did with the boy today has not gone unnoticed. Had a very clear communication about it. Very clear. Things will go much faster now. Time has made a shift. Those are the exact words. Spirit of the moon told me that time is breaking away from the laws of men. Returning to its natural flow. Which cannot be predicted by the human mind alone."

"Because I played the boy?"

"*How* you played him. Blocked his shots. Who could have believed such a thing? Only the very greatest have ever done that. It was a sign, you see. Proof of the shift. How else can you explain it?"

"Luck?"

"Doubt it," she says, clearing her throat. "But the reason I'm calling is to invite you again to the barbecue tomorrow night. In case you forgot. You and Greta. Will you come?"

"I'll definitely be there, but I'm not sure what Greta's up to."

"Tell her she can bring her friends if she wants. Gonna be a good party. Godfrey's gonna cook a huge king salmon. Sweet corn and fresh pumpkin pie. Moon nearly full. Should be a warm night, too. Now here's Spear. Hold on."

"My man," he says warmly. "My inspiration."

"Stop," I say, his praise painful to me. "I got lucky."

"Luck favors the well-prepared. Or something like that. At any rate, just wanted to let you know I got six or seven phone calls from guys saying you should play in the all-star game tomorrow. So on behalf of the other men, and myself, too, of course, I'm inviting you to join us. Will you?"

"God. Yes. Which team will I be on?"

"Any team you want. You'll see when we get there. Pick you up at the train at nine. We start a bit earlier on Sunday, go a bit longer. You're gonna like it, Vic. I promise. Nothing to fear. We'll make sure of that. Okay?"

"Yes," I say, bursting with joy. "I'll be there."

Now a silence falls between us, though there is nothing awkward in it. I'm smiling, and I sense that Spear is smiling, too, because today, somehow, we reached a deeper parity in our friendship. So now, before we say good night, we're just hangin' out on the phone for a little while, the silence a bond, not a burden.

17

 I am caught in a torrent of energy, running with nine other men to complete the sacred quorum, but I do not touch the ball. As I run, I feel a magnetic hum around me, around all of us, the park suffused with electricity. Spear floats through the air as if held aloft by invisible strings, his face ablaze with joy.

The game ends. Thomas takes my place. I sit down and Godfrey joins me for a blow. He is not at all like his brother. He is softer than Spear, inexhaustibly friendly, a lover of baseball and beer. He speaks of the San Francisco Giants as if they were family. "Pace a bit brisk out there for us old-timers, huh, Vix? Can't see myself running with this pack much longer. I turn thirty next month. They gonna call me old graybeard pretty soon. High school kids coming out here to bang against Spear. They all want to try him, one time at least, but nobody's gonna get by him for a long time."

"It's wild out there," I say, gaping at the fast-flowing play. "I feel like Buster Keaton caught in a time warp. I turn to go on offense and we've already scored and they're attacking again. No brakes today."

"Exactly," says Godfrey, reacting with a hoot to a sweet give-and-go between Juanishi and Wild. "You know, I been meaning to tell you, Vix, I always liked your columns. Always made me laugh."

"They did? I always felt so serious about them."

"Didn't seem that way to me. Seemed full of all kindsa inside jokes only a ballplayer would get. Like I would sometimes say to Spear, 'This is a man who knows the game inside out.'"

"Appreciate that," I answer, touched by his compliment. "Except for when my friend Alexi calls me, I've never really had any feedback about my writing from a really great player. Which you definitely are, Godfrey."

"Play with Spear all your life, you're bound to get pretty good." He nods slowly at his baby brother coming out of the game. "Not easy to stop this man."

Spear squeezes between us, rubbing shoulders with Godfrey. "Swatted my shot that one time, God. Where did that come from?"

Godfrey shrugs. "Got elevated. Some days these things happen. And I thank my lucky stars they do. Felt just fine."

Spear nudges me. "You didn't handle the ball, Vic. My fault. I should have gotten it to you, but Pogo needed to blow off some steam early. You see that one where he dunked going side to side? Up in the air forever."

"Spear, I'm happy just to be running out there."

"But, see, that's not what today is, Vic. On this day, no man is thought to be less than another. Nobody is denied the ball. Pogo *must* involve you. Where is that little man? I'm gonna set him straight on this."

"Wait, please," I say, fearing Pogo's wrath. "Please, don't bother him. Please. He's fine. He knows how to win."

Godfrey laughs and pats my knee. "This is Sunday, Vic. No numbers on Sunday. No commerce, no gambling, no keeping score. Play until you feel the need to sit down."

"You don't keep score?"

They shake their heads.

"How do you know who wins? How do you decide who makes the *final* all-star team?"

They laugh, slapping each other's palms, having a good old time.

I turn to watch Juanishi launch his huge muscular body above the rim, and I realize there must be twenty other guys *on* the court. Just watching him. The game has disappeared. Juanishi dunks again and again, each flight to the hoop more magnificent than the last.

When Juanishi is spent, we all gather in a big half-circle around the hoop, watching Godfrey and Pogo go one-on-one. Pogo vaults from the foul line and slams the ball home over Godfrey's enormous hands, the men chanting, "Pogo! Pogo!" In answer to this, Godfrey rises slowly on his toes from twenty-six, releasing the ball high into the air, and the chant becomes, "Godfrey! Godfrey!" as the ball tumbles true, clicking through without a hitch.

Now I feel that huge hand on my shoulder, Spear's hand. "Your turn, Vic. Your solo."

"My what?"

"Solo," he says, leading me onto the empty court, placing a ball in my hands. "Kind of like your initiation, this being your first Sunday here. Just groove with whatever comes into your head. Maybe someone will join you, maybe not."

The sun is at my back. A slight breeze pushes in from the south. There's a pleasant little nip in the air and fifty black men standing all around me, waiting to see what I'm going to do. It takes me back to the only high school play I was ever in. I was understudy to a boy in *The Tempest*, but I hadn't learned my lines because I never believed Stephano would get too sick to play his part. But he did, so I went on, clinging to Caliban and spouting gibberish whenever he poked me. And no one in the audience seemed to mind. Indeed, at curtain's fall, I received the loudest and longest applause.

But this is not high school. This is Tillsbury Park, and I'm
alone with a basketball, my audience full of masters. So what
should I do? Move. I shoot from twenty, the ball passing cleanly
through, igniting a most extraordinary response in me. I begin to
announce a game aloud, becoming each of the players as I announce them, something I used to do while playing alone as a
boy. "The ball comes off to Magic, he back dribbles, flips to
Erving eighteen on the right side. Boom. Drains it. Out it comes
to Worthy, he drops to Bird, and here comes Mr. Jordan taking
the pass at the top of the key, quick release. That's down!"

The brothers watch, frozen and silent until I call out, "Jabbar
sky hooks from eight on the right side, Ewing in his face."

The ball falls through and they cheer. Some of them shake
their fists. I'm stunned by their response, and the ball kicks off my
toe and flies out of bounds. I start to trudge after it in disgrace,
but Thomas passes me another ball and says, "Don't stop, Vic.
You're just catching on. Keep going."

So I return to the top of the key and explain, "That was Jerry
West kicking the ball. Kind of an obscure reference."

They laugh. All of them. Deep hearty laughs. Nothing I do
could possibly be obscure to them. Basketball is their heritage,
their continuum. So I monologue a bit more, mixing my favorites
from every era, disregarding the actual order of things, running
and babbling and shooting, the ball falling more times than not,
my Cazzie Russell rebound drawing a big guffaw, and now I'm
about to uncork a sweet John Havlicek fallaway when I realize
I'm in a game, Thomas snaking the ball away from me and firing
to Pogo for a skywalking jam.

The barbecue at the house of Rashan is a mellow affair, a few
dozen people drinking beer and margaritas in the evening cool,
Chaka and Godfrey working the big wood-fired grills, razzing
each other over salmon steaks and sweet corn and slabs of zucchini from the garden. I feel very relaxed in this company, no
longer the intruder. I move from group to group, jabbering hap-

pily with men who wouldn't talk to me a few days ago, and I feel more included than I've ever felt before. I showed them my most private game today, and rather than ridicule me, they honored me with praise.

Chaka makes big eyes at me over the sizzle. "You look cute tonight, Vic. Nice shirt. Turquoise is a good color on you. Greta here?"

"No. She's gone to some sort of moon ceremony on the Lost Coast. With her 'womens,' as she calls them."

"Wish she'd invited me," says Chaka, flipping the zukes. "I could use a good moon this month. Spear says you were magnifico today."

"He's just being nice."

"Spear wouldn't say it if he didn't believe it." She sticks a juicy slab of zucchini in my mouth. "You and Greta live together?"

"No. I . . . we . . . no."

"Say no more," she says, waving the question away. "Forget I asked that."

Wild joins us with his girlfriend, Cecily. "Hey, God," he says, hoisting his beer, "tell old Vix about the time Julius Erving came to Tillsbury."

Godfrey turns down the flames and wipes his brow. "He wasn't gonna play at first, just came to watch, but the taste got to him and he had to come in. I was nine years old. One of the greatest moments of my life, seeing him play. Man could levitate. Like Spear. Smiled just a little bit when he shot, so in love with the game."

"Tell him about the pass you made," says Wild, clutching Cecily. "Listen to this, baby. This is all true. I was there."

"Well," says Godfrey, swelling with pride, "I wasn't actually in the game, you see, being too young, but the ball came out of bounds and rolled right up to me, and I picked it up, and there he was, standing maybe ten feet away, holding his hands out to me, his veins all swollen like they get, his eyes going right into mine."

"This is true," says Wild, nodding at me. "All true."

"So I pick the ball up," says Godfrey, deeply stirred, "and I make a pretty decent chest pass to him."

"Perfect pass," says Wild, pointing at Godfrey. "Snapped it right to him."

"Yeah," says Godfrey, closing his eyes, "and when he said 'Good one,' I coulda died right then and been content."

I follow Spear upstairs to a spacious family room where five children in white pajamas are watching a video of Disney's *Pinocchio*.

Spear turns on the lights and steps in front of the screen. "Agnes, would you please stop the movie for a minute? I want to introduce you all to a new friend of ours, Victor Worsley, a writer and athlete."

They stare at me, wide-eyed, the two smallest children holding hands to gain courage. Five absorbent souls. Three boys and two girls, Isaac the only one I know.

"Hello," I say, feeling pleasantly ill at ease.

"Hello," they say as one.

Isaac leaps up and dashes into an adjoining bedroom, hurrying back with a sheaf of colorful drawings. "From looking at that book you gave us. Van Gogh."

The first is of a sunflower towering over a house, the colors lush Crayola, a fine imitation of Van Gogh's thick smears of paint. "This is beautiful," I say, smiling at him. "You're very talented."

"I know," he says, sighing impatiently. "Look at the next one."

A portrait of Spear, remarkably true to his essence, his eyes full of trust, his proud bearing suffused with sorrow.

The biggest boy, his skin as black as Spear's, offers me his hand. "I'm Lester. I just got a haircut. Usually it's not so short. I'm almost eleven. Isaac's only nine. I don't draw so good as Isaac, but I'm good on words."

"I'm happy to meet you."

Spear nods slightly, and the other children stand. The oldest girl, an inch taller than Lester, her hair in short braids, shakes my hand. Her face is exquisite, expressionless, her voice a monotone. "I'm Agnes June."

The smallest boy, his eyes averted, holds out his hand and mumbles, "Rama. Spear my daddy, Chaka my mama."

Lastly, the smallest girl comes near and bows, touching her forehead to my hand. "I'm Miranda. Rachel is my mama. Rashan my papa."

"I don't want to interrupt your film," I say. "It's very nice to meet all of you."

"We've seen it before," says Lester, frowning at me. "You play ball with my papa?"

"Yes," I say proudly. "I do."

Rama whispers something to Miranda. She giggles.

"No whispering in front of guests," says Isaac, glancing at his father. "You know the rules."

"Please share your secret, Rama," says Spear, gazing fondly at his youngest son. "There's nothing to be ashamed of."

Rama covers his mouth with both hands and shakes his head.

Spear sighs to express his disappointment. "Will you share the secret, Miranda?"

"It's not nice," she says, staring wide-eyed at Spear.

"Please share," he says, looking into the little girl's eyes. "You know how sad you get when somebody keeps a secret from you."

"He said . . ."

"Don't tell!" cries Rama, shoving her. "Don't say it!"

Spear takes hold of Rama's hands. "That was very rude of you to push your sister, Rama. I'm very unhappy that you're being so selfish. Please go to bed."

Rama's jaw trembles, but he does not cry.

Agnes June takes Rama's hand. "I'll put him to bed."

"Thank you, Aggie," says Spear, bowing to her. "Miranda, too."

"Good night," she whispers, leading the younger children away.

Miranda looks back at us and shouts, "He said your poop is white!"

"Did not!"

"Did, too!"

"Quiet," says Agnes June, yanking them both down the hall. "Just be quiet."

"As a matter of fact," I say, "my poop runs a wide gamut of colors."

Isaac and Lester burst out laughing, slapping happily at each other.

Spear glares at them until they stop. "When you two get done with your fairy tale, brush your teeth and go to bed."

Lester pouts. "I thought you said us older kids could come down to the party for a while if we were good. Isaac and me didn't do anything wrong."

"Isaac and I," says Spear, softening. "And you may come down for a little while. I'm glad you reminded me, Lester. Thank you."

Camille is shockingly white and tiny next to Spear. Her eyes are a brilliant blue, her red jeans very tight, her white shirt cuff-linked with enormous rhinestones, her dainty feet shod in blue cowboy boots encrusted with silver sequins. Her golden brown hair tumbles around her cherubic face, flawed only by a bitter downturn at the corners of her mouth.

"Camille, Vic," says Spear, smiling sheepishly. "Vic, Camille."

" 'Lo," she says, gripping my hand. "Sorry I can't stay. Got a gig tonight."

"You're in a band?"

"Camille Carson, that's me. Country rock. You like country?"

"Some. Your son is Isaac?"

"Yes," she says, nodding. "Thanks so much for the book about van Gogh. He really loves it. Reads it out loud. I don't like to read much, so he must have gotten that from Spear. Anyway, you should come hear us sometime. We play all over. I gotta run. Nice to meet you." She turns to Spear and gives his hand a squeeze. "Bye, honey."

Spear's face is lined with worry as he watches her leave the room.

"She's lovely," I say, finding it nearly impossible to imagine living under the same roof with more than one wife. And all their children. "Good band?"

"Tight," says Spear, his anguish about Camille palpable. "If you like that sort of thing. I'm more into jazz, though sometimes I like to listen to musicals. Lucinda does, too. For the standards. Blows my mind where certain songs come from. Ever heard Aretha do 'As Long As He Needs Me'? Who would have thought that was from *Oliver!*? Not me. That's how I met Lucinda. Saw her in an all black version of *My Fair Lady* at the Free Church. Changed my life. *Had* to get her into my bed. You know what I'm talking about? Lerner and Loewe? Come and meet her."

Lucinda is also small and devastatingly lovely, her skin honey brown, her black hair done in braids threaded onto big yellow beads. Her sleeveless blouse is fiery red, her skirt jet black, her feet in golden sandals. She looks me in the eye and says, "So here you are. The great white hope."

"White, yes," I say, hypnotized by her.

"I thought you'd be a foot taller." She looks me up and down. "So?"

"So," I say, sensing a comrade. "I do more with less. Or fail. But it's certainly thrilling to try."

"You stringing us along? Or can you really do something for him? Man should have turned pro five years ago. You gonna expedite that?"

I'm mesmerized by her displeasure, by the bulging muscles in her arms. I've always been a sucker for openly hostile women.

"Hey, come on, Loose," says Spear, holding out his hand to her. "Vic's my friend. This isn't a money thing. May never be. You can be sweet, please?"

"Bullshit," she sneers. "And *he's* bullshit. And now he wants to fuck me, don't you?"

"No," I say, wishing I were home in a bath, "though I do think you're attractive."

"See?" she says. "Bona fide asshole. Chump change."

Spear sighs heavily. "I apologize for her, Vic. She's not very happy today."

"I wonder why," she says, her eyes narrowing. "You got Camille playing music and you playing ball, and all us black women workin' our butts off to pay for it. He'll tell you he works, and he does, but the truth is, Chaka and I bring home the bulk of the bread, while old Rashan and him drive around helping people for nothing. Year after year he tells me, 'Just one more season, baby, and I'll be ready. Just one more year, that's all I need.'"

"This is the year," I say. "This is the month."

"How so?" she asks, her eyes full of suspicion.

"He's ready," I say, desperate to please her. "We'll get him a tryout."

"You hear him, Spear? *This* is the year. Your white savior says so. You believe it now? This is the month. Are you ready?"

"I'm ready," he murmurs, bowing his head.

"You better be," she says, gripping his wrists. "You goddamn well better be."

Wending our way through the ginkgo forest, Spear says, "There's so much I haven't told you, Vic. So many things happening all at once."

"Where does Lucinda work?" I ask, dizzied by all this new information. "She really is stunning. She could be in every movie I'll ever want to see."

"Secretary at the high school. Ugly job. It's a war zone over there. And you're right about the movies, Vic. That woman was

made to be recorded. When you hear her do 'On the Street
Where You Live,' your life is gonna change. Wrench your soul."

"And Chaka?"

"Teaches second grade. A little private school. Through the
Baptist church. Fifteen kids so far, and two old ladies to help. Not
a bad gig. She likes it."

"How about Rachel?"

"Two days a week for the phone company, long distance op-
erator. And she's our main home schoolteacher along with
Rashan."

"How did you all come to live together?" I ask, unnerved by
his seeming nonchalance in the face of such enormous complex-
ity.

"Lucinda and Camille were my lovers before I met Rashan," he
says, stopping beside an old apple tree, reaching high to pick us
the ripest fruit. "I didn't see them anymore after I hooked up with
him, and then about three years later I married Chaka and Rashan
married Rachel. Big double wedding. And it was a year after that,
on our anniversary as a matter of fact, that we made the decision,
as a group, that I would try to find my children and take responsibility for them."

"Where were they?"

"Lucinda was living with her mother in a little apartment on
the freeway, stuffing envelopes fifteen hours a day to pay for
Lester and Agnes June. She was happy to come on over here.
This is way better than what she had before, despite what she
said tonight."

"And Camille?"

"Horrible place. Crank house. Isaac sleeping in a closet off
her one little room. Mattress on the floor. No hot water. Playing
her guitar on the street for money when she wasn't too strung
out. Mean old white men using her whenever they wanted. No
offense about white people, but that was the worst hellhole I've
ever seen. I went in with Pogo and Godfrey and Thomas and
Juanishi. We scared the crap outta those old men and brought my

little Isaac home, Camille, too, though she doesn't like it much here."

"Wow," I say, imagining Pogo kicking the door down, Thomas and Juanishi rushing in behind him.

"And when I picked up my baby Isaac, it was like getting a piece of myself back, a piece of my soul I'd lost." He sighs. "Now, if I could just stop worrying about money and trust that everything is gonna work out."

"So how about that tryout?" I say, touching his arm. "That might solve the money problem in a big way."

"This month? Seems kinda soon, doesn't it?"

"This week if I can swing it."

"No," he says, shaking his head. "We gotta take you through the zoo one more time."

"Why? For what?"

"It's important to me," he says, putting his hand on my shoulder. "Now, let's go talk to Ruby."

We find her sitting in a rocker on her back porch, chewing baby carrots. "Just out here listening to the sounds of the party. Close as I want to get anymore. Brew you men some tea?"

"Please," says Spear, gesturing to the open ground. "Sit wherever you like, Vic. My favorite place is on that little patch of grass, lying on my back looking up at the clouds and the moon. Care to join me?"

Ruby rises from her chair. "Might see some shooting stars. You feel that chill in the air? Good night to make a wish."

"May I help you?" I ask, following Ruby to her door.

"No," she says, shooing me away. "I like to mix my potions in private. Go on, relax."

I lie down beside Spear, and we gaze silently at the few faint stars, hoping to see a blazing fragment streak across the sky.

"Reminds me of a poem I never finished," I say softly, almost hoping he doesn't hear me.

"Did you memorize it?" he asks. "Like to hear it."

I close my eyes and clear my throat, amazed at the force of my old feelings.

> *"We had to make a god more obscure than God.*
> *It was the mandate of science.*
> *We had to say there was a ladder,*
> *on top of which sat a man*
> *who looked like Albert Einstein.*
> *We had to write it down and put it in books*
> *and make our children memorize it.*
> *But here on this hill, the stars dripping with light . . .*

That's all I can remember."

"Good to write that anger down," says Spear, stretching his arms to the sky. "That's one of Rashan's techniques. We have people write down what they're feeling, or we take dictation if they'd rather not write, and then we read it aloud to them, and they get to hear what *they* think is happening to them. And it always helps. Things always get a little bit clearer afterward."

Ruby emerges with a pot of tea and three mugs. "I think you're gonna like this brew," she chuckles. "Help you remember those dreams."

"Money," says Spear, hugging his knees to his chest. "I can feel it coming, Ruby, and I'm afraid it's gonna kill my love for the game."

"It will if you try to hang on to it," she says simply. "So you must spread it out among all your friends and go on with your life. That's the only sensible way."

"Lucinda wants it," he says, anguished. "She's so cruel about it. Makes me sick to hear her be so cruel."

"Pray for what you need," says Ruby, filling the cups. "Say

what you want and the spirits will hear you. Then they'll think about it, and give you what you need."

"Could you talk to Lucinda? Please? She listens to you."

"No, my child, I won't. That's for you to do."

Back at the big house, I fall into conversation with Thomas and Godfrey. "Going to the Claremont later on when my lady gets off swing," says T., blindingly handsome in a sharp black tuxedo. "Big tango thing happening."

Chandler joins us, highball in hand, his T-shirt silk-screened with a snarling Tina Turner. He glances diffidently at the few unclaimed women and says, "Hey, Godfrey, you got a sweater? This cotton ain't shit against the chill."

"Better than that," says Godfrey, holding out his hand for a slap. "Take you where you won't need a sweater. No chill where we're going."

I follow with some trepidation, breaking a fine sweat as we file into the bathroom, little old me with two black giants and the man I've recently usurped on Spear's starting squad. I'm usually asleep when I have this sort of dream. Godfrey brings forth a bomber of a joint. "This is fine fresh green bud," he proclaims with authority. "No side effects but bliss. Wake up tomorrow refreshed. Guaranteed."

Chandler groans. "Man, I can't do that. What if I get a call to play and they want to test me?"

"Chan, my man," says Thomas, igniting his lighter, "been two years since they called, and I'm not puttin' you down, but you only been playin' weekends and even then your knees swell up like balloons. So get real. Have a hit."

"My knees are fine," says Chandler, eyeing the joint. "I've been going to the Berkeley Y twice a week, in case you wanted to know."

Godfrey spits smoke. "Berkeley Y? Nobody there. You just like to dominate."

"They got a good floor. Gotta stay in shape on wood, you

know." He watches the joint come to me. "Playground is one thing, wood floor's a whole other story. I'm keeping my shot fresh."

I want them to know I'm not afraid, so I toke twice and pass the joint back to Godfrey. He shakes his head. "Give it to Chandler. He wants it more than anything in the universe. Don't you, Chan?"

"No," says Chan, his hands trembling. "Not 'til after the season."

Thomas loosens his tie and squints at me. "You know something, Vic. I was gonna kill you when Spear bumped me for you. I was gonna kill Spear, too. Went home, loaded my gun, and borrowed my sister's car. And I think I probably would have shot you, except on the way to the park, thinking about it, you know, I saw how it wasn't what I thought it was about."

"No," says Godfrey, blowing smoke. "Never is."

Thomas smiles cunningly. "It was the opposite."

"Yes," says Godfrey, humming his assent. "The *exact* opposite."

"See, he loved me better than anybody, and he knew that I would under*stand* better than anybody, and that's why he chose me to make the sacrifice, you see. Pogo would have killed you. Plain and simple. Dead." He slaps Godfrey's proffered palm. "Whereas I love it now. And you know what I love most? Going up against him. Taking it to him. Seeing what happens when I do."

"It's good," says Godfrey, exhaling an enormous cloud of smoke. "I been going against him since he could barely walk. Never forget the day he got better than me. Clear as a bell. I was seventeen, he was fourteen, and he went up and I went up, and I came down, and he was still up there, lookin' around. Like a big old bird."

"Can I do this?" I say, scrutinizing the joint as it comes to me from Thomas. "And still get myself home?"

"Of course not," says Thomas, putting his arm around my neck. "Which is precisely why you must toke, motherfucker. You little white motherfucker. You're automatic out to twenty-three now, aren't you? We gonna keep you hostage over here, Vic, 'til you tell us your secret."

"Yeah, I've played my whole life against Spear," says Godfrey, continuing his thought. "Which is why I love it when I'm on his team. Nobody ever gonna be as tough to guard as him. Ain't that sweet gravy, Mr. T.? When you take that shot knowing he's there to pull the boards?"

"Wonder if he can do it?" asks Thomas, his voice trembling with emotion. "Wonder if he'll get a chance?"

"I have a plan," I say, thinking of Alexi, my giant Russian friend. "I'm fairly certain I can get Spear a high-level tryout."

"A tryout is nothing," says Chandler, grabbing the joint from me. "It's whether they let him play enough to get over his fear."

"What do you mean? Why wouldn't they?"

He tokes deeply, relishing the smoke in his lungs. "I thought you knew."

"I do, but . . ."

"You don't know shit," he says, glowering down at me. "You don't know what it's like to dominate somebody in practice, crush them, and then sit on the bench while they start. You have no idea how much they'll hate him, how they'll try to break his legs, pull his arm out of his socket, poke his eyes, smash his knees, take him out. Specially since he didn't pay his college dues, prove he can do what the boss wants him to do."

Thomas nods. "Man's got a point, Vic. Man's got a definite point."

"Spear's good enough," says Godfrey, sighing heavily. "I just don't know if he can get through all the crap to get there. But I'll tell you this, my little brother ever get his chance to go on at the Coliseum, and they let him play five minutes, ain't nothin' ever gonna be the same."

"Amen," says Thomas, slapping Godfrey's palm, slapping mine. "You in on this, Chan?"

Chandler tokes again and offers his hand. "Yeah, I hope he gets his chance."

"It's his destiny," I say, smiling as I quote dear Ruby. "And ours along with him."

"I like the way you say that," says Thomas, shaking my hand. "I didn't tell you this before, Vic, but I like the way you stood up to Pogo. That was something else, man. That last shot you made? Unreal."

Godfrey laughs. "Old Pogo still talkin' about it. Says it musta been some of Ruby's witchcraft."

"Maybe you *do* know something," says Chandler, relaxing into his high. "And you think he'll get his chance?"

"He will," I say, envisioning Spear in the Warriors' home gold, lifting the ball to the rim. "He will definitely get his chance."

18

Little Rama, devilishly cute, shakes me awake in the morning. "Papa says time to eat breakfast. I saw you in my dream. You were chasing us."

"Playing tag, maybe," I yawn, surveying the walls of books, vaguely recalling Chaka making this bed for me last night. "Do you know what time it is?"

"Nuh uh," he says, turning to go. "Papa says you need time for digestion."

I drag myself to the bathroom and gape at my haggard face in the mirror. "Don't be a fool, Victor. You're in no condition to play today. You'll only make yourself sick."

Barely roused by an icy shower, I stumble into the living room, where Rashan and the children are busily drawing pictures.

"Good morning, Victor," says Rashan, beaming at me. "I hope your sleep was productive. Ruby said the moon was pulling hard to bring our dreams out."

Isaac looks up from his paper. "We're drawing our dreams. Everything was very very red in mine, even the trees, only they weren't on fire."

"Or we can write them," says Lester, cocking his head quizzically. "You gonna live here?"

"No. I live in San Francisco."

"He stayed up very late," explains Rashan, "and since he had to be here this morning to play basketball, it made no sense for him to go all the way home just to come right back."

"You *could* live here," says Isaac, concentrating on his work. "Then you'd be right here to play basketball every day."

"You'd save lots of money," says Lester, seeming quite concerned.

"Thanks, but this was only for one night," I explain, feeling a twinge of sadness. "May never happen again."

I find Rachel in the kitchen preparing sandwiches for the children's lunch, her red Chinese robe embroidered with fierce yellow and white dragons. She stretches her arms toward the ceiling. "Morning, Vic. Your breakfast is in the oven. Spear went to get Camille. Said he'd be back soon."

I inundate my stack of broccoli pancakes with maple syrup and brewer's yeast and sesame butter, knowing I'll need thousands of calories to survive on the courts today. I haven't had such an enormous appetite since I was a fast-growing boy, when my mother's question, "Are you hungry?" always struck me as an absurdity.

Rachel brews a pot of tea and sits down with me. "Is it true you can get Spear a tryout?"

"True," I say sleepily. "I'm very good friends with Alexi Stepanaiovitch. I'm gonna call him today."

"Good old Alexi." She nods in recognition. "The king of slow, as Godfrey calls him."

"You've seen him play?"

"A couple times at the Coliseum, but mostly on television. I go over to Godfrey's to watch 'cause we only have a screen for videos here. Godfrey's got cable. Gets all the games. I'm kind of a basketball addict, actually. Chaka, too."

"Spear watch with you?"

"No, he hasn't looked at a television in nine years." She sips her tea, disarming me with a smile. "Some party, huh? How come Greta didn't come? I like that woman."

"She was having a moon ceremony on the Lost Coast with her 'womens,' as she calls them."

"Womens," she says, her cheeks reddening. "That's what we call each other, too."

"You know," I say, blushing as I speak, "you remind me so much of someone I used to know. A woman I grew up with, though you don't really look like her. There's just something so familiar about . . ."

Camille barges in from the garage, sobbing and swearing. "We just need to *play*," she cries, waving her arms. "I can't be a housewife *and* lead a band. It's insane!"

"You're right about that," says Spear, following her in with four bulging bags of groceries. "What you're doing to yourself is definitely insane."

Camille's face is streaked with remnants of eye shadow, her jaw trembling. "It was fine. I can handle it. It's part of the gig. These people are connected."

Spear answers breathlessly. "How are they going to help you, Camille, if you're dead? But then maybe your next overdose won't kill you. Maybe it will just fry your brain. Are we supposed to take care of you then? Push you around in a wheelchair? Change your diapers?"

"Look, I'm gonna get the band so tight, they'll *have* to let us record. I've got six good songs now and I met somebody who can get us on TV, once we get a decent video. I have to *work* on this stuff." She glowers at him. "I want out. You keep Isaac. I did my stint. Nobody likes me here anyway."

"What are you gonna live on?" he whispers. "How you gonna feed yourself?"

"Stop it, Spear," says Rachel, rising to intervene. "She's not helpless. You don't need to *keep* her anymore. She can do whatever she wants."

"Thank you," says Camille, nodding tentatively to Rachel.

Spear takes a menacing step toward Camille, his fists clenched. "Is that what you think I've been doing? Keeping you?"

She trembles at his show of force, and so do I. The room literally shakes with his immense emotions. "No, honey," she says, deflating. "No, of course not. Let's not talk about it anymore. You're right. Okay? I'll stay. Just don't hit me, okay?"

"I've never hit you," he says, unclenching his fists and stepping back from her. "Not since I met Rashan. And I never will again." He wipes his eyes and lowers his voice. "Go if you want to. I have a thousand dollars you can take. Saved it for Isaac's art lessons. But you take it."

Spear and I walk the thirty blocks to Tillsbury. The day is cold and dirty, litter tumbling in a bitter wind, the sickly lawns dotted with dogshit.

He shoves his hands in his pockets. "Why is it that just when things are finally calming down, all hell breaks loose again?"

"You mean Camille?"

"Yeah. She can sing, no question, but I feel like there's something mean in her that keeps people from trusting her all the way. Kinda like I used to be. Desperate under all that brag."

"Aren't we all?" I murmur, flashing on the pompous proclamations I used to write. "How will it be for Isaac if she leaves?"

"They're pretty distant," he says, nodding to convince himself. "He'll be okay after a while."

We turn the corner and six junkies block our way, a huge bleary-eyed guy growling, "Money. Gimme some money, man."

"Let us pass," says Spear, his voice deep and threatening. "We have no money. We're gonna play ball, that's all. Now move aside. I'm in a bad mood today."

I'm shaking in my shoes, ready to run.

The big guy blinks. "You the one they call Spear?"

"I am," he intones. "Now move, my friend. Now."

The man steps aside and we jog past, Spear's arm around me, trembling.

We do our stretching before we start to shoot, Spear as flexible as a child. He is so beautiful, I can't help but stare as he rises onto his toes, his arms raised skyward, his hands clasped directly above his head, his index fingers forming a single spire pointing to the sun. He holds this pose every day for fifteen minutes. I try to do it with him, though I can only hold it for a minute or so.

"So tell me, Vic," he asks, closing his eyes, "when you have fantasies about the game these days, what's going on?"

"Lately, I've been driving the lane," I say, watching him for signs of disapproval. "I take it to the hoop and lay it off the glass. Or I pass to Juanishi for a jam. Or I sneak one around Thomas and kiss it in."

His face remains expressionless, focused on centering. "And?"

"It feels wonderful," I whisper, seeing myself hovering in a thicket of arms. Unafraid.

"Yes," he says, opening his eyes. "That's good to dream about. But you aren't actually gonna drive the lane in a game. That's a metaphor, right?"

"It's not a metaphor in my fantasies. I actually take it to the hoop. Here at Tillsbury."

He arches his eyebrow. "Won't they crush you like a bug, you get that close?"

"Isn't that what you told me? Didn't you explicitly warn me to stay out of the key?"

"Yeah, but that was your first day here. And you said you were afraid you'd get hurt. So I said if you didn't try to play in close, no one would touch you."

"And nobody has. Because I've been given a special dispensation by the king. Right?"

Spear cocks his head, reminding me of his son Lester. "Are you serious? With the swatters who come to play in this park?

Come on, Vic. I have some reputation here, but you've been fair game all along. In the key or not." He chuckles. "You actually thought I could guarantee you wouldn't get bruised?"

"I actually did," I say, staring at him in disbelief. "So what you're saying is, you tricked me into playing."

He opens his eyes and grins at me. "You're something else, Vic. You really are."

"It's just hard to imagine," I say, scooping up the ball and shooting a long jumper. "That I could do any of this without you."

The ball climbs high into the blue sky, Spear rising to catch it above the rim, placing the ball on top of his head, nodding gently as he descends, dropping it through the hoop, obliterating all my previous notions of what a man might do with a basketball.

Everything is different today. Men I barely know stop by to tell me how much they enjoyed my solo yesterday. And miracle of miracles, I am chosen to play on a team with four men I have never played with. For the first time since coming to Tillsbury, I will be opposing Spear. He has Thomas in my place at shooting guard, Pogo playing point, Juanishi at power forward, and Wild at small forward, though "small" is a grievous misnomer in Wild's case.

Spear points to me. "I'll be guarding Vic. Gonna shut him out."

A most humbling game ensues. I attempt five shots and Spear bats them all away. Truth revealed. After that, I can barely get myself to run up and down the court. I leave Thomas free to shoot. He misses only once. But even so, my team does well, and with the game on the line, Spear runs close and whispers, "You can shoot over me. It *can* be done."

He leaves me slightly open and I get a pass, the basket thirty feet away. I launch a shot before I truly have the ball, sneaking it over his hand, missing badly. Spear snags the rebound and brings the ball across the mid-line, returning fire from forty feet, the ball climbing so high it shrinks to the size of a tennis ball before whistling down and clanging off the rim, a rare miss for my master.

We rush back the other way and I fire from thirty again, shooting it almost straight up in the air to get it over him, the ball stinging the backboard and zipping through to bring us within one of them.

Spear takes a lob from Pogo and falls away from thirty-five feet on the right side, the ball hitting high on the backboard and caroming through for the winner, the players on both teams dumbfounded by his astonishing display.

I walk off the court, half-proud and half-humiliated. Not a terrific combination. Thomas follows me to the bleachers, staring at me open-mouthed. Wild comes close and glares, while Juanishi and Pogo stay on the court, frowning in my direction.

"What did I do? Something wrong? Took too many shots?"

"Shot *over* Spear?" says Thomas, sitting beside me. "How'd you do that?"

"Luck. I was literally shooting straight up. I never expected it to arch like that. I certainly wasn't *aiming* for the backboard."

"Nobody shoots over Spear," says Wild, shaking his head. "I can't remember the last time anybody did it without two guys blocking him. The boy can't even do it anymore."

"But I can't do it either," I say, anxious to set them straight. "That was pure luck. I just threw it. I have no idea why he didn't block it."

"Pogo says Spear let you shoot," says Thomas, unsure of what to believe. "But you could see he was trying with all his might. He's never jumped higher. So how'd you know how to shoot like that?"

"Maybe my driveway," I say, remembering the old cracked concrete. "It sloped to a drain about thirty feet away, sixteen feet lower than the rim, and there was a telephone wire that ran across at about twenty feet high between the backboard and the drain. I'd shoot from there all the time because the ball would always roll back down. For like ten years. Every day. Hundreds of times a day. Maybe that's it."

Driving us to Ruby's in his baby blue Volvo station wagon, the front seats mounted on special tracks to accommodate hugeness, Godfrey regales us with details from the Warriors-Knicks game he saw last night on television. "Just an exhibition game maybe, but there it all was. Warriors loaded with gunners, Knicks playin' great defense and workin' for the wide open two. Warriors win by five, but if it had been in the regular season, Knicks woulda won by ten."

"How did Thurman look?" I ask, wishing I'd been there to see for myself.

"He's tough on the boards, but he's afraid to shoot from outside. Has that rookie hesitation. Watch him warm up, he's got a sweet twenty-footer, but he gets in the game, he won't take it, always lookin' over at Hathaway to make sure he's not doing anything wrong."

"The mark of Hathaway," I say, shaking my head. "The great puppeteer."

"Oh, I wouldn't blame him," says Godfrey, pulling up in front of Ruby's house. "These poor kids come out of college scared to death."

"Did you say something to me?" asks Spear, coming out of his daze, realizing we're home.

"We were talking about Hathaway and Thurman," says Godfrey, frowning curiously at his brother. "You know? Does the coach change the players, or do the players change the coach?"

"I'm sure it's both," says Spear, opening his door. "Almost always is."

"Is that what Rashan says?" asks Godfrey, climbing out, too.

"I don't know," says Spear, waving vaguely to both of us. "I'm supposed to be watching the kids. See you tomorrow."

Godfrey leans back against his car and watches Spear vanish behind Ruby's house. "Haven't seen him spaced-out like that since the old days when he was high all the time. Didn't care for anything but basketball and women and dope. I had to bring him food or he'd forget to eat. And then one day I said, fuck it, I can't take care of him anymore."

"How old were you?"

"Nineteen. I was already makin' pretty good money fixin' cars, you know, and then I got trained on Volvos, and I've been makin' *fine* money ever since. But first I had to let my baby brother go. And then he found old Rashan." He nudges me. "And now he found you, huh? Gonna take him to the top."

"He hardly needs me," I say, shrugging. "I might open a door or two."

"That's all anybody can do," he says, looking up at the clouds. "Meanwhile, I'm gonna run out to Point Richmond and get some fishin' in before I go to work. What are you gonna do? Go home to that beautiful woman?"

"Actually I've got a date with Ruby. I bragged about a particular pasta, and she . . ."

". . . asked ever-so-sweetly if you'd cook it for her." He laughs. "She may be pushin' eighty, but she still almost always gets her man."

I throw together dinner in the soft kerosene glow of Ruby's kitchen. She watches me intently as I grate the Parmesan cheese. "Damn stuff is nothing but a plug in our veins. Not even good for kids. But I eat some every now and then to remember why I used to love it. The richness. So buttery."

"Would you rather we didn't use cheese?" I ask, dropping the linguini into the boiling water. "It's not essential. This sauce, taught to me by my father's mother, is every bit as good without cheese. For the French bread, we'll sauté a few dozen garlic cloves and smear them on with a big sploosh of pesto. No cheeses need apply."

"No cheese in your pesto?"

I feign indignation. "And compromise the basil? Never."

"Then just a sprinkle," she says, nudging me. "Don't deny me my wicked pleasure."

"I'm so glad you persisted with me, Ruby." I take her hands in mine and smile into her eyes. "You're a wonderful soul."

"The time has come," she says, inspecting my palms. "I had a vision last night. You see how fat the moon was? Very clear communication. All the great forces of change are converging, and Spear must help to lead us through these troubled times."

"But what if he hates being a pro? What if he decides not to do it?"

"Then we won't ever have to wonder again," she says, tracing the lines in my palm. "Everybody has this idea that once you start doing something you have to do it all your life. People said to me, 'Now, Ruby, you can't stop teaching school. Nine more years, you get retirement.' But I told them that nine more years in that jail they called a school would turn my blood sour and kill me."

We amend the sauce with mushrooms and cayenne and rosemary, a dash of cumin, a splash of balsamic vinegar. As our pasta roils in the big pot, Ruby sits in her rocker, an old one-eyed tabby on her lap. I sit cross-legged by the fire, dangling a stick in the flames.

"We all knew who Godfrey and Spear's father was," she says, rocking slowly. "Put away in San Quentin for life. But he died after six years in there, too wild to stay alive in a cage. Big man, but no bigger than their mother. She was six-foot-five and stronger than any woman I've ever known. Wanted her boys to be safe. Knew she was dying. Didn't want them to see her shrivel up. So she came to me and asked if I would take them. And you know what, Victor? I had just been praying for a baby. My children all grown and gone away."

"How many kids did you have?"

"None from my own body," she says without a trace of sorrow. "Four girls I raised as my own, and six of their babies, too. Believe me, I thanked God when the last one moved out. Loved that peace and quiet for a year or so. But then I got so lonely, I was happy to take Godfrey and Spear. It was sweet those first few years. They were good little boys until I made them go to school. Then the other little boys started coming around, and pretty soon some of them were sleeping here, too. You know Wild and Thomas? They both spent some years here with me. But it got to be too much when they all got older and started bringing girls around, going out into the weeds to smoke and do who knows what. Loud music all the time. I was almost seventy. Couldn't take it anymore. So after Spear moved out to live with Rashan, I chased everybody away but Godfrey, kept pretty much to myself after that, until one day, about this same time of year, the ginkgo leaves just starting to turn, Spear came walking in here with a deed to the big house. Wanted me to come smudge the rooms with my sage and call in a communication from the spirits."

"What did they say? The spirits."

"Said Spear and his family were right where they needed to be."

"So . . . what exactly do you hear when you get your communications?"

"Voices." She places the palms of her hands on her chest. "Each spirit has a different voice. Just like each person does."

"How many spirits are there?"

"Millions and millions," she says, rising from her rocker, dropping her cat to the floor. "My mouth is watering, Victor. That pasta has got to be done."

19

Home for the first time in two days, I sleep fitfully, waking again and again to a replay of my shot over Spear, my heart in my throat as the ball finds its way through the hoop.

Greta arrives at seven in the morning, dazzling in a white cotton dress, her radiant black hair piled high on her head, tiny red feathers dangling from her ears. I stand at my door in a worn, gray bathrobe, groggy from lack of sleep, my body tingling in recognition of how eager and ready for love she is, her skin aglow. Yet I feel oddly distant from her, as if months, not days, have passed since we last touched. She seems so sure of herself, while I am sure of nothing. Before either of us can speak, the phone rings.

"Vic Tor! It's Alexi. I'm calling from the team jet. We are coming to land there in two hours. I have arranged for us to use my favorite gymnasium in North Beach. For my game with your man Spear. I'll call you from my hotel. You should see this view of the Grand Canyon. They are tipping the plane for us. Very dramatic. Good-bye."

Greta presses close. "I can't stay long. Just wanted to say hi and tell you about this beautiful place we found. It's only a five-mile hike into this lovely little meadow with a creek leading down to a black sand beach, the aspens turning silver, deer in the willows, the air full of swallows. I'd love to take you there. Is that a possibility?"

"I don't know," I say, my mind too full of men shooting fallaways to think about meadows and aspens and deer. "I have to stay completely focused on Spear right now and . . ."

The phone rings again. As I grab it, I admit to myself that I'm afraid of Greta, afraid I'll give too much of myself and disappear once more.

"Yo, Vic. It's Nolan. Confirming for tomorrow. Two hours of film enough?"

"That's plenty. Thanks. I've got another call coming in. Lemme get back to you with the details." I click on the next caller. It's Greta's assistant with two hot tickets for the Warriors game tonight. "Thanks," I mumble, my mind racing from Tillsbury to the Coliseum to North Beach and back again. So many *details* to keep track of.

Greta clears her throat. "Excuse me, Mr. Worsley, but when you have just the slightest smidgen of time, would you give me a call? I'd love to hear about what's going on with you, but I gotta get to work right now."

"Sorry things are so crazy," I say, wrapping my arms around her. "I missed you."

"Why do I doubt that?" she says, bemused. "How about if I come over this afternoon?"

"Sure, if you want. I have to go to the game tonight with Spear, and then he's gonna spend the night, but yes, this afternoon would be ideal."

"Now we're talking," she says, kissing me. "That should get me through the day."

• • •

At Tillsbury, the sun at its apex, a stench from a ruptured sewer filling the air, my mind grows hot with anticipation and my game falls apart. I hit a stumbling shot from twenty-six and my legs lock up. I topple to the concrete, frozen from the waist down. Wild and Pogo drag me off the court, and Thomas subs for me. I lie on the sidelines caught between now and tonight, Alexi and Spear already battling each other on the court in my mind.

I have never seen Spear play so poorly. He bobbles the ball and dribbles it off his knee. He drops three alley-oops. He shoots hideous air balls. His passes are too low to Wild, too high to Juanishi, too far ahead of Pogo, too far behind Thomas. With the game hinging on a single shot, he fails to block a puny jumper, and five insufferable teenagers win the game, their shouts of triumph resounding through the park.

My legs come back to life, the blood returning so swiftly my muscles scream. This has happened to me several times in my life, the strength leaving my legs at a critical moment, returning when the moment has passed. I'm always deeply ashamed when it happens, but powerless to prevent it. I stand up carefully, the pain all but gone now as I rejoin my unhappy teammates clustered around Spear.

"What's *wrong* with you?" asks Pogo, furious about losing to these pompous teens. "You let *them* beat us?"

Godfrey waves his hands in front of Spear's face. "Hellooo?"

"He's not all here, that's for sure," says Wild, shaking his head. "Since when you pass so low to me? You know I like to stretch for it high. You got the flu?"

Thomas squints at Spear. "You feelin' okay, bro? I haven't seen you miss like that since the first day you picked up a ball."

"Leave him alone," says Juanishi, perhaps the most deeply wounded by our loss. "He's gonna go up against the biggest man in basketball tomorrow. That Alexi guy from the Clippers. Give him some room, huh? I got winners. I'm gonna smash these boys. Who wants to stay?"

Pogo punches Spear's arm. "You'll *eat* Alexi. Don't worry about it. Gonna eat him alive."

"Shoot your outside, Spear," says Wild, nodding. "Pull him out and then fly on by. Drop it like you do from way up high."

"Crush him," says Juanishi, taking the court. "Just like I'm gonna crush these boys."

We only get as far as the duck pond before Spear has to stop and sit down. "Feel like I'm gonna faint," he says, blinking. "Didn't sleep last night. Nightmares every time I'd drop off. I don't know if I can do this pro thing, Vic. It's a whole other life. What's so wrong with this one? You know what I'm talking about?"

"We can call it off."

"But maybe I don't want to." He glares at the muddy water. "I don't know. What do you think?"

"We'll go to the Warriors game tonight, watch Alexi play, and then see how you feel about things after."

"Problem with me going to a game is I get hypnotized when I watch the pros. All I can think about is being down there with them. So maybe we shouldn't do this until I can see my way more clearly."

"Whatever you'd like, Spear."

"That's the problem. I don't know what I'd like. I don't see how to get from here to being a Warrior, making that my life. You know what I'm saying?"

"That's why Ruby came to *me*." I see her standing at my cluttered desk, searching my face with her fierce eyes. "It's the part of the process I know all about."

"So what happens?" he asks, rubbing his tired eyes. "After we go to the game tonight?"

"We film you playing one-on-one with Alexi tomorrow, show the tape to the Warriors coach, and get you an actual tryout. A scrimmage or something."

"And then?"

"Then you make a deal and go from there."

"To where?"

"The cover of every magazine in the world."

"If I'm going on covers," he says, putting his arm around me, "you're coming with me. I'm not doing that stuff alone."

"I've disappeared by then," I say, feeling a funny twinge in my chest. "I'm living on the coast in a little cabin deep in the redwoods."

"I want to live there, too," says Spear, climbing to his feet. "Let's go talk to Rashan."

"You okay to walk? Maybe Wild can give us a lift."

"I'll be fine," he says, reaching down to clasp his ankles for a good long stretch. "This is just fear. I can walk it off."

We find Rashan in their sprawling vegetable garden, weeding the beans and corn with Ruby and Rachel. The children sit in the shade of a young cherry tree, listening to Agnes June read a story. The day has turned generously warm. It feels more like spring than fall. And it occurs to me that I might, as Isaac suggested, live here quite happily.

"You both look bee stung," says Ruby, glaring up at us. "Come on over here and get your hands in the dirt."

We remove our shoes and settle down to work, freeing the weeds from the crumbly soil. I imagine Greta coming through the ginkgos to join us. Maybe we don't need to go any further than this. A big garden. A family of friends. Enough to get by.

"I can hardly think," says Spear, working close to Rashan. "I keep hearing gears grinding, like when you miss a shift in your truck, and I'm thinking, maybe this isn't my true path, taking my game to market like this. You know?"

"Now is the time," says Ruby, nodding emphatically. "I felt it all through the night. Like a hundred little earthquakes."

"Pulling weeds," says Rashan, bowing to Ruby, "is our path. If nothing compels you to leave, stay. If you turn professional, do so with devotion and compassion. That's the Buddhist way. If it's not meant for you to continue, you will step off that path onto another. No shame. No such thing as failure. For now, pull weeds."

"You should do it, Spear," says Rachel, her eyes glistening. "It'd be so fantastic to see you out there. We'd come to every game."

"I'm fixing you some tea, Spear," says Ruby, wincing at the pain in her hips as she rises. "Calm you down. Let you sleep some."

He exhales mightily. "But not too strong. I want to be sharp for the game tonight."

"Vic, you need some of this tea, too," she says, pointing at me. "It'll do the trick."

"You know how to calm yourself," says Rashan, holding aloft a tangle of dandelions. "You're not a victim, Spear. This is no more happening to you than you are happening to it."

"Tell him stories," says Rachel, winking at me. "That's the best way to calm him down."

The train ride home is little more than a blur, the crosstown bus almost empty. I leave the Japanese bank at the bottom of my hill, and though I'm unspeakably weary, my financial status now precludes the luxury of a taxi. I give myself to the motion of climbing, haunted by the blank look of the silent teller as she jotted my total on a white slip of paper. Barely enough for one more mortgage payment.

My front door is open, Greta's satchel on the futon, a vase of yellow daisies on the dining room table. It occurs to me that I could sell the table to pay yet another month's mortgage. Pure mahogany. Cost me a small fortune. I stride through the house, calculating how much I could make from all my things, how many months of my mortgage I could pay. But why save the house? Why not sell it to someone else and buy a few more years of freedom? Write those poems I've always wanted to write.

Greta greets me at the back door, her eyes wide with wonder. "You okay?" she asks, taking me in her arms. "Rough day?"

"Overwhelming. I'm feeling rather discombobulated."

She kisses my forehead. "I have something to show you. In your backyard. Come on."

We walk down the faint remnant of a path, stopping at the edge of a forest of tall weeds festooned with red and purple morning glories, the air alive with bees.

"Here," says Greta, gently parting a curtain of wild oats, revealing a nest of five large kittens, dark tabbies crowded together for warmth on a big yellow leaf.

"I was just thinking about getting a cat the other day," I say, reaching out to caress the kits. "Maybe one of these."

"Don't touch," she says, staying my hand. "Your scent will frighten their mother when she comes back, and she may abandon them. Besides, they're too old to take. They belong to this paradise you created."

"Created? I haven't been back here in years."

"And look what happened. Spontaneous wilderness."

"Poet," I say, kissing her. "I was just thinking of poems."

"I *do* like to write," she says, blushing. "And I love reading what you write. Miss your column in the *Chron*. Everybody does. I even heard Lucas on the phone saying something about maybe having you write a little freelance for him."

"No," I say, flinching at thoughts of my old daily grind. "Seriously?"

She shakes her head. "You're funny, Vic. How can you be so unsure of yourself after all these years of success?"

In the kitchen, her back to the cool fridge, her leg around my leg, I am suddenly gripped by a horrible sense of responsibility for my wild backyard. I *can't* give up the house. What if some rich person buys it and hires an exterminator and puts in a formal garden with box hedges and white gravel over black plastic? But how can I pay my mortgage?

"So," I blurt, ruining our prelude to a much deeper kiss, "you think Lucas might be calling me soon? No replacement yet, I see."

She bites my ear. "Vic. Let's not talk about that right now, okay? I'm feeling oh so certain we've got something better to do."

"But the cats," I cry, anguished by the thought of those kittens being murdered to make way for a proper garden. "If I sell the house, who knows what might happen to them."

She leads me down the hall to the bedroom. She closes the door and takes off her skirt, kneeling on the bed and moistening her fingertips with her tongue. "You'll sell to somebody really nice," she says, rocking forward to show me how she wants me. "Come on, darlin'."

20

On the bus, caught in a traffic jam two miles from the Coliseum, I look out the window and go on with my story, following Rachel's advice about how to keep Spear relaxed. "So I'm twenty-three, hitchhiking through Ohio, haven't played ball in two months, and I get picked up by a long-haired guy who says he's on his way over to some college to play, and a half hour later we're pulling up to the main gym at Ohio State."

"I knew a guy who played for them," says Spear, nodding. "Said the coaches were total control freaks. Maybe all coaches are. You play with anybody strong?"

"There was really only one guy who had pro potential, a white kid with a decent hook, about six-eight. But here's the story. We start to play, and I'm bringing the ball across the mid-line for the first time, and my legs lock up. Just like they did today. Had to drag myself off the court and lie there watching a bunch of farm boys having the time of their lives, playing on the main floor, the place I never got to play. My ultimate fantasy just inches away."

"Playing pro was my big dream," he says, nodding. "Until Rama was born. Never forget that night, Chaka pushing him out to me. Then I held him in my arms and looked around at Rachel and Rashan, their eyes full of tears, and Chaka so relieved. The little baby was breathing on my hand, and I saw that I didn't need to make a million dollars for us to be happy. I could play without that weighing on me. You know what I mean? It was like a huge burden was lifted from me, and from then on I played more and more in the moment."

Our bus inches ahead, game time fast approaching. "So you *really* don't want to be rich and famous?" I arch my eyebrow. "Money and power?"

"Some part of me must," he says, shrugging. " 'Cause here we are on our way to the Coliseum. Can't you just feel Ruby driving us?"

"Why does she want it so badly for you?"

"She's very wise," he says with no trace of sarcasm. "Told me I'm destined to be a leader. To use my power to help people, basketball being my path."

"We'll get there just in time," I say, checking my watch. "Everyone and his mother must be going to this game."

"New world religion," he says, grinning at me. "You know why that is?"

"As it happens," I say, affecting a slight British accent, "I was an anthropology major during my brief stint in academia, and I did quite a bit of research on what ancient Homo sapiens did, physically, with their time. It turns out, we mostly ran. For thousands and thousands of years. Several hours every day. Running. One scientist estimated that the super-athlete of today may only be one-third as strong as the *average* person living fifty thousand years ago."

"Can't imagine somebody three times stronger than Godfrey." He frowns at his hands. "Or Juanishi. He's very very strong, Vic."

"It's just a theory, but it confirms my feeling that basketball somehow satisfies a deep desire to experience primordial reality."

"Women, too?"

"Women even more so. They ran from all the same things men ran from, *and* they ran from us."

"That's an interesting theory, Vic. You oughta write a column about that."

"I don't write anymore," I say, clearing my throat. "They fired me."

"See," he says, grimacing. "That's the whole problem with turning pro. You're playing for somebody else, not for yourself. Who wants to live in a world like that?"

"Because that's reality," I say bitterly. "So what's *your* theory? Why do you think basketball is so incredibly popular now?"

His face brightens. "It's a model for a better way of living. A revolutionary paradigm."

"Are you serious? How so?"

"Because when the game is played properly, it's the ultimate blend of individual effort and self-sacrifice for the good of the whole. And completely nonviolent. Isn't that what we all want our lives to be? It's like we all know intuitively that unless we attain some sort of balance, we're doomed. That's why I think basketball is the game of the next millennium."

"We're here," I say, looking out at the swarm of people crowding into the great hall where the intense rivalry between the Clippers and Warriors is expected to yield an unusually brutal game. "Maybe *you* should write the column."

"Stay close," he says, following me off the bus. "I haven't been here in seven years."

We stand at the portal leading to the very best seats, Spear trembling at the sight of the glittering court surrounded by seventeen thousand fans. "Whoa," he says, clutching my arm. "There's some heavy energy floating around in here. You feel that surge? That's why I had to stop coming. Made me feel desperate about not playing pro. This is one tempting room, Vic."

"We'll be fine. Trust me."

We are centered on the north side of the court, twenty-nine

rows back, my favorite vantage point for watching Alexi. From here, as he moves easily among the other players, his control of the game appears to be rehearsed, his transitions from backcourt to the key like odd little dances that somehow predetermine the outcome of the play. He has won eight championships in his fourteen years in the pros, playing for five different teams. The Warriors were, in Alexi's own words, his "great catastrophe," the only team he failed to win at least one championship for.

"I'm gonna pray a little," says Spear, bowing his head. "You want to pray with me?"

"Sure," I say, feeling only slightly ridiculous. "Why not? I stand for the national anthem. I might as well pray."

"Great Spirit," he whispers passionately. "Thank you for the breath of life. Thank you for all that you give. Please help me stay in my body. Help me remain calm. Help me stay in harmony with you. Send health and help to my family, to Ruby, to Rashan, and to Vic and Greta. Thank you for all that you give."

"Amen," I say, remembering Greta's face during love, her sweet surrender. "Thank you for all that you give."

"There," he says, breathing a sigh of relief. "That's better now."

"Yes," I say, caught for a moment in a memory of my old Jewish grandmother standing in her garden praying for guidance. "That *is* better."

He glances around at the multitude of excited people. "I don't think I'll have too much trouble watching tonight, but I don't know if I could actually *play* here."

"Tomorrow will tell. Alexi in North Beach. My buddy Nolan running film."

"Seems so fast," he says, tensing up. "I don't know if I can do this."

"Spear, let me buy you a beer. It'll take the edge off."

"Okay," he says, closing his eyes. "Beer might be good."

On a whim, I turn to the young man to my right, a fresh-faced fellow in his late twenties. "Excuse me. Would you like to earn ten bucks?"

"You're Victor Worsley, aren't you?" He nods rapidly, his cheeks growing red. "You are, huh?"

"Yes," I say, surprised to be recognized. "And you are . . ."

"Allan," he replies, continuing to nod. "Allan Allan. I'm an artist. Video collage? But I actually want to be a sportswriter. You're kind of my idol. Actually."

"If you'll bring us four extremely large beers, and one for yourself, I would be most grateful." I dig out my wallet. So what if I'm running out of money? The world might end at halftime.

"Keep it," he says, rising quickly. "The beer's on me. It's a great honor."

Spear stares blankly at the Warriors warming up, his soul hovering down among the men he may one day do battle with, if only, to quote Chandler, he can get over his fear.

Someone calls my name. "Vic?" The voice is familiar. I turn to my right again, and here is Jim Hathaway, the Warriors' head coach, tall and straight-backed, six-foot-ten, still a relatively young man after twenty-five years in the game, his white shirt freshly starched, his trademark bow tie slightly askew.

He nods in Spear's direction. "Introduce me?"

"Spear," I say, nudging him. "I'd like you to meet Jim Hathaway, Warriors' coach."

Spear arises smoothly, causing a ripple of wonder at his astounding size. He locks hands with Hathaway over my head. "Pleased to meet you, Jim."

"Spear," says Hathaway, testing the word. "Born with that name?"

"No. I was given that name by a great point guard. Man we call Pogo for how high he can get. We named each other when we were twelve."

"Spear is a fabulous talent," I say, delighting in the truth of it.

"You have any tapes?"

"Tomorrow evening," I say, gambling on Nolan's genius. "Your office. Seven?"

"Perfect."

Hathaway disappears. Spear sits down. A silence rife with fear envelops us. Blessedly, Allan Allan arrives with six big beers. Spear gulps down two and grabs a third. "This is all going way too fast, Vic. Way way way way way too fast."

"More beer?" asks Allan Allan, overjoyed to be assisting us. "Wait 'til I tell my dad I met you. He'll die. He reads you religiously, Vic. May I call you Vic?"

"No more of this," says Spear, grimacing at the cheap beer. "Makes me stupid. But I could use some water, please."

"I'm off," says Allan Allan, skipping away.

"You know him?" asks Spear, frowning after the odd young man. "He looks a little crazy, doesn't he?"

"Of course he's crazy. He wants to be a sportswriter. So the question is, do I tell him to kill himself *now* or later?"

Spear straightens up as the Clippers take the court. "Jesus," he gasps, his nostrils flaring at the sight of Alexi. "I always forget how big he is. I mean, he's not just tall, he's . . ."

"What *is* he?" I ask, staring in wonder at the great Russian. "Every time I wrote about him I would struggle to find words other than 'giant,' 'huge,' or 'massive.'"

"Mountainous," he says, watching Alexi tap the rim with his hand, barely reaching up to do it. "Glacial. Overtowering. Beyond big. Gargantuan. Three men in one."

"Smartest big man alive," I say, nudging him. "Next to you."

"What makes him so smart?"

"Economy of movement and extreme foresight. He always seems to know what everybody else is going to do, but no one ever knows what *he* might do."

"Second sight," says Spear, nodding grimly as the buzzer sounds. "Thomas has that. Knows just where to be to make a steal."

"Or if Alexi doesn't *know*, then he's certainly a fabulous guesser."

"No," says Spear, shaking his head. "The great ones don't guess. No time to guess."

Alexi concedes the opening tip to a much smaller man. He is apparently in no mood to jump. He ambles through a few set

plays, barely breaking a sweat as he scores eight points before
coming out of the game. This is an exhibition contest, after all,
and the Clippers aren't about to risk injury to their franchise
player in a game that counts for nothing. Alexi sits down to mild
booing from the fans. He says something to his coach and they
share a laugh.

"What do you think he said?" asks Spear, squinting at me.
"Just now. To the coach."

"Oh, probably something like, 'Only in America do they boo
their heroes.' "

"We'd love him more if he'd stay in. Barely got going."

"True, but that's part of his game. Pacing himself from minute
to minute, game to game, year after year. Without injury. He's
over forty, you know."

"And he completely controls the game," says Spear, his eyes
fixed on the ball. "They might call him a center, but to me he's
the point. Whenever he's in, all the plays evolve from whatever
he decides to do."

"What do you think of this Warrior rookie Thurman? The
fans love him."

"Great rebounder," says Spear, bowing his head. "God, I'd
love to be down there playing!"

Alexi returns to the fray late in the fourth quarter, the Warriors up by seven. He trots onto the court and calmly steals the
ball, lofting it to his power forward for a stunning jam. He jogs
back on defense, blocking two shots in quick succession before
rambling the length of the court to take a sharp pass from his
point, hooking it in over two leaping defenders, the first of his
three unanswered buckets that give the Clips a win at the buzzer.

"Vintage Alexi," I remark, deeply gratified by his demolition
of the speedy young Warriors. "And to think that Hathaway
traded him."

"It's gonna be okay," says Spear, turning to me. "Gonna be just
fine."

"What do you mean?"

"The game tomorrow. Not a serious problem."

"How so?"

"There's no way he can stop me, Vic. He's too slow."

"Or so it seems from here."

"I'm not saying he's too slow to control a game. He's a master at that. But he barely jumps. So how's he gonna stop me?"

"I don't know. Maybe he won't. But if anyone can, Alexi will."

A pleasant surprise awaits us in my home on the hill. Spear's son Isaac is drawing pictures with Greta at the dining room table. His face is smeared with the sauce from their pizza, the house rich with the scent of warm dough and broiled mushrooms, the table covered with Crayola portraits they've made of each other.

"Hi, Papa," he says, holding up a picture of Greta, her eyes much bigger than her nose or mouth. "We just looked at a book on Picasso."

Spear leans down and kisses his son. "When did you get here?"

"Rashan brought me," he says, his eyes fixed on his drawing.

Spear touches his son's hand. "Look at me, please."

Isaac gazes into his father's eyes. "Chaka told Rachel I was missing Camille, and then Rachel told Rashan, so he brought me."

"Chaka called," says Greta, beaming at Spear. "I said I'd be here and that we wouldn't mind having him overnight with you. So . . ."

"Thank you," says Spear, bowing to her. "That's very kind of you." He kisses Isaac's cheek. "Past your bedtime. Way past mine, too." He looks at me. "Where would you like us to sleep?"

"In Vic's room," says Greta, sounding highly officious. "It's the only bed big enough, if you sleep diagonally. I moved a single bed in beside you for Isaac."

"Where will you guys sleep?" asks Isaac, frowning at Greta. "How many bedrooms are there?"

"We'll sleep on a futon by the fire. We often do."

"Wish I could sleep by the fire," says Isaac, looking up at his father. "We don't have a fireplace in our house. So we only have fires at Ruby's, huh, Papa?"

"That's right," he says, cradling his son's head in his massive hand. "Now say good night and go brush your teeth."

Isaac hugs Greta and skips down the hall to the bathroom. Spear bows to her again. "Thank you so much for taking care of him. You seemed to be having a pretty good time."

"He's fantastic," she says, squeezing my hand. "No problem at all."

"Must have caught him on a good night," says Spear, wrinkling his nose. "He can be a little terror, lemme tell you. I'll see you in the morning."

"Sleep well," I say, bursting with admiration for him. "Pleasant dreams."

I drive the lane, breaking the taboo, weaving my way through a forest of tall trees and jagged rocks, taking the ball to the hoop, scoring with a perfect finger roll, my momentum carrying me onto a path leading down into a deep valley.

Spear is ahead of me, running swiftly. We stumble through a dense jungle of shrunken trees, and sink down through swampy ground into a humid little room where my mother and father sit side by side on a beige sofa.

"You're naked," says my mother, scowling at me. "Put something on."

"Why aren't you alone?" asks my father, glaring at Spear. "He's naked, too."

"I'm sorry," I say, falling to my knees. "It's all my fault. You're absolutely right. Forgive me?"

My parents say nothing. Their faces are as rigid as stone.

Spear lifts me gently to my feet. "No need to beg," he says, touching the center of my forehead. "Nothing left to fear."

"You've changed," I say, staring in wonder at him. "When did this happen?"

"So have you," he says, turning with me to face a mirror.

We are exactly the same height, our heads shaved, our bodies streaked with red and black paint.

Spear bows deeply to my mother and father. "How great you are," he intones, "to have made such a man as your son."

My mother's face softens and she relaxes into sleep. My father's mouth takes on the barest semblance of a smile.

Spear takes my hand and we leap into the sky.

21

"Nice of Greta to watch Isaac again," says Spear, hunched over in the front seat of the cab. "She's a fine woman, Vic."

"I know. She's just . . . I can hardly believe . . ."

He grins back at me. "But enough about her. Tell me about Alexi. How'd you meet him?"

"Alexi came to San Francisco his rookie year," I say, recalling how much he meant to all of us. A true big man. The first to become a Warrior since Wilt Chamberlain at the dawn of professional hoops. There had been other tall men who could score, but no one great enough to carry the team all by himself, if need be. "I knew a smattering of Yiddish phrases from my mother's mother, and I'd heard rumors he might be Jewish, so I whispered them to him in the locker room one day and he laughed. Two days later he granted me his first interview in America. I ended up doing seventeen columns on him. It was the high point of my writing career, without question. He says he wants to do a book with me someday. *The Russianization of Basketball*. A bit grandiose, don't you think?"

"He *is* grandiose," says Spear, nodding to himself. "He's like gravity."

"The first Russian player to become an American icon."

"And why do you think he likes you so much?"

"He says my voice reminds him of his father. Whenever he sees me, he kisses my cheeks and says, 'Vic Tor. You great good soul. I think of you always.'"

"So he's Jewish," says Spear, pleasantly surprised. "I used to play ball with a guy named Billy Fitch. He had a great little hook, left or right. Didn't matter. His father was from Senegal, tall and skinny and black as coal, and his mother was a little speckled Jewish lady, had a diner in the Mission. Rosey's Cafe. Good buttermilk pancakes. We used to go over from Oakland on the F Bus after playing and eat tuna sandwiches and drink strong black coffee."

"You nervous about playing Alexi?"

"Not so much nervous," he says, frowning at the road ahead. "But a little sad. Don't know why. Just a little sad."

"We don't have to do this, you know."

"What would we do instead?" he asks, winking at our driver. "What would you do if you weren't driving cab?"

The chubby old man chews his lower lip and shakes his head. "I been at this forty years. Too late to change now."

Allan Allan, the odd young man who bought us beer at last night's game, stands on the littered sidewalk outside the North Beach Poetry Gym, a crumbling old club built of dark red bricks, its roof and walls splattered with fifty years of pigeon poop. He waves timidly to us as we roll up to the curb.

"Did you call him?" asks Spear, waving back at him. "Poor kid needs to eat more. Let's buy him some lunch."

I glare out at the strange young man. "I didn't call him. And the last thing we need is a disgruntled youth along for the ride."

"You never know," says Spear, laughing at me. "Maybe you got yourself an apprentice."

"Just what I need," I smirk, the money gauge in my mind hovering barely above empty. "I could pay him ten cents a day. Think he'd go for that?"

"Probably do it for nothing," says Spear, handing me a fat wad of twenty-dollar bills. "This is money I set aside to pursue my career. Use it however you think best."

"I can't take this," I say, handing it back to him. "I'm not doing this for the money."

"Operating expenses," he says, dropping the bills into my jacket pocket. "For cab fares and things like that. Our war chest, right? I'm sure you know how to spend it better than I do."

"God, Spear, this is . . . well-timed. I'll pay you back. Somehow."

"Whatever," he says, climbing out of the cab. "I've never played in a gym."

"Never?"

"Truly," he says, pushing open the big blue doors, only to freeze in disbelief. "Pretty rickety in here, Vic. Pigeons in the rafters. Backboards warped. Nets gone gray. I'm not complaining, but this isn't exactly how I imagined it. Kinda dark in here, too, isn't it?"

"Alexi insisted on this place. He learned his English here during the years he spent with the Warriors."

"No problem," he says, stepping onto the court, testing the give of the wood. "Has some spring to it."

Allan Allan darts inside, genuflecting to both of us. "I can help. I kind of overheard last night. I'm an excellent cinematographer."

"One's enough," says Nolan, jogging over to shake Spear's hand. "You must be Spear."

"You must be Nolan," he replies, liking my buddy instantly. "You play ball with Vic?"

"Off and on for almost thirty years. Since we were little more than pimples."

"You play pretty even with him?"

"I generally beat him," says Nolan, winking at me. "Though we haven't played much since he's been playing with you."

"You must be good."

"I couldn't get a shot off against you."

"*I* could," says Alexi, coming in behind us, swaddled in gray fox fur. "But only because I'm eleven feet tall."

"You made it," I say, laughing at the sight of my fabulous friend. "Looking positively czarist, aren't we?"

Alexi engulfs me, kissing my cheeks. "Vic Tor! My brother! You are thin. What is wrong?"

"I'm fine. I want you to meet Spear."

Alexi and Spear grip hands and give each other big toothy smiles.

"Alexiskaya Ilyich Stepanaiovitch. Alexi."

"Spear Rashan Benedentes. Spear."

"Alexi," I say proudly, "this is Nolan. He'll be doing the filming. And this is Allan Allan. He'll be helping whoever needs help, I guess."

Alexi glances comically at Spear. "Allan Allan? Is this a joke?"

"My mother's," says Allan, shrugging his skinny shoulders. "I suppose I could change it, but it's marketable. Odd is sometimes good."

"Oh, well," says Alexi, clapping his hands. "At least it's easy to remember."

The court is a pale rose patch of hardwood, brilliantly lit, surrounded by darkness. "I'm shooting movie film," says Nolan, his boyish face flushed with pride. "I have a hunch this might be rather extraordinary."

Alexi removes his coat and hands it to Allan Allan. His crisp white uniform and brilliant blue shoes stand in stark contrast to Spear's gray shirt and shorts, black sneakers, and red headband.

"He is very balanced," says Alexi, nodding in Spear's direction. "I have rarely met a man so powerful."

Spear makes his way to the free-throw line and rises onto his toes, centering on the ancient rim. "This hoop is about a half-inch low," he says, closing his eyes. "Might want to make that adjustment."

"Thank you," says Alexi, bowing slightly from the waist. "Also you should know the backboards are quite generous here. Soft in the corners."

"Mmm," says Spear, humming in tune to his balancing. "Thank you."

Alexi whispers to me. "What is he doing? Praying?"

"I guess you'd say he has a somewhat Buddhist approach to the game."

"Buddhist? He doesn't need to win?"

"I guess not. Although he almost always does."

"How good is he? Give me some estimate."

"Levitates. Ambidextrous. Incomparable."

"I see," says Alexi, sighing heavily. "Should have had more pancakes."

Alexi joins Spear on the court. There are three cameras running at three elevations, their angles and focus manipulated from a bank of screens and control panels hidden from our view. Nolan communicates with us over the gymnasium loudspeaker. Allan Allan rushes out onto the court, arguing that a subtle glare off the whitewashed backboard *must* be mitigated by a reflector. Nolan acquiesces and the peripheral darkness deepens.

Alexi completes his preparations with a dribbling drill as unhurried as thawing snow, bouncing the ball back and forth between his legs, back and forth and back and forth until the ball is charged with enough momentum to leave the floor and float gently into the hoop.

"Good one," says Spear, nodding his appreciation. "I've never even *tried* to do that."

"It's a Chinese technique," says Alexi, assuming the starting tai chi pose. "Taught to me by a man I coached with in Peking. Took me six months to make my first basket this way."

"This floor is not bad," says Spear, bouncing away from Alexi with his hands at his sides, the wood of the ancient gym like a

trampoline to his legs after twenty long years on the hard concrete of Tillsbury.

"This floor is dead," says Alexi, his jaw dropping at Spear's
elevations. "Are we filming? Please. Quickly."

"Rolling," says Nolan, waving to Alexi. "Spear? Could you
jump back to the well-lit side? Thanks."

Spear springs to the free-throw line, and Alexi feeds him a
pass that carries him high for a tricky banking spinner that snaps
through the net, Alexi catching and feeding him for a swish
from nine, a left hook from twelve, a right hook from thirteen,
a soaring jumper from seventeen, a scooping runner from
eight, a fallaway from twenty-one. On and on without a
miss.

Alexi holds the ball after Spear's fifteenth basket, shaking his
head sadly. "Don't worry, my friend. You'll do better once you
get warmed up. Now I shoot a few."

"May I feed you?" asks Spear, stepping nimbly to the baseline.
"You like bounce passes?"

"I like passes that get to me when I want them."

"See what I can do," says Spear, readying himself to catch and
feed.

"I love this court," says Alexi, tumbling toward the rim, pushing the ball through with his trademark delicacy. "I love how
cool it is in here. Like Russia in the fall." He hits a little jumper. "I
played here with teeny drunk poets. They could barely shoot the
ball, barely dribble. But, my God, could they talk. Every try, even
their misses, they rejoiced. Can you imagine?"

"How great," says Spear, zinging him a pass. "You about ready
to go?"

"Patience," says Alexi, popping the ball in from twelve. "I'm an
old man. Forty-four in August. Have pity."

Spear tosses the ball in from five feet out. "After what I saw
last night, I'm the one should be begging for pity."

"I wasn't begging," says Alexi, snatching the ball and banking
it in. "I was only making a suggestion."

They begin to play, Alexi going up with the ball and sneaking his shot under Spear's armpit. "My God you jump high."

"You gonna talk the whole time?" asks Spear, scoring unguarded from twenty. "Is that how you like to play?"

"I never know," says Alexi, dribbling in. "Some days I like to chat, others I don't. You object?"

"No," says Spear, swatting at the ball. "Just curious."

Alexi fakes one way and lays it in the other. "Now come close, Spear. It's too early for me to go out so far to guard you."

Spear drives the lane, going airborne from ten feet. Alexi times his leap to meet him at the rim, but the ball is long gone, touching high on the backboard and tumbling through.

"That was very beautiful," says Alexi, backing in and throwing up a ten-foot hook that Spear snags out of the air and takes beyond the three-point arc, where he turns to drill a no-frills jumper from twenty-four.

"You have guessed my timing," says Alexi, trying another hook. "Yes?"

"Doubt it," says Spear, rising to snag it again.

Alexi swipes it back and lays it in. "No one ever jumps as high as you."

They play hard for another ten minutes, Alexi toiling near the hoop, Spear ranging far and wide, the contest oddly even until Spear leaves the ground and turns full circle in the air, Alexi getting a hand on the ball, only to have Spear pull it free and score a soft eight-footer before he touches down.

Alexi holds the ball. "You stay up in the air longer than anyone ever has. How old are you?"

"Twenty-seven," says Spear, eager to keep playing.

"You're very good. In pros I would not guard you. Not by myself. If you would like, I would be very happy to show you to the coach of the Clippers." He glances off court at me. "Unless Vic Tor wants to doom you to Hathaway, the man who must control everything."

"I was born to play for the Warriors," says Spear, tapping the ball out of Alexi's hand and drilling a nineteen-foot hook. "I

figure I've got maybe three or four years of super-fast left in me.
Maybe more."

"Super-fast is a murderous illusion," says Alexi, lofting a floater
in from twenty-two. "It's the reason poor Hathaway always loses
in the end."

"We'll see," I say, walking onto the court, Spear feeding me
before I can decline, the ball flowing from my hands through the
net from twenty-five feet out.

"Aha!" says Alexi, clapping his hands. "I knew you played, Vic
Tor. Why have you always denied this to me?"

"He played in college," says Nolan, popping out of the con-
trol room. "Scored thirty-two points against Sylvania. I was there.
This was before the three-point shot, and all of his were threes.
So by today's standards we're talking forty-eight."

"Do *you* play?" asks Alexi, frowning at Nolan. "With Vic Tor?"

"We go way back," says Nolan, jogging onto the court with
us. "College. Girls. Pizza. Hoops."

"Then," Alexi shrugs, "we must now play a game with the four
of us. First two to make it are a team."

"Can we do this?" Nolan squints at me. "Given who we are
and given who they are?"

"Sure," I say, canning one from the top of the key. "It'll be
fine."

Spear feeds Nolan. He hits the same shot.

"Good," says Alexi, shaking Spear's hand. "We are now teammates. With distinct height advantage."

"Wait a minute," cries Nolan, grimacing at me. "*That* was
shooting for teams? Us against them? This is insanity, Vic."

"That's the fall of the ball," says Spear, thirty feet from the
hoop. "But we'll let you have it first."

"Maybe we should split you guys up," I say, watching Spear's
shot tumble through. "Height is not your only advantage."

"You made the shots, you picked the teams," says Alexi,
amused by our panic. "It's all part of the strategy. But don't worry,
the pain will not last for long."

We do badly at first, Nolan and I, forcing our shots and

fumbling on defense, but we soon realize that both Alexi and Spear wish to make a game of it. An actual game. They loaf around, shooting and rebounding flat-footed, leaving us open to shoot away our jitters until Nolan scores twice from the top of the key, and yours truly finally hits a clean jumper from the right corner just before Allan Allan cries, "Cut!"

In Little Joe's, with carafes of red wine all around and egg-plant Parmesan warming our noses, Alexi holds his glass aloft. "To my friend Vic Tor. A man of love."

"To you," says Spear, raising his glass to Alexi. "My teacher."

"What did you learn?" asks Alexi, drinking deeply. "Or are you teasing me?"

"You were just cruising," says Spear, clinking Alexi's glass. "This was no big deal for you, whereas it was my biggest to date. I played with everything I had, while you were already halfway to your game in Seattle tomorrow. But you still played me even. Almost effortless."

"Flatterer," says Alexi, clinking Spear's glass. "But it's only half true. You are excellent. No question. Magnificent." He downs his wine and rises gallantly. "Now I must leave you for the airport, where my team is no doubt waiting for me. Good luck, Spear. I look forward to playing with you again. Call me if you ever wish to speak about the game. Or anything."

Spear shakes Alexi's hand. "I learned more with you today than I've learned all year long playing at Tillsbury. No jive about this. You are my master."

"I'm touched," says Alexi, kissing Spear's cheeks. "I am also late. We'll talk."

"I'll walk you out," I say, desperate to hear his private reaction to Spear.

At his sleek silver limousine, Alexi turns to me, his face tinged with grief. "I must warn you, Vic Tor. If he is as good as I think he is, it could cause serious ripples in the great pool. You know what I'm saying?"

"Not exactly."

"Basketball at this level is not just sport." His chauffeur opens the door for him. "Corporations have a great interest, shall we say, in all the great players. There is a strategic balance of personalities connected to things they like to sell. I think you know about this, Vic Tor. Sometimes these things are far more important than the game itself, whether we like it or not. I'll call you tomorrow."

22

Spear sprawls on the futon, reading Kipling by the fire. Isaac sits cross-legged on the rug leafing through Toulouse-Lautrec. Greta is off running errands on her bike, while I brew yet another pot of Ruby's calming tea. We're killing time, waiting for Nolan to call with news of the film. My mood keeps swinging from sad to euphoric, my time at Tillsbury already transmuting itself into myth. My game against the boy, my battle with Pogo, my shot over Spear's outstretched arms, they all seem more like dreams now than reality. On the other hand, reality these days is seeming more and more like a dream.

"Alexi couldn't guard me unless I came close," says Spear, closing *Kim*. "He was tough inside, but outside I was free."

"He wouldn't be guarding you alone, Spear. He'd be one of many."

"I can do it. I'm every bit as good as he is. How much does he make?"

"Twelve million a year, base. Untold millions in endorsements."

He shakes his head. "I won't do endorsements, but twelve million would be okay. We could turn our whole neighborhood into a beautiful farm. Build a soft court at Tillsbury with good seats all around. Give the rest away."

"No endorsements? I'll have to ask Alexi how that'll go over with the powers that be."

"I'll put my name to something good, something that will help people. But I'm not gonna sell junk when people are starving to death."

"Toulouse-Lautrec," says Isaac, "was a *good* painter. Look at this, Papa." He brings the book to Spear and shows him a picture of a defiant woman in a green dress. "You know what else? Greta's gonna buy me paints and everything."

"Oh, yeah?" says Spear, tickling his son. "Caught yourself a patron, huh?"

The phone rings. It's Nolan. "Vic, this Allan Allan guy is amazing. Thanks for bringing him around. We'll run a tape over soon. Fasten your seat belts."

Greta breezes in, winded from her uphill ride, her cheeks ablaze. "What a glorious day! The air is like honey."

I stare at her in amazement. She is an angel descended from the clouds. How can it be that she loves me, that she wants to be with me?

She presents Isaac with ten tubes of acrylic paint. He bows awkwardly. "Thank you, Greta. Thank you very much. I'll make my first picture just for you." He dabs each color onto the back of his hand, showing them to Spear.

"We'll need special paper," she says, beaming at her protégé. "They told me which kind to get. Acid free."

"But that book says Toulouse-Lautrec painted on cardboard. Can't I try that?"

"Sure you can," says Spear, nodding to his son. "You're the artist."

"And these are for you," she says, handing Spear a pocket journal and a shiny black pen. "In case you need to write anything down."

"These are lovely." He bows to her. "I appreciate your taking care of Isaac. He'll make you a fine painting."

"What did you get for me?" I ask wistfully. "A grant? Say, fifty thousand a year for the rest of my life?"

She hands me a manila envelope. "Sorry. Just this column I wrote. It runs tomorrow in the *Chron*."

"What? He's running something *you* wrote?"

"I told you I wrote, Vic."

"But you never said anything about a *column*."

"I'm not supposed to write columns?"

"But you didn't *show* it to me first."

"Why should I?"

"So I could help you."

"Help your*self*," she says, grabbing her satchel and rushing out, slamming the door.

Isaac looks at his father. "We better go, huh?"

"No," says Spear, chuckling. "They're just getting used to each other. You know how you and Lester used to fight all the time when he first came to live with us? Well, now you're friends, right?"

"*Best* friends. Lester is my best friend."

"So, it's like that with them."

I rip open Greta's envelope and stare in horror at the title of her column.

What Women Watch at Basketball Games
by Greta Eagleheart

"Oh, my God," I say, handing the pages to Spear. "Look what she's done."

Spear's eyes race along the lines of her words and his face lights up. "This is good, Vic. The woman can write. Sounds a bit like you, a shade more romantic, different ideas, but definitely good."

"Read it to me," I say, falling listlessly into my armchair. "I can't believe this is happening."

" 'Women watch the way the men dance. We watch their legs, imagining those legs touching our legs, those beautiful, muscular arms holding us. We watch their eyes for signs of fear, for flashes of pleasure in the heat of aggressive play. We study each man until we know him, and then we marvel at his interactions, his airborne conflicts, his choices and posturing. And deep in our hearts, we hold on to the hope that this great game will be the shaping ground for those noble men we've all been waiting for, off the court as well as on.' "

"That's not bad," I say, a veil lifting from my eyes. "That's rather good, actually."

"Got a good feel to it."

"*Um,*" says Isaac, clutching a tube of red. "Have you got any cardboard? I need to get started."

I have to wait for Greta to get back to her house before I can call to apologize. To pass the time, I do something I haven't done since I was twelve. I make chocolate chip cookies from scratch, with Isaac as my able and eager assistant. "More sugar," he suggests, tasting the batter. "Definitely much more sugar needed."

"Don't tank up on sweets," says Spear, deep into *Kim* again. "Bad for your stomach. Give you bad dreams."

"But this is a special occasion, Papa." He smiles slyly at me. "This is like a slumber party."

When the cookies are done, I carry the largest five to the phone with me, eating all of them before I dial.

"Hello," says Sheila, sounding distracted.

"Sheila? It's Vic Worsley."

"She doesn't want to speak to you, Vic. You hurt her feelings."

"Would you give her a message for me? Tell her I'm terribly sorry. I've been a horrible ass."

"You read the column?"

"Yes. I loved it."

"Got a nice swing to it, doesn't it? Hold on."

Nolan and Allan enter, triumphantly waving the video.

"The mother lode!" shouts Nolan, doing a spontaneous jig. "The micro-sensation of the year!"

Spear frowns at them. "How long *is* it?"

"A tiny masterwork," says Nolan, shaking the video at me. "Where's your VCR?"

"In my office." I wave them down the hall. "Just past the room where Isaac is painting. I'll be there in a second."

"Hurry up," says Spear, glowering at me. "I need you for this."

" 'Lo," says Greta, coming on the line, sounding far away.

"Greta, I'm sorry. I'm a pompous, pathetic . . ."

"Stop. You were being territorial. I forgive you." She takes a deep breath. "So what do you think?"

"It's wonderful. It's savvy and seductive and informative. It's bound to cause a sensation."

"Stop," she says eagerly. "Please."

"I can't wait to see it in the paper tomorrow."

"You really like it?"

"I love it. Come on over. We're just about to watch Spear's film."

I jog down the hall, stopping to look in on Isaac, the floor of the guest room covered with newspapers. He has a tube of yellow paint in his right hand, a tube of black in his left, and he's glaring fiercely at a large piece of cardboard pinned to the wall.

"How's it going?"

"Not so good," he says, squinting at his canvas. "Doesn't go on like crayons."

"Using a brush?"

"Not yet," he says, daubing on more yellow. "Not quite yet."

In my office, while Nolan and Allan fiddle with my ancient television, Spear stares down at the city, lost in thought. Nolan rolls his eyes at me. "Had I known the prehistoric nature of your set, we could have shown this at my studio."

"No biggy," says Allan, inserting a final prong. "We have attained functionality. The tape, please."

Spear hands him the video. "Thank you for all your hard work."

"No, no," says Nolan, shaking his head. "The pleasure was all ours. Just watch."

The film begins.

                              ALEXI
                    (staring into the camera)
Are we filming? Please. Quickly.

Spear soars high above Alexi, giving the ball to the hoop, a grateful smile on his face.

Spear snags Alexi's towering hook, clears it with a snappy dribble and leaps high to hit a jumper from twenty-five.

                              ALEXI
You stay up in the air longer than anyone ever has. How old are you?

                              SPEAR
Twenty-seven.

                              ALEXI
You're very good. In pros I would not guard you. Not by myself.

Spear vaults over Alexi, turning full circle in the air, placing the ball in the hoop, landing lightly on his toes.

                         FREEZE FRAME.

"Whoa!" I cry, dazzled. "Succinct."

Spear stares at his frozen image. "That was me?"

"Most beautiful thirty seconds of film ever glued," says Allan, nodding at Nolan. "It will conquer every short film festival on earth."

"We've already got the title." Nolan winks at Allan. "Shall we tell them?"

"Please," says Spear, deeply interested. "What will you call it?"

"It's subtle," says Allan, arching an eyebrow. *"Alexi and Spear."*

"We tried *Spear and Alexi,*" Nolan explains, "but it didn't sound quite right."

"I can see that," says Spear, drumming with his fingers on my desk. "The cadence isn't right."

"Exactly," says Nolan, giving him a high-five. "Precisely correct."

We replay the tape for Isaac. He shrugs. "Nice, but it seems too short. What about your fallaway? That's my favorite shot. The way you just fall and fall and fall."

Greta arrives with Sheila, both of them wearing great floppy hats. They crowd around the set and we show *Alexi and Spear* once more.

"What a rush," says Sheila, flaring her nostrils at Spear. "Nothing halfway about you."

"Shouldn't there be more?" asks Greta, frowning at me. "Seems so short."

"Thirty seconds is the dominant communication duration of our time," says Allan, wrinkling his brow. "I majored in thirty-second spots. Rule number one. If your audience wants more, you've succeeded."

Spear frowns. "It's definitely good, but why not just run three or four minutes of what actually happened? I want to see everything. Real time. Where's the rest of what you filmed?"

"It's my gift to you," says Nolan, grinning at Spear. "But as a selling tool, this little baby is optimum. Believe me."

"Shall I order Chinese?" asks Greta, putting her arm around me. "It's a dominant way to not have to cook."

"Chinese," I say, clapping my hands. "And then we're off to see Hathaway, the moodiest man in basketball. Oh, please let him be mellow tonight."

"No meat in ours," says Isaac, looking to his father for approval. "We're vegetarians."

"So are we," says Sheila, holding out her hand to him.

"Whereas I eat virtually nothing *but* meat," says Allan, smiling sheepishly. "So could you get a little box of beef for me? *Por favor.*"

"Make it a large," says Nolan, clapping Allan on the back. "You're hired."

23

 The wind is blowing furiously through the financial district, the streets nearly empty, the markets closed until morning. We abandon our cab five blocks from Hathaway's office. Spear stretches his arms to the sky. "Those little cars were not built for people like us. Need to loosen up before we talk to the man."

"I'm nervous," I confess, finding it hard to breathe. "This could be it, Spear."

"*It.*" He frowns at the word. "What do you think he'll say when he sees our little film?"

"He'll give you a tryout. He loved Alexi. Begged him to stay. Begged him to learn set plays. But Alexi, as you know, must be free to improvise. Fixed plays are only useful to him when they're used by the opposing team. He's a master of disruption, and when he got away from Hathaway, he became a champion."

"So when Hathaway sees me flying over his favorite big man, who knows what he might do." Spear takes a deep breath to calm himself. "What kind of player was he? Hathaway, I mean. I never heard much about him. He ran before my time."

"He was not fast," I say, remembering the glory days of big white men, most of them too slow now to compete with the African giants. "He only had maybe five good seasons, but he was unique. I saw him in his prime with the Pistons in a game against the Lakers. He had seventeen boards in the first half, no points, and twenty-six points in the second half, no boards."

"You said he was moody."

"He'll love you on Monday and hate you on Tuesday and love you again on Wednesday. He used to grant me interviews, cancel at the last minute, and then call me at home to apologize. He once proclaimed me a genius on national television, and two days later he said I was the biggest idiot to ever wield a pen. When I criticized him for trading Alexi, he wrote a column of his own rebutting every point I made, and then the day after it ran, he sent me an autographed basketball and season tickets. 'Split personality' might be a more appropriate term."

Spear watches the waning moon traverse the narrow gap between two skyscrapers. "Who knows what his life must be like? I can't imagine living in a world where everybody wants to rob you blind, take your best players. All the time. I wonder how he stays sane."

"By cultivating the belief that only *he* is right," I muse, thinking of myself. "That everyone else is a fool. It makes one feel quite superior—and very much alone."

We stop at the baronial entrance to Warriors' Tower, a spire of gray granite soaring into the night sky. Spear gazes up at the neon crown and sighs deeply. I watch his proud face and feel astonished to be partnered with such a great man, to be standing beside him at this mythic portal, the air alive with promise.

"So tell me this, Vic. If it's so lonely, why do I want to be in a world like that when I can work as a counselor with Rashan? Expand the garden. Do my reading every day. Yoga. Meditate. Love my children. I don't need to prove anything."

"We can cancel," I remind him. "No problem."

"Oh, let's hear what he has to say. I'm curious. I admit it, I'm dying to hear."

. . .

I am cowed by the shimmering opulence of Hathaway's do-
main, an accumulation of wealth beyond all reason. The black
granite walls are trimmed with wide strips of chrome. The floor is
fine white marble. The famous paintings on the walls are by
Matisse, Chagall, Miró, Kandinsky. The real things. Yet they
seem mere affectations in this corporate vortex, proof of power,
little more.

Hathaway greets us cordially. He seems quite relaxed. We sit
on black leather sofas and sip flavored bubbly water served by a
lovely Japanese woman wearing black slacks, a white shirt, and a
black bow tie, her feet shod in silver high-tops.

Hathaway smiles sadly at me. "So, I hear they fired you for
blasting me. I had nothing to do with that, you know. I don't care
what *anybody* writes about me." A flicker of pain colors his
cheeks. "You know nothing of my work. How you got a job as a
basketball critic is beyond me, though sometimes you make me
laugh, I admit it. The piece you did on Cosmo Carter's knees
may have been the funniest thing I've ever read. But his knees are
fine. We're close to signing him, just between you and me, now
that you can't write about it."

"It was time for a change," I say, swallowing my fury. "For
what it's worth, I'm sorry I wrote that last column. It was inexcus-
able."

"So you're an agent now?" He squints at me. "I wouldn't have
expected that of you."

"I'm not an agent. I'm not getting any money for this."

"We're partners," says Spear, nodding to me. "We'll share
whatever we get."

"So tell me about yourself," says Hathaway, turning to Spear.
"You happy with the tape?"

"It's a surprise," I say. "We'd rather let it speak for itself."

"I don't like surprises," Hathaway says, inserting the cassette.
"Never have."

A large screen descends from the ceiling. The room darkens.

Spear and I settle back in our seats. The film begins. Hathaway leans forward at the sight of Alexi. We've got him now. He's done for. He holds his breath for the entire film, exhaling audibly as Spear soars above his foe and gives the ball down into the net.

We sit in silence for what seems like a very long time before Hathaway brings the lights up. "This is amazing. Why haven't you been playing? Were you in prison?"

"I play every day. In Oakland. Tillsbury Park."

"Never played semi-pro?"

"No."

"You're twenty-five?"

"Twenty-seven."

"You want a ten-day contract? League minimums? I'll sign you right now."

"Vic handles that stuff," says Spear, sitting back. "Whatever he says is fine with me."

I shake my head, feeling deliciously shrewd. "A ten-day would be a silly thing for you to do, Jim. The minute people see him warming up, every team in the world will want him. How about a year at league minimum? What is that, three hundred thousand? With a five-million-dollar bonus if he wins you the championship."

Hathaway sneers in derision. "From a thirty-second videotape? You're insane."

"From a full scrimmage with your best men," says Spear, his voice so deep it startles me. "Tomorrow. Your *best* players. The Coliseum." He begins to rise, but sits again. "Oh, yeah, and one other thing. My primary condition for signing is that Vic comes with me."

"What? Vic?" He splutters indignantly. "In what capacity?"

"Whatever capacity he wants," says Spear, winking at me. "So I have somebody along I can trust."

"What? Assistant coach?" He leaps to his feet and paces the room, glaring fiercely at me. "Go fuck yourself, Vic."

"Fear not," I say, enjoying his extreme displeasure. "I have absolutely no interest in coaching."

"So let me get this straight," he says, snarling at Spear. "If you impress me sufficiently at this scrimmage, I sign you for almost nothing. And if we win it all, I give you five million dollars. And Vic accompanies you as some sort of mascot?"

"Oh, yeah, shoot," says Spear, slapping his forehead, "I forgot one other thing. At that scrimmage tomorrow, I'm bringing my own team, and from what I've seen, we'll kick your butts. What time?"

"Hold it, Spear! What are you . . ."

"Eleven in the morning," says Hathaway, his eyes narrowing. "No cameras. No media. Promise me, Vic?"

"Absolutely, but . . ."

"You swear?"

"I swear."

On the street, waiting for a taxi, Spear claps his hands and hoots at the top of his lungs. "We did it, Vic! Gonna get our shot at the Coliseum."

"With what team?" I ask, disgruntled. "And why didn't you consult with me first? I thought we agreed I was going to handle this part of things."

"I'm sorry, it just seemed like the perfect moment for me to take charge. You know what I mean? I don't know the business, but I know the game, and I saw that crack in his defense, so I went for it. Forgive me?"

"But what team? Who—"

"What are you talking about?" He stares at me, puzzled. "Our team. Pogo, Thomas, Wild, Chandler, Juanishi, Godfrey, you, and me."

"Me?" I say, blanching. "Don't be ridiculous, Spear. Let me make some calls. I know some great semi-pros who would cream to play the Warriors."

His mighty shoulders sag. "But don't you want to play with us, Vic? Hit your automatic from twenty-five?"

"In my dreams." I flag a cab. "But you know goddamn well I'm not good enough to walk on the same court with the pros."

"That's not true," he says, straightening up. "We'll just have to let that idea settle in for a while. You've got until tomorrow to decide."

"I've decided," I say, hearing the sorrow in my voice. "It'll be thrilling enough to cheer you on from the sidelines."

We find Greta in the kitchen making apple cobbler. Sheila and Isaac are snuggled in front of the fire, looking through a big book of African sculpture. Isaac smiles dreamily at his father. "I'm gonna need something to carve with, Papa." He yawns. "We staying over here again tonight?"

"No," says Spear, squatting down beside him. "Get your stuff together. We're gonna catch a train home."

"After dessert?" He nods hopefully. "We've been waiting very patiently, huh, Sheila?"

"Yes, we have," she says, mussing his hair. "And if your papa tries to make you leave before you get some, he'll have to deal with me."

Spear laughs uproariously. "I won't be sleeping much tonight anyway. So get your things packed up and we'll leave right after dessert."

I cling to Greta in the kitchen, hoping to calm myself in her arms. "Oh, I'll be glad when this is over and I can just hang out with you and have nowhere else to go."

"You love it," she says, feeding me a warm chunk of cobbler. "You never want it to end. Admit it."

"I wonder if I could keep playing at Tillsbury, even if Spear isn't there."

"You can do anything you want," she says, holding me tight. "Just try to have a good time while you're doing it."

"Did Vic tell you the news?" asks Spear, engulfing us both in his huge embrace. "We're gonna play the Warriors tomorrow.

The gang from Tillsbury is gonna take on the pros. Now won't that be fine?"

"You'll be great," says Greta, looking fearlessly into his eyes. "I know you will."

"Hey, Papa," says Isaac, rushing into our midst. "Let me and Sheila be in the hug, too."

It's long past Isaac's bedtime when Rashan picks us up at the station in Oakland, his face creased with worry.

"What's wrong?" asks Spear, hugging his friend. "Rama hurt himself again?"

"No. Lucinda left. She took Lester and Agnes June."

"Where did she go?" asks Isaac, clutching his father's hand. "When are they coming back?"

"No one knows."

"But she can't take them away," he says, starting to cry. "They live with *us*. Papa, she can't do that. Can she?"

"God," says Spear, pressing his palm to his forehead. "Why now? Why not the day after tomorrow?"

"There's more," says Rashan, shaking his head. "Camille must have taken a check. She withdrew three thousand dollars from the group savings. That's why Lucinda went away."

We arrive at the big house, rain threatening. Rashan turns off the engine. Isaac runs inside, crying for Lester. We stay in the truck, sitting in silence. Rashan stares out into the night. Spear closes his eyes and sinks into meditation. I am overcome by a vision of Lucinda seething with anger, hiding somewhere with Lester and Agnes June. But now the vision changes. Her fury has passed and she returns to their house, and Lester and Isaac are reunited, the wounds healed.

Spear opens his eyes. "It's good Lucinda went away. She needed to. She'll come back when she doesn't have to do that hateful job anymore. After the basketball money comes in."

"She *chooses* that job," says Rashan, glaring at him. "You are not responsible for her happiness."

"I don't know, Rashan. I think maybe you and I part ways there. I couldn't feel good about myself if I didn't put back what Camille took. Lucinda works hard for her money. And we're all in this together, aren't we?"

"Yes, of course," says Rashan, opening his door and climbing out. "We ordered several pizzas. Your men will be here soon."

"Hey, Rashan," says Spear, calling after him. "You're not mad at me, are you? I know money won't bring Lucinda happiness, but it might bring her a little relief. A little time to think about what she really wants to do. That's a gift I'd like to give her."

Rashan softens. "There are no errors, Spear. You do what you must."

At midnight in the living room, Pogo counts bodies. "Okay, we got Spear at center, Godfrey at power, Juanishi pumpin', me at point. Where's Thomas? He gonna run the two spot, right?"

"Thought I'd start Vic at two," says Spear, fumbling with a can opener. "Hey, where's the *good* opener, Chaka?"

Juanishi whines. "Vic? He barely been in a zoo. How you gonna run him with the slicks? We might as well play five on four." He glares at me. "No insult, man, but you ain't much. You know what I'm saying? You're short and you're slow."

"Held the boy," says Godfrey, wagging his finger. "Besides, we got Thomas and Wild and Chan coming off the bench."

"Actually," I begin, "I don't think I'll . . ."

"Key word here is 'team,' " Godfrey continues. "Team needs a bench. Team needs depth. Team needs bodies to throw at the slicks."

Spear points at Pogo. "So Vic plays. Agreed?"

Pogo shrugs. "What can I say? Your team."

"That's right," says Spear, relaxing into his big armchair. "I got winners, and I pick the team I want to run with."

Chaka enters the room, Isaac clinging to her. "Gentlemen, your pizza is now sliced and ready."

In the kitchen, wedged between Godfrey and Spear, I look across the crowded table at Pogo. "Look," I say to him, "I know you think I'm a liability to the team, and I actually was considering not playing, but now I think maybe I can help. I think I can hit some threes."

"Vic," he says, trying not to scoff. "You have no idea. Not a clue. But Spear's right. He's got winners, so we'll do the best we can with what he picks. But if you think you can pop threes off these guys, you know less about the game than I thought."

"Or maybe he knows a little more." Godfrey grins. "After all, he got us this gig, didn't he?"

"Yeah, and I'm a virgin," says Juanishi, shaking his head. "Vic won't do shit. Anybody want to bet me on that?"

"This is gettin' old," says Godfrey, turning to his brother. "Say what's what."

"You want to answer Juanishi?" asks Spear, looking at me. "Before I say what I have to say?"

I look at Juanishi and Pogo, and it occurs to me that the pressure of tomorrow's game has thrown them back to the beginning of our time together, that I have returned with them to my first hours at Tillsbury when they saw me as nothing more than an interloper, unproven and unworthy. "I'll do the very best I can," I say, nodding to Juanishi. "I'll play with all my heart."

"So here we go," says Spear, nodding his thanks to each of us. "The Warriors as quick and fast as men can be. But we can play with them. And you know why? Because we're a better team. I've seen these Warriors play. They lack cohesion. They have no identity. We're tighter, sharper, way more together. We cannot forget this. We've been working for this moment every day for our whole lives, whether we knew it or not, and now Vic has gotten us this gig. Tomorrow is a chance to play against the best in the world. By tomorrow night, we'll have done things we'll never forget. And none of us will ever be the same."

. . .

When Juanishi and Pogo have gone, Spear and Godfrey and I walk through the ginkgos to where Ruby is squatting by a small fire, throwing a handful of tiny bones onto a plane of dust. She has five black feathers stuck in her hair, an old tattered shawl over her shoulders. Godfrey and Spear squat to her right, I kneel to her left.

She frowns at Godfrey. "Come on around this side of Victor. Get this circle balanced."

He obliges her, sitting to my left. "This good, Mama?"

"Perfect," she says, nodding to him. "Crows been here all day. Five, six, seven, all day long in the apple tree. Come to bring the natural law. Time to throw the bones."

"What do they say so far?" asks Godfrey, looking for signs in her dust. "Good news, we hope."

"You'll do well tomorrow," she says, reaching across my knees to touch Godfrey's hand. "Be strong on the boards. See this little round bone here? That's you shooting from way outside. Easy as pie."

Godfrey sighs with relief, his faith in Ruby unshakable. "What else, Mama?"

"Just now throwing for Spear." She gathers the bones and smooths the dust. "May the spirits guide this fall."

The bones touch down close together, save for the longest, which bounces into the fire.

"My God!" she gasps, shaking her head in wonder. "That hasn't happened but twice in all my seventy-nine years. Into the fire, Spear. You're going into that fire, and you know what they say. Only way to survive the flames is to be pure of heart."

"Not take any money?"

She looks at the remnant bones, clustered tightly. "No money," she murmurs. "Not a cent for yourself alone."

"There's a minimum he has to take," I say, squirming. "It's an actual law."

"Then he can just give that minimum away," she says, nodding to her bones. "Must get the ball to his brothers, play this game as a team. But don't forget to prove yourself close to the hoop. They want to see if you can dominate. Once they see you can score inside, you can do anything you want."

She gathers the bones and smooths the dust. "I'll need something small of yours, Victor. Something to take the place of the bone that burned."

I reach into my pocket and find a small chunk of pink tourmaline that Greta found on her trip with her womens to the Lost Coast.

Ruby puts the stone in her mouth, rolling it around on her tongue. "That's a good rock," she says, adding it to the bones. "Has a strong, clean energy."

The bones tumble onto the dust, my tourmaline nestling close to a chicken vertebra. Ruby glares down at the configuration. "Thank goodness she gave you that stone, or you might not even be here at all. Something over there to the west about changing where you live, but I don't see any basketball in here."

"He's playing," says Spear, gathering the bones and throwing them again. "Read what that says."

The bones make a circle, the tourmaline at its center. Ruby squints at my rock. "You believe this? Pretty little pink thing in the center of a perfect circle? How many times do I have to tell you to keep your hands off my bones? You still don't know how to let them go. They must leave your hand like falling water. They are not to be forced."

He bows his head. "I'm sorry, Ruby. I thought you were trying to keep him out of the game."

She gathers the bones and smooths the dust. "You know me better than that, Spear. Do you want to say something, Victor? Before I throw these again?"

"The truth," I say, bowing to Ruby. "Tell me the truth."

"Okay," she says, scattering the bones and stone in a wide circle with nothing at its center.

I see only the emptiness. "What does it mean?"

"Things are lined up," she whispers. "Something very big is up for you."

I feel a tingling in my loins. "What?"

"Don't know." She shakes her head. "I've never thrown a thing like this. Not even a little bit like this."

"But you can tell it's big? Whatever it is?"

"Gigantic." She hands me Greta's tourmaline. "Don't lose that."

24

 I am standing on my parents' driveway, twenty-five feet from the hoop. I release the ball in a high arc, deeply pleased with myself as it settles into the net. But the ball doesn't fall through. The net has become a nest of twigs. I climb the pole and scale the backside of the backboard, dropping lightly down onto what I think must be a bed of basketballs. Upon closer examination, I find they are eggs, huge brown ones, and I am seized with panic. What enormous bird must have laid these?

Now I see her, a giant raven, descending out of the sky. I move to the edge of the nest, preparing to jump, only to find that I am no longer ten feet above the ground, but hundreds of feet above a raging sea. Sick with fear, I begin to climb down the pole, which becomes the trunk of a tree, and now I hear something breaking the branches below me. I look down and see a huge serpent!

I try to scream, but I'm mute. I scramble back up into the nest, and as the great bird glides closer, I burrow down between her eggs, bracing myself for death. But death doesn't come, for the raven snatches the serpent in her beak and drops him into the ocean.

I wake to sounds from the kitchen, Godfrey singing "I Feel Good" as he flips buttermilk pancakes, Chaka and Rachel pouring coffee and orange juice, the guys razzing each other as they mill around waiting for breakfast. And though my dream has left me drenched in sweat, I climb out of bed feeling remarkably calm.

As I come down the hall, I catch Chandler downing a beer to calm himself, and he says, "Don't worry, I'm not an alcoholic, okay? Just need somethin' to knock the zoom."

At the kitchen table, Pogo smiles sheepishly at Godfrey. "I had a dream we won this thing. Just a dream, I know. But I woke up thinking . . . who knows."

"Maybe we *can* win," says Juanishi, nodding at Pogo. "How they gonna stop Spear?"

Thomas laughs. "They're gonna triple-team him, that's how."

"Then I'm loose to jam," says Juanishi, slapping Thomas's hand.

Spear comes down the stairs with bad news. "Just got off the phone with Wild. Says he's too nervous to play. Sick to his stomach. Running a fever."

"Well, then I guess it's a lucky thing we got Vic," says Pogo, snickering at Juanishi. "You gonna pull some boards, Vic?"

Chandler grimaces at Spear. "We gotta get somebody else. You're not seriously gonna run this little shit, are you?"

"I'm not only gonna run him, I'm gonna cut you." Spear points to the door. "Get outta here. I'm not having a drunk on my team."

Pogo flinches. "Hold it, Spear. They'll eat us running. Without Wild we *got* to have Chan. We need him."

"They won't eat us," says Spear, stacking flapjacks high on his plate. " 'Cause we're gonna change the tempo. Slow it way down, drive old Hathaway mad. Right, Vic?"

"It's something to try," I answer, grateful to be asked. "These guys thrive on speed. So if we can make one or two extra passes, they'll have a hard time staying in their rhythm."

Godfrey ponders this. "But don't go passing up open shots. If you're in the clear, do it."

"Here's the thing," says Spear, looking at Chandler. "If we help each other, we'll be fine. There's no way we can play one-on-one ball with these guys. They're big and fast and mean. We juke and jive, they'll crush us. We play team, we'll get open shots. And they *will* be keying on me. They'll open with this rookie Thurman on me, but he won't do, so they'll double-team me. That means Godfrey's open. That means Juanishi's free. That means Pogo can take a pass and put it up clean."

Juanishi claps his hands. "This could be juicy. Could be very nice."

Spear grins at Thomas. "But you know what? More than all that, I want to see you tomorrow, Mr. T., and say, 'What did you do with yourself yesterday?' "

Thomas shrugs nonchalantly. "Oh, we went on down to the Coliseum, ran a game with the Warriors, smoked they ass."

Spear laughs, smothering his cakes in syrup. "Yeah, remember I went up on the right side, two guys hanging on me, and I dropped a pass to Juanishi, he looked about to tomahawk and then dished to God for a thunder stuff? Left those poor fools gasping for breath."

"Yeah," says Thomas, seeing it all. "And that ten-footer I made off steam from Pogo."

"Which I got from Vic," says Pogo, kissing the air in my direction. "You gonna feed me all day long, right?"

"No," I say, taking careful aim with my words. "I'm gonna be too busy driving the lane."

Godfrey chuckles, but no one else finds it funny.

Pogo stares grimly at me, stung by my rebuff. "I don't know what it is, Vic, and I didn't *want* to know, but now I do. Why does he start you? What do you do better than Thomas?"

"Nothing," I reply, liking the sound of it. "At least nothing that I know of."

Pogo glances at Spear. "So then why do you play him? He hurts our game. He takes a jump shot off two three pics. We can't do that against these guys. How's he gonna play defense? They'll just walk around him."

Juanishi grimaces at Spear. "It's true, man. He's pathetic."

"I disagree," says Godfrey, nodding to me. "I like the way you play, Vic. You get me some sweet old passes nobody else thinks to try."

Pogo shoots Spear a horrified look. "You play him because you like his *passing*? You crazy? Motherfucker passes like a girl."

"What girl was that?" Spear squints at Pogo. "What if I told you Vic was gonna lead us today?"

"Lead?" says Pogo, cocking his head. "Point? Wait a minute. *I* play point. *I* bring the ball up. *I* start the play."

"You alternate," says Spear, nodding slowly. "Why not?"

"Don't do this," says Pogo, hopping mad. "Get real, Spear. These are the Warriors. He won't get the ball over half-court against these guys. They'll pick his shit clean."

"He's right, Spear. I'm not the guy to bring it up. That should be Thomas or Pogo or you. Not me."

Spear takes a deep breath. "Okay. You bring it up, Pogo. But every other time, try to get the ball over to him. At least to start. Just trust me on this, okay?"

Juanishi shakes his head in disgust. "Any other handicaps? Shall we tie our ankles together? Or do you just want us to suck his dick after the game?"

A dense silence falls, yet I feel surprisingly unalarmed. This seems more their business than mine, the angry posturing of fierce young men.

Spear puts his fork down and gazes steadily at Juanishi. "My friend," he says softly, "I respect and admire you, but I need you to know something, or I won't have you play today either. You listening?"

Juanishi looks away. "Yeah."

"This would not be happening without Vic. Do you understand?" Spear hesitates, struggling to contain his emotion. "He came out here every day and took your abuse. Your constant abuse. He played his best and he got us this gig. And I doubt very much, as strong as you are, that you could have stood the garbage you dumped on him. I truly doubt it. I'm sick to death of you treating him like he's somehow less than us."

"I'm sorry," says Juanishi, nodding to me. "He's right. Off the court, I guess you're just as good as anybody."

"Played the boy like a demon," says Godfrey, trying to lighten things up. "I say let him guard Nosler to start. Keep that shit from gettin' the ball in the first place."

"Nosler ain't the boy," says Thomas, ever the pragmatist. "The boy's a freak. Nosler's a fast pro. *I'm* gonna have trouble staying with him. What's Vic gonna do?"

Chandler calls from the corner. "Hey, anybody gets tired, I can come in and give 'em a breather. Just a breather. Mostly I pass to you, Spear. Sorry about the beer. Only had two. That's it. I'll be bone dry by game time."

"Then Chan comes in," says Spear, not missing a beat, "and hits that inside banker he loves."

Chaka salutes us all. "I'm off to work, fellas. Have a good game. Wish I could be there."

"You should be, honey." Spear takes her in his arms and kisses her. "Get a substitute. I'd love you to see it. Rachel's coming."

Rachel winks at me. "Wouldn't miss it for anything. Things like this don't happen every day."

"You serious?" says Pogo, staring wild-eyed at Spear. "Fans? We can bring fans?"

Spear grins mischievously. "Why not? Only condition he made was no cameras, no media. Didn't say anything about fans."

"Might be good, actually, have some peeps watching," says Godfrey, picking up the phone. "Let's make some calls. Get a little friendly noise going on."

"Exactly," says Spear, rubbing his hands together. "Think of it like this. Buncha guys from out of town come to test our turf. We gotta show 'em what's what, right?"

Chandler smiles impishly. "You're gonna love that floor. Played in a college tournament there. Like walking on a cloud."

Spear points at Pogo. "Gonna loft you an alley-oop, Pogo, so you can blow their minds."

"One time I ran out on that court after a game," says Juanishi, shaking his finger at Chandler. "You were there. You saw me. I grabbed the game ball from some little dude and slammed it home. This was in my street clothes. No problem. Can't wait to do it with my actual shoes on."

Spear grabs Thomas and wrestles with him. "Gonna be nice. Gonna set you some sweet old pics."

"Got to be automatic today, Vic," says Thomas, breaking free of Spear. "Every chance you get."

Rashan's truck becomes the team bus, Spear our driver. The day is breezy and cool, the clouds white and billowy above the gates of the Coliseum, the vast ramparts bedecked with hundreds of corporate banners. Spear slows our bus to a crawl. "There she is. Home of the brave." He winks at me. "Greta coming?"

"Yes, and Sheila, too."

"Maybe Sheila wants to play," says Spear, grinning at Pogo. "How about we bring a woman on with us?"

Pogo forces a dry little laugh. "No comment."

My dear friend Willard Yates, a grumbling old Slav with a loud bark, steps from his guardhouse, clipboard in hand, appraising Rashan's vehicle with great disdain. I join Spear in the window.

"Hello, Vic," says Willard, chewing on his yellow pencil. "You're early. They said to let you in at ten. It's only nine forty-five. Nobody told me anything about an entourage. You know you're being followed?"

"It's fine, Willard. Family and friends. Hathaway gave us carte blanche. Besides, what's fifteen minutes and a few dozen friendly spectators?"

"Few dozen?" He reddens. "I could get in big trouble for this."

"Mr. Yates," says Spear, reading Willard's name tag. "If I do well today, I could make the team." He holds out his hand. "Then I'll be seeing you every day, and you'll just be waving me on through, right?"

"Right." Willard shakes Spear's hand. "But for today you haven't made the team, so I'll need a preapproved guest list."

The line of cars continues to grow, snaking out of sight around the corner. "Not possible, Willard. Hathaway will be furious if we make him wait. There's no time to make a list."

"I'm only doing this for you, Vic," he says, reluctantly waving us in. "And I'm holding you personally responsible for anything that goes wrong. Any damage, you pay for it."

"You're a great man, Willard."

Thomas nudges Chandler. "This Vic is seriously connected."

"Maybe so," says Pogo, unsure of what to think. "But how's that gonna help him get his shot off against these guys?"

Juanishi shakes his head. "I still say he won't be able to. No offense, Vic. Nothing personal. I just don't think you can."

We walk out onto the brightly lit court, all of us staring in wonder at the enormity of the place, the otherworldliness of it. Hathaway's gregarious assistant, Richard Enrox, greets us with clipboard in hand. "Jim wanted me to let you know he's decided to run this like a real game. Four twelve-minute quarters. Five time-outs each half. Six fouls, you're gone."

"Who calls the fouls?" asks Spear, stripping off his sweatshirt. "Anybody we know?"

"Hathaway," says Richard, pumping up his grin. "Wears the uniform and everything. You got a problem with that?"

Spear shrugs at the question. "I'm Spear Rashan Benedentes. You played in the final sixteen-some years ago. Didn't you make a three-pointer at the buzzer against Missouri?"

"Wow." He blushes. "You remember that? Amazing."

"You tell Jim something for me." Spear puts his huge hand on Richard's shoulder. "Tell him I'm absolutely certain he's gonna call a fair game. You tell him I trust him. Okay?"

"Sure will," he says, scurrying away. "Good luck."

· · ·

We gather together before we begin our warm-ups. The first twenty rows are already filled with raucous fans. Chaka waves to me and points to the east where Sheila and Greta and Lisa are coming down the aisle, and I feel a jabbing pain in my lower back that brings sudden tears to my eyes and blurs my vision.

Rashan joins our circle, nodding to each of us. "Well, here you are. Exactly where you always wanted to be. I'm very proud of you, though there are those who believe that pride is a vice. But I *am* proud to know you, to be your witness today. You are every bit as great as the Warriors. This game is the fruit of your labors, so enjoy yourselves."

I trot out onto the court and Pogo feeds me. I shoot an air ball. His return pass hits me in the chest and I stumble and fall. I start to get up, but my ankle gives way and I sink to the floor, a chill running down my spine, my legs going numb. Oh, well, I tell myself, as my old familiar depression settles in, they didn't really want me to play anyway.

Spear yanks me to my feet and leads me to the free-throw line. "You forgot something, Vic."

"My legs are shot," I mumble, clutching his arm. "I can barely stand up. Help me to the bench."

"You're fine, my friend." He puts his arm around my waist. "Not a thing wrong with your legs. Not a thing wrong with you. Now center with me on the hoop. This is the main floor, daddy-o. Time for the big fun. I'm not gonna let you miss it again."

"Spear, I can't walk."

"Rise with me," he says, lifting me up. "Rise onto your toes and see the center of the ring. See it?"

My vision clears and the blood gushes back into my legs. "Yes, I see it."

"Now focus on the very center of that space, and in case you didn't remember, *two* basketballs can pass through there side by side. You see?"

"Yes!" I cry, the hoop a ring of golden light. "I see it."

Spear lets go of me and places a ball in my hand. I release it. Swish. Again. Swish. "Do you see what I see, Spear?"

"I don't know," he says, handing me the ball again. "What do you see?"

"A big basket of light."

"Yeah, that's what I see." He takes a pass from Pogo and hooks it in from fifteen. "Beautiful, isn't it?"

I shoot again, the hoop enormous. I aim for the right edge. Swish. Left edge. Swish. Center. Swish. I move to the top of the key, the pool of light still huge. Twenty-five feet away, I'm dropping shot after shot, my legs charged with strength, Thomas feeding me and feeding me and feeding me.

The Warriors enter in their stylish gray sweatsuits, a bit perplexed by all the fanfare for a little scrimmage against a bunch of park players. They strip off their sweats and watch us shoot, and when they laugh uproariously at Godfrey's air ball, our hoop becomes smaller than *one* basketball, so none of us can score.

The Warriors run their layup drills, moving with practiced ease. Chandler hurries over to Spear. "Shouldn't we be doing something like that? Form two lines?"

Spear dishes to Juanishi. "Why? Won't help us now."

"We gotta do something," says Thomas, spinning around in frustration. "We're dying, Spear."

Pogo stands at the top of the key, gaping at the growing throng of fans. "Jesus, Spear, I didn't know we knew this many people. Kinda scary, huh? How many you think there are, Vic?"

I look around with my sportswriter eyes. "The second tier is filling, so there must be close to a thousand."

Spear sinks a clean twenty-footer. "Let's play a little three on four. Me and Godfrey and Pogo against the four of you. Half-speed."

Thomas shakes his head violently. "You crazy? They'll see our moves."

"Let's play," says Spear, no-nonsense in his voice. "Just like we're playing at the park. It's the only way we're gonna stay loose."

So we begin a game, and the Warriors stop their drilling to watch us. They point and laugh and criticize, until Juanishi comes to slam and Godfrey rises to deny him, Pogo catching the feed at the free-throw line and drifting *over* Thomas to dunk it. The crowd roars, and the mighty Warriors shake their heads in wonder.

Hathaway appears resplendent in an old-fashioned referee's uniform. Black shoes, black slacks, white shirt, black bow tie, big red whistle. He hands me a pile of ragged jerseys. "You'll need numbers for the scorekeepers." He smirks at me. "We've got a crowd, might as well make this semiofficial."

"Thanks for allowing the fans," I say, passing the jerseys to Thomas. "Most kind of you."

Hathaway leers at me. "You're actually gonna play? Don't you think that's taking things a bit too far?"

"I always take things too far," I say, looking into his eyes. "But I don't have to tell you that, do I?"

"You don't have to tell me anything, Vic. Let's just have our little game. Shall we?"

The buzzer sounds. Spear gathers us in a tight circle and we pile our hands in the middle. "Say whatever needs saying," he says, nodding to each of us. "Here we go."

"Watch out, they'll slap your rebounds as you bring them down," warns Chandler. "Make sure you got it solid."

"Shoot too hard, try a fallaway next time," says Thomas, nodding to Juanishi. "We're coming to you early, Juanja. Establish yourself."

Spear takes a deep breath and looks at me. "Vic? You know these guys better than anybody."

"They aren't real comfortable passing to each other yet." I look at Thomas and Pogo. "They all want to shoot more than they want to pass, so if you can stay tight on your man and force him to dish, we should get some steals."

"But don't be gambling," says Godfrey. "Stay tight on your man even when he doesn't have the ball."

"Don't be afraid to talk," says Juanishi. "Shout your switches and call if you need help."

"Somebody give me one more alley-oop," says Pogo, breaking the stack. "Just one more time, dear God."

Tip-off. Hathaway tosses the ball up and Spear reaches above Titus, the Warriors' center, and taps it down to me. I grab it frantically and hang on until Pogo takes it from me. I move to the right wing, the swift and famous Nosler ignoring me, his attention focused on Spear launching himself high above everyone from ten feet out, dropping the ball cleanly through, the crowd roaring.

I sprint down the court, straining every muscle to keep up with Nosler. Titus puts up a hook, but Spear snags it out of the air, baseballing it full court to Pogo, who leaves it for Juanishi to snatch and jam.

Nosler glides by me, cruising into the lane with the ball, weaving around Pogo and Godfrey to put up a silky shot that Spear blocks to Godfrey. He fires it to me and I turn and heave it toward our goal sixty feet away where Spear materializes in the air beside the ball, guiding it with his right hand deep into the cylinder. Six nothing, us.

Hathaway doesn't say a word, but his Warriors quickly adjust to neutralize Spear on the boards. Nosler rises above me and buries a jumper from beyond the three-point line. Six to three. Us.

Pogo hits Godfrey in the corner and he pumps in his patented set shot. Eight to three, us.

Nosler blows by me, dodges Juanishi, passes to Thurman, and here is Spear again, batting the shot away, a whistle blowing.

"Foul on Spear."

Pogo rushes up to Hathaway, fire in his eyes. "That was clean! You blind?"

"And that's a T," says Hathaway, slapping a technical foul on Pogo.

"Calm down," says Spear, gripping Pogo's arm. "We all know the truth. Don't we, Thurman?"

"Yeah," says Thurman, going to the line. "The truth is, I make my free throws. All three of them."

Eight to six. Us.

The pass comes to me from Pogo. Nosler swarms me, but I get it back to Pogo and he passes to Juanishi who skies for a jumper. He misses badly, but Godfrey gets the rebound and goes up with it, Thurman pounding on him—but there's no whistle! Spear grabs the rebound and slams the ball home, glaring at Hathaway for missing the call. Ten to six. Us.

Titus wheels on Spear and shoots from eight, but Spear bats the ball to Juanishi who fires to me and I lob a pass high to the right of the hoop, where Pogo walks the air to snatch the ball and jam it home, the crowd up and dancing. Twelve to six. Us.

"Nice dish," says Hathaway, running alongside me. "Been watching your old Bob Cousy tapes, huh?"

I try to ignore him, but I simply can't resist giving him what I hope is a rakish grin. After all, it's not every day one gets an assist against the Warriors. No. Wait. I've got two assists, my absurd toss to Spear. What more could I want?

Juanishi fouls Vogel and I realize I'm about to faint. "Sub!" I shout, nodding eagerly to Thomas. "Please."

I collapse on the bench beside Chandler, gasping for breath. Vogel makes both free throws. Chandler looks up at the scoreboard and says, "Twelve eight. This can't last. No way this can last. They're just toying with us."

"Chandler," I say, buzzing with satisfaction, "cool it, okay? We're having a good time out there. A real good time."

"Sorry," he says, biting his fingernails. "Guess I'm just horny to get in."

•   •   •

At the end of the first quarter, we're ahead twenty-four to twenty-one. We stand around in sweaty disbelief. "Get the ball to me, please," says Spear, bumping fists with Pogo. "I want to do some stuff inside."

Play resumes. The Warriors are scalding from outside, but Spear simply will not be stopped. He takes eleven shots from near and nearer, high and low, off glass and straight through, making ten of them, his only miss a flagrant foul Hathaway refuses to call. Spear dishes six assists, steals twice, and blocks five more shots, and we find ourselves up fifty-nine, fifty-one at the half.

Hathaway beckons to me from the center of the court. "Vic." He smiles warmly and shakes my hand. "I'm convinced. Let's not damage the merchandise. Three years. Two million a year. A bonus schedule you'll love. Assuming he passes his physical."

"One year, Jim," I sigh, sensing we might be done for the day. "You two may not get along."

"Three years. Three million a year, assuming he's medically sound and drug-free. He is, isn't he?"

"Let's talk after the game."

"No more game," he shouts, chasing after me. "Enough is enough. We've got a game against Portland tomorrow night."

"So we win?" Chandler stares in amazement at Spear. "That's it? We win?"

The Warriors explode off their bench, refusing to quit.

"This is to the finish," Nosler growls, glaring at Hathaway. "You let us play this out, or I'll quit this fuckin' team."

"Okay, okay," says Hathaway, snarling at me. "We'll play a second half. Only this time we destroy you."

We huddle, a few more minutes to rest, and Thomas says to me, "Hope you got some legs left, Vic. No way I can play a whole other half."

"Me either," says Pogo, putting his hand on my shoulder. "You and Juanishi gotta play guard some of the time. Damn that Wild. He's just what we need now."

"Okay," I say, scanning the crowd, my heart thumping at the sight of a certain little boy. Or so he seems to be. "My God, the boy is here."

"No." Spear shakes his head. "I don't play with the boy."

"Why not? They won't be ready for him."

"Because we don't need him. You can do everything he can do. When Pogo and Thomas sit down, I'm gonna play guard, and you're gonna play guard, and Godfrey's gonna jam the middle, and Juanishi and Chandler are gonna sweep the boards, the one or two we might miss."

Pogo touches my wrist. "This is when we need your automatic, Vic. If you only make one bucket, it can change the whole game. Give us the edge."

"I'll try. First chance I get."

The Warriors have a new strategy. They've diagnosed us perfectly. They *triple*-team Spear, leaving our weary guards open to miss all but a few of their long-range jumpers. Chandler nails a banker, Juanishi two, and Spear breaks free a few times, but midway through the third quarter the Warriors quietly pull ahead sixty-seven to sixty-one. Spear calls time out.

"Okay," he says, wiping his brow. "Plan B. Pogo, you and T. sit down. Godfrey, you fresh?"

"Feeling okay." He rises stiffly. "Fresh, no. But I can play."

"Vic?"

"I'm out of my body, but . . . sure."

"Go to the line and center. Hurry up."

I jog to the free-throw line, the crowd murmuring. I haven't played since the first few minutes of the game. I go up on my toes, centering on the center, and someone shouts, "Do it!" and the hoop grows large. I turn to see who shouted, and it's Ruby, standing on her seat, waving to me, Lucinda and Lester and Agnes June beside her.

I take the inbound pass from Spear and turn to the hoop unmolested, releasing a long three-pointer that splashes through. Sixty-seven, sixty-four. Them.

Spear steals a pass and hurls it to me. I pull up behind the three-point arc and sink a perfect rainbow to tie the score, just like that, and the crowd is on its feet, roaring for me. My heart is pounding so hard, I wonder if I'm about to die.

But I stay in seven more minutes, watching Spear walk in the sky. He hits seven threes and three long twos without a miss. Hathaway is so stunned, he stops even trying to ref. We finish the quarter up by eleven, exhausted, our heads bowed in prayer for the strength to finish.

In this fourth quarter, this final twelve minutes, Thomas and Pogo play out the last of their strength, and the Warriors pick up the tempo and run us down. With three minutes left, despite Spear's heroics, the score is tied.

Time out. I'm deaf to what anyone is saying. I look at the fierce faces of my friends, and I know only that I love them.

And now I'm in the game, Spear playing point, dishing to me for an open shot I miss by a mile. I have nothing left. The Warriors roar by me, passing around Spear, scoring easily, going up by two.

Spear hits me again. They don't even bother guarding me. I launch for three and clang it off the back of the iron, Spear rising to tap it in. Score tied.

The Warriors rush back and score, stealing the inbounds pass and scoring again. Godfrey calls time out. We're on the ropes. Down by four.

"This could be the last point we ever play," says Spear, his eyes brimming with tears. "Let's go good."

I take a deep breath and center on the center of the center of the center of the center. Now we're running and the ball comes to me and I drive the lane, taking it to the hoop, floating through the canyon of bodies, rising on a cloud of energy, twisting away from a hand reaching to take the ball from me, releasing the ball to Juanishi for a demonic jam that brings us to within two of them.

We dance back on defense, Nosler slipping by me. I lunge in pursuit, *knowing* he'll pass away from the direction he's facing, a no-look dish to Vogel. I swipe at the air and the ball is there! It flies off my fingertips to Spear, and he starts his run at center court, building to blurring speed, leaving the floor at the top of the key, eluding the swiftly closing blockers, releasing the ball to kiss the glass and tumble through, tying the score with twenty seconds left.

The Warriors rush back at us, Nosler determined to shoot. I can do nothing against him. But Spear and Juanishi rise together and tip the ball to me, seven seconds to go. And as I push the ball ahead of me, desperate to drive the lane once more, I am blind to the open man. Vogel picks me clean from behind and races in ahead of Spear to score.

So the Warriors win, but you wouldn't know it from the way we mob each other, from the crush of joyful friends, from the Warriors wading in among us to gather around Spear, Nosler shouting, "Where you been, man? We been waitin' a long time for you."

Epilogue

[I Saw Myself]

I saw myself
a ring of bone
in the clear stream
of all of it

and vowed,
always to be open to it
that all of it
might flow through

and then heard
"ring of bone" where
ring is what a

bell does

LEW WELCH

25

 It is Tuesday, and on Tuesdays I like to visit Ruby. She brings her pillow and a blanket and a pot of tea out to the clearing on the edge of the ginkgo forest, and we settle down with a view of the young apple trees.

"This tea is sharp and tangy, good for the brain," she says, handing me my cup. "Helps me organize my thoughts."

There are no fences for a long way in either direction, the backyards melding into a continuous farm, a community of ninety-seven people, nine more on the way. The soil and sun bring forth vegetables and fruit, the ponds swarm with fish, the ducks eat snails and lay eggs, a cow and five goats give milk, their surplus sent to a kitchen for the poor.

I sold my house to a piano player. She's building a recording studio where my office used to be. She loves the wildness of the backyard and promises to leave it alone, save for sometimes walking on the faint path to the old oak. I imagine the cats and birds and whatever else lives out there enjoying her music.

I'm renting a small garden cottage not far from Greta's in Noe Valley. My bedroom has a splendid view of a tiny backyard lush with red clover. I work three mornings a week at a used bookstore in the Haight, two afternoons making coffee drinks at Cafe Trieste in North Beach. The rest of the time, I garden at Greta's and scribble and hang out with my womens and my mens. I play ball three times a week with Nolan, once or twice a week at Tillsbury. A good life, all in all.

"Did you go to the Lost Coast with Greta?" asks Ruby, handing me the morning's sports section. "Read me anything good in there."

"How did you know we went camping? We didn't tell a soul."

"Drink that tea," says Ruby, wagging her finger at my cup. "Calm you down. You always get so worried when I know things from the spirits. You like everything to come through your ears and eyes, don't you?"

"Speaking of which, did you catch the game last night?"

"I went up to the big house and watched a little. It hurts my eyes the way they jump those cameras around, but I did see one slow motion that was fabulous. Spear got fouled by everybody on the other team, and he still made it."

"Says here he finished with forty-two points, twenty-three rebounds, nine blocked shots, and thirteen assists."

"Turnovers?"

"Four."

"Wonder how come so many? How much they win by?"

"Only five. They've now won sixty games and lost twelve. Ten more games left until they face Boston in the first round of the play-offs."

"Bye-bye, San Antonio," says Ruby, shaking her head. "Now read me what they say about Spear."

It was the usual unusual business last night for the Golden State Warriors, Spear Rashan Benedentes scoring the last fourteen points of the game, capping his show with a stupendous banker at the buzzer from thirty feet, a pop that left the Phoenix Suns deflated and mystified. It was an average game for Spear, nothing like his seventy points and forty rebounds against Houston, but sufficient to keep the very best teams quaking at the prospect of meeting the Warriors in the play-offs.

Godfrey Benedentes played a vivacious seven minutes, hitting five baseline threes, much to the delight of the jubilant crowd. This team may not know *how* to lose anymore, their last loss coming twenty-nine games ago.

After the victory, Spear was brimming with info about the festival he's sponsoring in the new Tillsbury Amphitheater, with its intimate seating for two thousand. "It's going to be a great show," he proclaimed. "We're bringing together pros and playground players from all over the world for games and contests, and that's just the half of it. We're going to have the best food and every kind of music and dancing on earth. Hope everybody can make it!"

Asked for the umpteenth time if he plans to sign a long-term contract with the Warriors, Spear smiled enigmatically and quoted his friend, Rashan de Witt: "Live honestly and openly and the machinations of the money men shall not impede you."

Coach Hathaway outdid himself in his praise for Spear, calling him, "the most complete player the game has ever seen."

A complete player, yes. But more than that, he is a complete human being, and we are blessed to watch him in full flower.

"I like that last line," says Ruby, sipping her tea. "Doesn't sound like the usual thing they put in the paper. More poetic."

"Yes," I say, smiling at the funny photo above my weekly column. "I always consider it a subtle victory when words like 'flower' appear in the sports section."

About the Author

Born in San Francisco in 1949, Todd Walton composed his first story, "Albert the Alligator and Billy Brown," when he was six years old and he has been writing ever since.

Walton's fiction began to appear nationally in 1975 with the publication of "Willow" in *Cosmopolitan*. In 1978, while living in Seattle, Walton published his critically acclaimed first novel, *Inside Moves*, which was made into an Academy Award–nominated motion picture. His second novel, *Forgotten Impulses*, was published in 1980 and chosen by *The New York Times* as one of the best novels of that year. He is also the author of *Louie & Women* (1983), *Night Train* (1986), and a self-published novel of stories, *Under the Table Books* (1995).

A musician, performer, and backpacker, Walton lives in Berkeley and is at work on a new novel and an album of songs.